A MOTHER'S RUIN

When 18-year-old Eve runs away to start a new life in the city, she quickly discovers that Leeds is not everything she expected it to be. Wandering the cold streets, timid Eve can only find work as a barmaid at the Bluebell Inn. Serving ale and cheap gin to the rowdy crowd, Eve eventually catches the eye of dashing Sergeant Joseph Oates — but his intentions are not honourable, and he will leave her with more than just a broken heart . . .

GRACIE HART

A MOTHER'S RUIN

Complete and Unabridged

MAGNA
Leicester

First published in Great Britain in 2020 by
Ebury Press
an imprint of Ebury Publishing
London

First Ulverscroft Edition
published 2020
by arrangement with
Ebury Publishing
Penguin Random House UK
London

A catalogue record for this book is available
from the British Library.

ISBN 978–0–7505–4836–6

Published by
Ulverscroft Limited
Anstey, Leicestershire
Set by Words & Graphics Ltd.
Anstey, Leicestershire
Printed and bound in Great Britain by
TJ Books Limited., Padstow, Cornwall

1

'I forbid you to go, Eve! You'll leave this house over my dead body!' Margaret Reynolds screamed at her headstrong daughter as she stood in front of the kitchen doorway, barring Eve's way from leaving the family home, with her arms held out over the exit.

'Stop it, Mam, you can't keep me here anymore. There's nothing for me in Rothwell — I'm sixteen and don't want to stay and be made to go into service for those nobs at the big house at Temple Newsam. I just won't! I'm not going there — I'm going to Leeds, whether you and Father give me your blessing or not!' Eve Reynolds raged back at her mother as she grabbed her shawl and a few of her belongings that were airing on the rack above the kitchen fire, shoving them into her already bulging carpetbag.

'If your pa was here he'd take his belt off to you, my girl! You're only doing this because he's not. You know you hardly make any money with the little bit of washing you take in for other people, and it gets in my way in the kitchen. He's lined you up with the position of parlour maid, thinking you'd be grateful and now you're throwing it back in his face. You know Hugo Meynell-Ingram is the next thing to royalty here — you should be thankful for the position offered to you. But instead, here you are turning

1

your back on everything, for absolutely nothing, not even a roof over your head.' Margaret folded her arms, still blocking her daughter's way. Her face was flushed and her breath short as Eve came towards her. 'You're not going to Leeds, my girl. You know nobody there, you've no money and no work awaits you. Sometimes I think that you're simple in the head! Why throw away the life you have for nothing?' Her mother still stood her ground, but now tears were beginning to flow down her cheeks. She loved her daughter with all her heart, but Eve had always been headstrong and when her mind was set on something there was no changing it.

'I'm not going to be tied to a pompous oaf like Hugo Meynell-Ingram forever, and have to curtsy to him every time he passes and do the same for all his fancy guests. And from what I hear from other village girls, that's not the worst of what he demands of his staff. I'll make my own way in the world; that's why I have to go to Leeds and not stop in this pitiful little village. I love you, Ma, but Father doesn't understand that there's more to life than being in service and I aim to plough my own furrow in life.'

Eve put her bag down on the spotlessly clean stone-flagged floor of the small worker's cottage and looked with sympathy at her mother's face as she wiped away her tears. Her father was dependent on the Temple Newsam estate for his living — and the cottage itself was tied to his job.

'Please, Mam, let me go. I'll be all right; I'll find somewhere to stay before the day ends and I'll find myself work in the morning. Jenny

2

Tomlinson says there's plenty of work if you're willing to do long hours — and at least I'll not be tied day and night to a family that can't even remember your name, let alone care about you. Father's been gardener there since he was a lad and they still treat him like the dirt he handles every day. I don't want to waste my life running after that sort.' Eve calmed herself down, she knew her mother was partly right in her worries, but if she didn't leave her home this minute, her father would soon be back and, as her mother had warned her, that would mean a good hiding and him forbidding her to leave the house.

'Think about it, lass, your father will never make you welcome at home again. He's already said to me that he doesn't know what we've done to deserve such a wilful creature as you. Since you've turned sixteen you've a mind of your own. He despairs that you no longer attend chapel and that you won't join us in taking the pledge against the demon drink. This will push him too far, Eve; he'll turn his back on you and, worse still, he'll forbid me from ever seeing you. Please, unpack your things and stay, for my sake if nobody else's.' Margaret walked towards her daughter and held her arms out to hug her. Eve was her only child, born to her late in life when hope had nearly gone of her ever being a mother. Because of that, perhaps, they had both been too strict with her and now she was rebelling against her upbringing, belittling her life with them at home and it hurt Margaret deeply.

'No, Mam, I'm going.' Eve picked up her bag and, taking advantage of her mother being off

3

guard, made for the front door, opening it quickly and looking around hastily as her heartbroken mother sobbed in the dark interior of the cottage. 'I'll send word as to where you can find me. I'm sorry, Mam . . . I love you.'

Eve shed tears too, as she set off down the road that led out of the small mining village of Rothwell, not daring to look back at her mother, who was now standing in their front garden, shouting for her to return home. It would only take a second of weakness and she'd be running back to her mam, begging her forgiveness. She had to be strong and look forward to a new life away from the strict upbringing that she had endured with her Methodist family. Although she had always been shown love and kindness, Eve yearned for some excitement — dances and young men courting her and frivolous dresses instead of being told to be demure and not to be too forward in the company of village boys she'd known all her years. A life in the growing town of Leeds, with its many shops and trades, was an opportunity to see something of the world. Something far more alluring than being a parlour maid to the gentry at Temple Newsam and having to be subservient to all around her.

Determined to reach the bustling centre of opportunity called Leeds before nightfall, Eve walked quickly, her tears diminishing the nearer she got to the town. She needed to find somewhere to stay the night and in the morning she would set off on her quest to find work. She'd read in old copies of the *Sheffield Telegraph*, passed on to the family by their minister, that industries were springing up daily in the town, that girls like her were needed to work in factories and shops and that there was no end of possibilities once you had made your way into the bustling heart. That you could buy a pie for next to nothing and that on every street there was something called a doss house, where you could lay your head for a penny or two. Eve smiled to herself; she'd saved up a penny here and penny there over the last few months and now she had as much as two whole shillings safely placed in the pocket of her skirt. That would see her with a bed and her stomach filled for at least the next few nights, just until she had found herself employment and then she would look for a more permanent place to stay. Having lived with her mam and dad all her life, she was eager for her own home, where she come and go as she liked and not have to listen to sermons from the good book and be quiet as her father chastised her for not paying attention. Life was going to be good, she thought, as she climbed the brow of the hill and looked out into the distance at the town that lay in front of her.

Eve stood for some minutes, looking at the scene: the many houses and factories, mills with their tall chimneys belching out smoke enshrining the town in a magic cloak of mystery. There were canals that twisted and meandered across the land, busy with barges filled with goods of all kinds and, from this distance, the town folk looked like ants, busy going about their work. There were pedlars travelling to and from Leeds with laden packhorses or carts brimming with wares, all part of this thriving place where wealth and opportunity lay. She breathed in and sighed, shaking her head and trying to forget the vision of her mother crying and begging her not to leave home. What did her mam know? She'd never wanted any other life than the one she had in Rothwell; she'd never felt how Eve felt, stifled by the mundane life of being a country girl. But, even so, Eve could feel the tears welling up in her throat as she remembered her mother's loving words and kisses; she loved her mam and she hoped that one day Margaret would understand her need for freedom. Her father, on the other hand, she knew would simply be furious that she had gone. Knowing him too well, she also knew her mother's warning would come true: she would not be welcome if she were to return home. From now on she was on her own and she would have to make the best of it; but it was a challenge that she was determined to embrace with open arms, she thought, and she went on her way, smiling at her fellow travellers as she walked the last four miles to her new life.

* * *

Eve stood on Crown Point Bridge as she took in the sights of the busy town. She had been to Leeds just once before with her parents but only as a child when she had found the town an exciting place, full of wondrous things, and now, at just sixteen, she was even more enthralled by the business of the place. In front of her stood the busy market street of Briggate and behind that was the magnificent building of the Town Hall; to the east and southeast were countless mills, forges and factories while the most fashionable of Leeds made their homes at Headingley and Chapeltown. Of course she knew that the poor of Leeds still lived in squalid conditions with poor sanitation in the back-to-back houses of Holbeck, New Wortley and West Leeds, where death and illness made no exceptions in the crowded streets and money was scarce, too scarce to pay for a doctor's attention if you were taken ill. Eve, however, was too awe-inspired to notice the beggars in dark doorways and the prostitutes, showing their wares along the canal-side. She saw only the monkey on the organ grinder's back and the woman selling flowers and fripperies, the likes of which she had never seen before. The air around her was full of the noise and smells of a busy town and it was intoxicating. She took in all the sights and sounds and vowed to herself never to return to Rothwell to live; this was going to be where she would make her living and home from now on and nobody was going to stop her.

'Hey, watch what you are doing! You nearly knocked me flying.' A young lad stopped her in her tracks, scowling at Eve, who hadn't realised that she had even touched him, let alone nearly knocked him down in the street as she had been taking in the sights. He glared at her, pausing to pick up his hat from the ground before dusting himself down.

'I'm sorry, I didn't realise you were there,' Eve said apologetically. The lad was no more than ten or twelve and he was dressed in a jacket and breeches with a spotted muffler around his neck. His face was streaked with dirt and grime but his eyes were of the brightest forget-me-not blue.

'Bloody well watch what you are doing next time,' he mumbled and then went on his way, whistling as he pushed through the crowd.

Eve bent down and picked up her bag, walking on and looking in the windows of the many shops, admiring all the latest fashions and accessories that Leeds had to offer as she walked up through the busy market street. She became aware that the day was coming to an end and that the stallholders and tradesmen were preparing for the evening, tidying their patches up and swilling down the pavement where blood and fish guts had been dropped from their stalls. She looked around her; finding a place to sleep was her priority now, somewhere she would be safe for the night. To her left, she saw a sign on the wall just to the right of an archway leading to a yard, which read:

Bed and Board available here, no drink allowed.
Respectable people only. 6d per night.

Eve stood at the entrance to the yard and looked down the dirty flag stoned alleyway. On one side was the Binks Hotel and, on the other, a tea room called Morley's, but right at the very back of the yard was a double-windowed small cottage with a notice of VACANCIES in its window. She picked up her skirts and made her way down the yard, passing the hotel, which was full of rowdy market traders having a gill before they returned home and then lifted the door knocker in the shape of a gloved hand on the green-painted cottage door. Her stomach churned as she waited for the door to be opened; she'd never stayed the night away from home before and she had no real idea of what to expect. Eventually, a stout man came to the door and looked her up and down.

'I'm looking for a bed for the night, preferably a room of my own, although I wouldn't mind sharing with another woman.' Eve looked at the red-faced man and felt even more vulnerable.

'Aye, well, we've got a bed you can have, but we'll not be wanting you to be bringing men back to entertain and we don't encourage drink on our property. There's enough of that goes on at that bloody place.' The man scowled and looked across at where cheering could be heard coming from the Binks Hotel and echoing around the yard.

'No, sir, I'll not be doing either. All I want is a bed and perhaps a bite to eat if you can provide that also,' Eve said quietly.

'Aye, well, you look respectable enough. Now show us your money; it'll be sixpence for a bed and a further penny if you eat with us this evening. I like to make sure we get paid before you enter our home because we've learned from experience that it's better to take for folks' keep when they arrive rather than when they leave — that's when you find out they've not a penny to their name,' the owner of the cottage said with a sigh.

'Of course, sir, I wouldn't expect any different.' Eve put her bag down; her arm ached from carrying it and she was just relieved that she had found a good honest house in which to stay the night. She put her hand in her skirt pocket and reached for her small purse with the two shillings that she had so diligently saved. It didn't come to her hand and she felt deeper into her pocket, her face flushing in embarrassment as panic set in. The purse wasn't there! Her skirt pocket was empty, which meant she'd not got a penny to her name.

'I-I'm sorry,' she stammered. 'I can't find my purse! It was in my pocket when I left home and now it's gone!' Eve felt tears welling up in her eyes and she looked for sympathy from the man, who just shook his head and turned his back on her.

'It's always the same; you young lasses think we were born yesterday. You come into Leeds with no money, thinking you can make it by selling yourselves to any Tom, Dick or Harry, like the whores you are. Well, it'll not happen under me and my old woman's roof. No brass, no bed.'

And with that, he slammed the door shut, leaving Eve in tears on the doorstep. She'd no bed, her stomach was empty and, worse still, she had no money to her name and all she could hear were her mother's words of warning going around in her head. What she was going to do now she didn't know, but the prospect of being in a large town at night and on her own scared her terribly, especially as she passed the rowdy hotel and made her way back onto the wide street of Briggate. She couldn't return home — she just couldn't. It would mean losing face and her father would beat her for not obeying him and her mother. Suddenly the vibrant and exciting town of Leeds looked dark and foreboding; she was now on her own with no family and not a friend in the world as she wandered down the now-deserted market street.

'Hello, dearie, just come from the country, have you? You'll not get any trade looking as miserable as that.' A woman dressed in a low-cut bodice and a vibrantly coloured skirt leaned over Eve as she sat in a darkened doorway, resting her aching feet. 'Your face is bonny enough, mind, but you need more swagger.' The prostitute looked down at her and laughed. 'You're on Bert Bradshaw's patch too, so mind he doesn't catch you, else he'll take you for what he can get out of you and then you'll soon not be looking so prim and proper.' She stood up and looked Eve up and down. Under her scrutiny, Eve stood silent and clutched her bag tightly without replying.

'Too posh to talk to an old tart like me, are you? Well, you'll not be so high and mighty after a night or two on the streets. You listen to me: this is no place for a fresh-faced slip of a thing like you. Go back home and think yourself lucky that you bumped into Bonfire Nell on this night and followed her advice. Lord knows I should have done the same myself a long time ago.' Nell watched as Eve still said nothing but picked her skirts up and started to nearly run down the street, just to get out of the way of the outspoken whore.

'Go back home, lass. It's never too late to do that rather than end up on the streets like me!' Nell yelled after her as she watched Eve disappear into the darkness.

Eve shivered and shook as she turned the corner down into Warwick Street, the words of Nell the prostitute ringing in her ears. Perhaps she should return home; a belting from her father and a lecture or two would surely be better than having nowhere to spend the night and no food. How had she lost her money? She thought that she'd been so careful, had put it deep within the pockets of her skirt and it should have been secure there. If she'd had her money, it would have made all the difference; she'd have been safe and secure in the rooming house and not be wandering the streets being mistaken for a woman of the night. Then she remembered her incident with the young urchin boy on the bridge. Had he picked her pockets while she stood engrossed in the new scenes? He must have done. Oh, how could she have been so stupid as not to have looked after her money more carefully? She knew that no one was to be trusted in the town. Eve hung her head; nothing was turning out the way she had imagined it would and everything that her mother had warned her of was coming true . . .

Eve lifted her head as the clock in the church tower struck midnight. She was ravaged by hunger, not having eaten since her breakfast early that morning so she'd walk the streets until morning and then return home, like the prodigal daughter she was and just hope that her parents

12

would forgive her. She walked down the cobbled Walker Street, stopping for a second outside the Bluebell Inn, gazing through its mucky windows and noticing that it was empty except for the landlord sitting down at a table enjoying a late supper. She could smell his plate of beef stew as the steam from it escaped out of the open window above her head. Her stomach growled and she felt pangs of hunger as she stood on her tiptoes looking in at the empty inn, her nose pressed against the window and her mouth dribbling at the sight of the landlord dipping a hefty slice of bread in the broth. She stepped back quickly as the man spied her and turned to walk away when she saw him get up from the table and make for the inn's door.

'Hey, not so fast,' the burly man shouted after her. 'What are you doing out at this time of night? You don't look the kind to be wandering the streets. Stop, lass. Don't run away.'

Eve ignored his shouts, walking quickly down the street, not daring to look backward, her heart beating faster when she heard the man striding out behind her. Suddenly his hand was on her shoulder.

'Just stop for a second. I'm not going to hurt you but there's plenty out there that will.' Theodore Lambert pulled on Eve's shoulder and turned her around. 'I saw you looking in and I want to know what a sweet young lass like you is doing out here in the night?' Theodore looked at the fear on Eve's face.

'I didn't mean to disturb you,' she said. 'It's just that I saw your lamps were still lit and I smelt the supper you were eating. But I'll be on my way now.' Eve looked up into Theodore's kindly face and saw that he meant her no harm.

'On your way to where? I can't help but notice the bag you are carrying — have you left home?' Theodore stood back and looked at the pretty lass in front of him. She wasn't the sort who stood on a street corner at that time of night like so many in Leeds. She was a fresh young thing, straight from home if he knew the signs, but she'd be at the mercy of any man who decided to take advantage of her if she wasn't careful.

Eve hung her head; this was the first time since her arrival in Leeds that someone had actually shown any true kindness towards her. 'I left home first thing this morning and I aimed to find lodgings and work,' Eve began, trying to control the tears that were welling up in her eyes. 'But I lost all my money and now I'm going to have to return home and admit that I was foolish to think that I could make a new life for myself here in Leeds.' She snivelled and then looked at Theodore, hoping that he really was not the sort of man to take advantage of her.

'Have you eaten? Are you hungry?' Theodore looked at the young lass standing in front of him and felt pity — as well as knowing that she was just the sort of lass he needed, desperate and on her own.

'I've not eaten since early this morning, sir. That's what attracted me to your inn, the smell of your supper.' Eve dared not look at the man as he smiled at her.

'Then we can soon remedy that; there's more

14

than enough beef stew in the pan in my kitchen. Come and fill your belly at least.' Theodore had seen plenty of young women come into the growing town of Leeds — and he'd seen plenty of them fall upon hard times and enter the oldest trade of all. He'd made it his business not to encourage them at the Bluebell — he was trying to build the reputation of the place and prostitutes dallying for trade around its doors wouldn't help him do that. At the same time, a bonny face behind his bar was always appreciated by his mostly male drinkers.

'I thank you, sir, but I shouldn't enter an inn; it's against my family's beliefs.' Eve looked at the man who was offering her food that she was desperate for and was sorely tempted by his kindness.

'And would your family want you to go hungry and cold and to wander these streets putting yourself at risk? I can offer you some supper and even a roof over your head for the night if you are happy to stay in such a heathen place as the Bluebell. If you are worried that my attentions are not honourable, I can assure you that they are. My wife, Mrs Lambert, runs the inn with me and ourselves and our four children live above the bar. We have a spare room in the attic that you can sleep in, so at least you will be safe with us tonight and then you can be on your way in the morning, if you wish.' Theodore looked at the lass who should never have left home and hoped that she trusted him enough to accept his offer. Although he was nowhere near perfect himself, he knew that the notorious Bert

15

Bradshaw, who ran and owned many a whorehouse down by the canal docks and preyed on those who came looking for their fortune in the growing town, would soon get wind of her arrival and take her under his so-called protective wing.

'I don't know ... I shouldn't. I don't know you. How do I know I can trust you?' Eve wavered in her thoughts as the temptation of something to eat and a bed for the night swayed her into giving the offer time of day.

'Trust me, I might like my gambling and run an inn, but you'll be safe while you are under my roof. My old lass will see to that and she'd want me to bring you back with me, instead of seeing you wandering the streets. I'd get a right earful if I told her that I let you go on your way. Come, give me your bag and come in and get warm and fill your belly and then, if you want to stay the night, you can and be on your way in the morning.' Theodore reached for Eve's bag and smiled as she handed it to him hesitantly.

'I'll welcome some supper, sir, but I will reserve my thoughts on staying the night if you don't mind.' Eve wondered if she should be trusting this burly but apparently kind-hearted man; after all, she wasn't a naïve girl — he might have other plans for her if she stayed the night under his roof.

'The devil will not get your soul for one night's stay in my abode. Now, what's your name? It would help if I can tell my old lass that and assure her that you are of good character.' Theodore walked her back up the badly lit cobbled street to where the oil lamps of the Bluebell shone brightly out into the gloom.

'I'm Eve Reynolds, sir. I'm from Rothwell, my father works for the Temple Newsam estate and I can honestly say that I am from a good upbringing.' Eve nearly had to run to keep up with Theodore as they reached the Bluebell Inn's steps.

'Well, Eve Reynolds, look after your soul because you're very welcome at the Bluebell Inn. We might serve drink here and have the odd gambling night and I'm known as a hard man, but I'll not have the low of the old town taking advantage of such a bonny little thing like you. Too many young lasses go that way, but at least tonight you'll be safe.' Theodore climbed the two steps up into the main bar of the Bluebell Inn and held the door open for Eve to join him in the low-ceilinged, wooden-floored barroom.

Eve had never been into an inn before and as she looked around her, she felt as if she was committing a terrible wrong and could only think what her parents would have said. She'd heard many a time that drink and those who served it were the implements of the devil and yet, there she stood as bold as brass, in the bar area of the Bluebell. The walls were brown with tobacco smoke and the smell of beer and food mingled together in the air. The inn did not look quite as inviting as it had done from outside when she'd wished for the warmth of the dying fire. The long wooden bar had a tall mirror behind it, surrounded by various bottles of drink in all shapes and sizes and ale jugs stood along

17

the length of the bar while an array of spittoons lined the wooden floor, placed at regular intervals for easy use of drinkers.

'I shouldn't be here,' Eve said as she turned around, looking like a frightened rabbit that wanted to bolt into the safety of its burrow.

'Nay, you are all right. I'll yell for my Nancy; happen the sight of my old woman will calm your nerves and then you can sit and eat some stew with us.' Theodore pulled out a chair from beside one of the many tables and motioned for her to sit down upon it. 'Nancy! Get your arse down here! We've a visitor,' he bellowed as he made his way behind the bar and pulled a long curtain to one side that obviously led to the inn's living quarters.

'For lawks sake, Theo, keep your voice down, the baby's only just settled,' a voice called back from behind the curtain. 'What are you doing, asking folk in at this time of night? Don't they know we want our sleep like any other decent souls?' Nancy Lambert emerged from behind the curtain with her hair in rags and her nightdress on. She was as broad as she was tall and waddled as she walked towards Eve. 'Who's this, then? And what is she doing sitting there?' She looked at Theo and then at Eve and put her hands on her ample hips.

'This is Miss Eve Reynolds and she has fallen upon hard times while visiting our great town of Leeds. She's lost what money she had when she started out and has nowhere to stay tonight. And I, being the good soul that I am, have offered her supper and board — that is, if she will accept my offer.' Theodore slapped his wife on the back.

'Eve, is it? Well, you match your pretty name, just look at those bonny red cheeks and those long golden ringlets! No wonder my Theo saved you from the streets.' Nancy smiled a sickly smile at Eve and then gave a warning glance at her husband.

'I really shouldn't be here. I'm grateful for your offer but my parents would not —' Eve stopped in mid-sentence.

'Get her some stew, Mother, and a chunk of that bread. Here, come nearer the fire, it may be only September but there's a nip in the air.' Theo insisted Eve move her chair nearer to the fire and Nancy spooned a dish full of beef stew from out of the pot that was bubbling on the range, passing it to her together with a spoon before going behind the curtain yet again and returning with some crusty bread, which she put on the nearest table.

'Here, you look half-starved, get this inside you and then see how you feel. My Theo is a devil for wanting his own way and he's such a big brute of a man nobody dares say no to him. But really, he's as soft as muck once you know him.' Nancy sat down next to her, while Theo went behind the bar and tidied the empty drinking tankards that still needed his attention.

Eve looked at the stew; she was so hungry and the smell tempted her so much, making her mouth salivate. She looked across at Nancy, who urged her to pick up the spoon and eat.

'You could do with a good dinner in you by the looks of you,' Nancy chuckled as Eve could

19

resist no longer and started to eat quickly.

'Not everybody wants a fine figure like yours, my old lass. You leave Eve be, she'll catch many a man's eyes looking like she does.' Theo winked at them both.

'Aye, that's the trouble, Eve. If you go back out there tonight, who knows who will take a fancy to you and not all are as kind and generous as my Theo here. Why don't you stay the night? The top attic bedroom's spare and the bed's aired. Up until yesterday, our barmaid was living in it, but she decided to run away with some soldier from the barracks, without so much as a by-your-leave. The little madam!' Nancy growled.

Eve ate her supper quickly, deciding it was the best stew she had ever tasted and she suddenly felt warm and content as she looked around her and pondered her situation. 'But I've no money to pay for my stay and you've done enough by feeding me . . . ' She felt sleepy and the temptation of staying a night at the inn instead of on the streets was beginning to win her over.

'Makes no difference to us, lass, whether the room is empty or slept in and you are better in here with us than out there.' Theo moved her empty plate away and smiled.

'Stay, just until the morning and then you can be on your way. At least then I can sleep tonight, knowing that you're safe under our roof — and I'm sure your mother would also want that, even though we may not be the kind of company you're used to keeping.' Nancy patted Eve's hand and smiled.

'I *am* tired and I must admit I'm not relishing

the idea of sleeping on the streets. And I promise I will repay your kindness when I'm able to.' Eve looked at both her hosts and admitted that what they said made sense.

'That's settled then, Mother, so show her to the attic room and let me make safe the bar for this evening because it'll be light before you know it and Thwaites brewery will knock on my door with a new delivery of ale,' Theo said loudly and grabbed his tea towel again, looking at the dirty tankards that he still had to wash.

'Come, Eve, we aren't the biggest of places but we keep a clean house and bar and there's all you need in the attic bedroom, so you make yourself comfortable for the night and then we will see what tomorrow brings.' Nancy took a lighted oil lamp from the bar and led Eve up the creaking dark oak stairs to the bedroom in the loft. The room was sparsely furnished but there was all that she needed there: a bed, a washstand with a jug and bowl filled with water upon it, a small wardrobe — and she spied a chamber pot under the bed. There was also a bolt on the inside of the door, Eve was relieved to see, for although the Lamberts seemed friendly enough, she didn't want any unwanted intrusions from either of them. She watched as Nancy lit her a candle by the bedside.

'I'll leave you with that; try not to burn it too long for candles cost money and we are always trying to save the odd penny here and there.' Nancy smiled and then left, closing the door behind her and leaving Eve deep in thought.

Eve sat on the edge of the bed and looked

around her, then stared at the bag full of the only possessions that she had in the world. With no money and no job, she would have to go back home, there was nothing more that she could do. She got up and bolted the door, then undressed and washed in the cold water on the washstand before climbing into the bed that lay directly under the skylight. There she lay watching the dark clouds of the night scuttle across the sky by the light of the moon. Her parents had warned her about Leeds and they had been right, in part, but seemingly they had been wrong when it came to innkeepers, at least in the case of the Lamberts, who had shown her nothing but kindness. She would have to try and repay them in some way come the morning, she found herself thinking, as the long day got the better of her and her eyes began to droop and feel heavy. She was warm, safe and off the street, that was all that mattered. Tomorrow was another day and she'd decide what to do then.

★　★　★

'What have you gone and brought a bloody Bible-bashing do-gooder into the likes of this house for, Theodore Lambert? It's like bringing a lamb into a den of wolves!' Nancy, her face an angry red, stood at the bar and swore under her breath at her husband as he put everything back in its place for the next day, pouring himself a generous measure of gin while he did so.

'You know very well why I've brought her; we've lost our bloody barmaid and have you not noticed her looks? If we can persuade her to work for us here, the men will flock in their droves to see her pull a pint. She's the bonniest thing Leeds has seen in a long time — and so innocent.' Theo leaned back and downed his tot of gin while he watched his wife get even more annoyed.

'Aye, well, you make sure she stays that way. Don't you be sneaking up those stairs and knocking on her door, I can tell the difference between the rats having a game of dominoes and you having your wicked way astride the barmaid. I don't know why I don't up and leave you as any self-respecting wife should. Well, I would if I had somewhere else to go to and enough money to feed and dress our children. For God's sake, let's try and keep this one if she agrees to work for us, so don't you rock the ship,' Nancy sighed.

'Oh, she'll be staying; she's nothing to go home for and she'll soon be leaving her Bible-reading days behind her, that I'll swear. We'll soon show her the error of her ways.' Theo laughed as he blew the oil lamp out and followed his wife's ample body up to the stairs to their bedroom.

2

Eve lay in the bed high up in the roof space of the Bluebell Inn. Downstairs, even though dawn had just broken, she could hear beer barrels being unloaded from the dray cart and bounced on the cobbled street down into the cellars of the inn. The smells and atmosphere were completely different to those of home. She looked around her at the small room that had obviously belonged to the barmaid before her arrival. There were still hairpins on the dressing table and a dying posy of dog daisies beside them. Had she been happy working here? Eve wondered as she eased herself out of bed and started to dress. The Lamberts certainly seemed an amicable couple, judging from how they had treated her the previous night, but today she would have to decide what to do next.

After finding herself penniless and demoralised by her adventure in Leeds, returning home with her tail between her legs looked like the most obvious solution. She put her head in her hands and sighed. She didn't want to return home; even though Leeds was not all that she had expected it to be, she would rather stay than have to listen to the lectures of her father and be in service in the big house. She wanted more than that. She wiped back a tear and then shaking her head, refreshed her face with cold water from the jug before dressing and looking at herself in the long mirror of the wardrobe. She was young and pretty with a good figure — she could see that — so surely there would be a worthwhile job out there for her this morning; she just had to find it.

★ ★ ★

Nancy Lambert looked up from breastfeeding her youngest next to the newly lighted fire of the inn's kitchen. 'Don't mind me, I'm obliged to feed him as usual, else he'll scream the whole blinking pub down. There might not be much of him, but his lungs certainly work well enough.' Nancy hugged the baby to her and grinned up at Eve before looking down at the guzzling baby. 'My Theodore says I could take a fella's eye out with my breasts! I've always had too much up top, not like you — there's hardly owt there. That'll change once you've had children, everything changes when children come onto the scene.' She concentrated on feeding the baby, not noticing Eve blushing and not knowing quite where to look as Nancy slid her left breast back into her bodice, leaving the ribbon on her top unfastened before placing baby Albert on her knee and gently patting his back to relieve him of wind. 'Sleep well, did you, dearie?' she asked.

'I did sleep well, thank you. How can I repay you before I go on my way home? Now that I'm penniless, I'm not sure how I can.' Eve sighed and watched as baby Albert regurgitated some of his mother's breast milk down onto her hand and apron. Nancy quickly wiped her hand and scowled at the little soul as she placed him to sleep in a cot at the side of the fire.

'Now, not so quick, young miss, we'll not have you going on your way just yet.' Nancy walked to the curtain that separated the kitchen from the bar and pulled it back, yelling Theodore's name down into the dark hole of the cellar, the hatch of which lay open on the floor next to the bar.

Eve felt a moment of panic. What were they going to ask her to do? What if they demanded money? Or even worse, demanding payment in kind.

'Theodore, get your arse up here, our guest says she's leaving!' Nancy bellowed, making the baby momentarily flinch before closing its eyes again to sleep. She turned around to look at Eve and her bag before folding her arms as Theodore climbed up the steps from the cellar. His face trickled with sweat and his striped shirt was wet and stuck to his back as though he had climbed out of hell. He brushed his hands together and stood just inches away from Eve.

'Now, you can't leave us this soon, I need to have a word with you.' Theodore smiled slyly at his wife and then at Eve. 'Right, me and my old lass got talking last night — and I know it's not what you are used to, and it's definitely not something your parents would approve of . . . ' Theo stopped for a moment, watching the horror appear on Eve's face. 'Well, we wondered if you would perhaps consider becoming our new barmaid? You're a bonny enough thing and you'd soon learn the ropes — that way, you'd be helping us out as much as we're helping you out.' Theo looked at the expression on Eve's face

26

and waited for an answer.

'Oh . . . Oh, I do thank you, sir, b-but I don't know what to say. It's not that I don't appreciate your offer, it is just that my family are sworn against the evils of drink and for me to be working here, well, it would break their hearts.' Eve looked around her and thought that she could do a lot worse but everything in her upbringing told her this was not where she belonged. She hung her head and felt disheartened. She had come to Leeds to break away from her family — and yet, here she was saying no to a roof over her head and a job. And the Lamberts might be rough and ready, but their hearts were obviously good.

'Aye, well we expected you'd say as much. If that's the way you've been brought up, we understand. But I can't say that I'm not disappointed, you'd have been just right for the job.' Theodore nodded his head and then made his way back towards the cellar steps to carry on with the job in hand. Before going back down into the darkness, he turned and smiled at Nancy. 'I tried, Mother, but I told you what her answer would be. She's too good for the likes of us.' Theo shook his head and then went back down to the depths of the beer cellar.

'You'll be leaving us, then? You can tell my Theo is disappointed, he really thought that you'd be right good for us and that we would be helping you out at the same time.' Nancy scowled a little at Eve as she reached for her bag and turned to leave the inn.

'Yes, I'm sorry, but I'm truly thankful for my

27

bed for the night and my supper, you've been really kind to me.' Eve hesitated as she stepped out into the busy Walker Street with traders shouting of their wares and early morning shoppers going about their business.

Nancy looked down at Eve from the doorway of the Bluebell. 'Are you going home, then? Or are you looking for employment elsewhere in the town? If it's the second, just be careful about who you talk to, not all are as understanding as Theo and me. And you can always change your mind and come back to us if you decide differently.'

'I don't know, I might have a walk around the town, see if there is any work out there, and, if not, I'll have to go home and admit that I'm wrong and that I should have been grateful for what I had already,' Eve explained, worrying that she seemed ungrateful to her host for the night's stay.

'Well, before you go wandering off, just stay there a minute; you'll need something to eat and I can hear the baker's lad coming in at the back door with our usual delivery. I can at least make sure that you've something in your belly on your walk home.' Nancy turned into the inn and soon came back with a loaf of bread wrapped up in a napkin. 'That'll keep you going, seeing you've not got a penny to your name. We might be unruly, beer-swilling publicans but we do have a little bit of Christian in us.' She came down the steps onto the street and placed the bread in Eve's hands. 'Now, you know where we are if you change your mind.'

'Thank you, you've been nothing but kind and I'll tell my parents that they are wrong to judge so hastily.' Eve looked at Nancy. Her low-cut blouse was still not buttoned up properly and her long, greying hair was not even brushed, let alone made tidy, but still, she could see there was kindness in her eyes.

'Aye, well, it takes all sorts to make a world and you have to make a living where you can. Now, you take care and come back if you decide that you *could* live with us.' Nancy climbed the two steps back into the darkness of the Bluebell, leaving Eve surrounded by the bustling town.

Eve found a quiet place near a water fountain to eat a chunk of the bread Nancy had given her before deciding her plan of action. She didn't want to return home. She knew that her father would gloat in knowing that his and her mother's words had been true — that Leeds was no place for the likes of her; that evil lurked in every corner and that you couldn't trust anybody. She also knew that she would be in for a belting if she was to go back, a thing that she had often experienced when stepping wilfully out of line and not following her father's rules. He would take his thick leather belt from around his waist and, with the buckle end wrapped around his clenched fist, beat her with the leather strap and leave welts across her bare buttocks. No, she couldn't go back! She *wouldn't* go back; she'd find work and lodgings in Leeds somewhere or she would return to the Lamberts at the Bluebell Inn and take up their offer. In fact, the more she thought about it, the more she thought how foolish she had been not to have accepted. They had shown her only kindness and the room that she had slept in was not too bad; in fact, it was not unlike the one that she had left at home.

The thought of serving alcohol and spirits made her smile — that would be the final insult to her father. If he ever found out, he would never want to see her face again, of that she was sure. It was just the thought of her mother bearing the brunt of his wrath that made her hesitant about returning straight away and accepting the Lamberts' offer.

As she tucked into her bread, Eve took notice of her surroundings. By the fountain were children in rags, begging, and women selling posies of heather; further down the street, towards the market that stood on the broad thoroughfare of Briggate, tradesmen were shouting. The town was full of life, more life than she'd see in one year back home in Rothwell. It was almost as if it was begging her to stay, she thought, as she watched customers come and go from the gin shop on the street corner. She watched as an obviously well-to-do woman came out and stopped just outside the shop, so desperate for a drink that she opened her small bottle of gin and took a swig out of it. Eve turned and looked at a man who was shaking his head as he watched the same woman, before he drank from the water fountain.

'Aye, it's a sad sight to see, well-to-do ladies going to the gin shop for their daily dose of Lady Geneva; some can't even wait to get home before they have a tipple,' the old man sighed and wiped his mouth with his jacket sleeve.

'I've never tried it, sir, so I wouldn't know why they do it,' Eve said as she looked up at him.

'They are desperate, lass, and it helps them through the day. It's about time the government put a tax on Lady Geneva to regulate the sellers — at least then it wouldn't be for sale on every street corner or brewed in many a house. Women would have to go to the public houses that are now springing up, which men enjoy so much, instead. They'd think twice about that, for a public house is no place for a lady. Chandlers and stallholders even distil gin and sell it for just a few pence. It's time for sanity to return to this country — even those who can barely afford it rely on gin to get them through the day. Just look at her, a well-to-do lady visiting the gin house to get her tonic, a little pick-me-up to wrap the soul in a comforting blanket and to let her throw caution to the wind. It will be the downfall of this country, you mark my words. Families in this town can't live without it and, as for the streets of London, I believe gin-drinking is even more prevalent there and that all sense has been lost.'

Eve pondered the man's rant. 'I've never drunk anything alcoholic in my life,' she explained again, 'my family does not permit it.' She looked across at the well-dressed woman who was now tucking her bottle of comfort into her posy bag and walking off down the street. Eve watched her weave her way through the crowd and thought that as long as it gave her strength to face the day, what harm was there in it?

'Aye, well keep it that way, don't let the devil

get your soul. Those that drink gin dance with the devil, and then you're of no use to anyone.' The old gentleman tapped his stick on the cobbles of the street and looked down at Eve. 'What brings you to Leeds? You look like a country lass to me. Are you here to make money and your way in the world?' He knocked her bag with his stick and looked at Eve with a gleam in his eye.

'Yes, sir, I'm in need of employment and a place to live,' Eve said innocently, thinking that an elderly sober man would mean her no harm.

'If you are desperate, I can't offer you a place to live but I can offer you a little money for services rendered, if you know what I mean.' The old man leaned down towards her and smiled. 'A whole sixpence for you to lift up your skirts and relieve me of this itch. That alleyway over there will do just fine, no one will see you.' He grinned as he saw Eve take in his words.

'I'm sorry, you've got me wrong, I'm not that sort of a girl! And at your age you shouldn't be taking advantage of my position. I bid you good day, sir, I don't wish to be in your company any longer.' Eve stood up and grabbed her carpetbag, looking at the dirty old man who clearly had conflicted morals; he was quick to judge those who needed a drink to get through the day, but at the same time would take pleasure from forcing himself on someone vulnerable like herself. She walked off across the square towards the market and Briggate, almost running to get out of his earshot as he yelled at her.

'Bitch! Go and ply your trade with someone with the pox and not with a respectable man like me,' the man shouted after her as he turned her rejection around upon her.

Eve could feel her eyes filling with tears as she fled into the market street and hid in the throng there. No matter where she went in Leeds, she had been set upon by horrible people, but surely there were some good people here too, like the Lamberts, the only ones who had shown her kindness since her arrival. Perhaps she should have taken up their offer, she thought again, at least she would have had work and a room of her own.

People jostled her as she walked through Briggate and took in the sights and sounds of the market. The air was filled with the smell of food and was abuzz with the calls of the competing stallholders' voices, all of it making her head dizzy. As she walked towards the end of Briggate, she began thinking that she really would be better to return home. A belting from her father would soon be over and done with, and then she would just have to learn to accept her lot and knuckle down to a life of servitude at Temple Newsam. It really seemed that Leeds wasn't for her. Momentarily distracted by a stall selling tempting oysters, she heard a voice that she recognised call her name.

'Any luck, then? Have you found somewhere to stay and work? There's always the mills out on the outskirts of the town, you know — they're always needing lasses.' Nancy Lambert, a full basket of produce fresh from the market on one arm and her baby balanced on her hip in the other, patted her on her shoulder. She appeared more presentable now, wearing a clean dress and with her hair plaited upon her head.

'No, nothing. I don't think the town is for me, Nancy. I'm beginning to realise that I'm just a country girl and I should go back where I belong,' Eve said and looked at Nancy as she jiggled her baby into a more comfortable position on her hip.

'Well, our offer is still there; we've got that room empty and my Theo will pay you well as long as you're prepared to work and keep yourself to yourself. It might not be what you're used to, but we'd look after you and there's something to be said for a barmaid who doesn't drink. At least we wouldn't have to watch our profits!' Nancy smiled. 'You can come back with me now, settle into the room and start work in the kitchen, cooking with me this afternoon. Theo will teach you what to do behind the bar and you'll soon get used to it.' She smiled again. 'I could do with another set of hands right now! I need some of those turnips from off that stall and was just wondering how to carry everything back.'

'I don't know . . . It isn't what I expected to be doing and there is still the problem with the position not pleasing my parents.' Eve looked at Nancy and her baby.

'Then don't tell them what you're doing! Tell them you're in service at a big house and they'll not know any different unless they come to visit you. Nobody will tell them anything, because your Methodist sort doesn't usually frequent the Bluebell, and so none of them will know that you're working for us.' Nancy noticed Eve's hesitation and urged her to take baby Albert for a moment as she took advantage of Eve's indecision. 'Besides, look at Albert's face, he's taken to you.' Nancy grinned at her youngest offspring as she thrust him into Eve's arms. 'You'll need to work hard and keep secrets when the drink gets the worse of some of our customers, but you'll be fed and homed and you'll be your own woman at least one day a week. You'll not do much better than that for an offer.' Nancy tickled Albert's cheeks and wiped his dribble before it fell on Eve's clean lace collar.

Eve looked at her new ward and then at Nancy, trying to come to terms with her offer. She smiled at baby Albert as he chuckled in her arms. She'd had no dealings with children before and she felt her maternal instincts stir within her as his chubby hands played with the lace on her collar.

'I might regret this . . . but yes — you've got yourself a new barmaid. I don't know the first thing about ale or liquor or how a public house runs, but I can but learn. I'm not exactly in a position to turn your offer down and you've shown me the most kindness since I left home for which I'm truly grateful, so yes . . . I *will* work for you.'

'That's settled then! You are to be the new barmaid at the Bluebell. It's sometimes a noisy house but my Theo keeps it orderly — mostly!

You'll soon get used to the customers and our ways and we will keep our own counsel and expect you to do the same, no matter what goes on behind our walls,' Nancy said, pleased, walking off to the vegetable stall and leaving Eve holding Albert and struggling to pick up her bag to follow her.

'Now, I need some good firm turnips because there's no need to waste that much on expensive meat for pies when they are being fed to drunken men — a bit here and there does, for they know no difference when there's a few gills inside them.' Nancy turned and smiled at the expression on Eve's face. 'You'll soon get used to our ways and it will all make sense.'

As Eve looked on, Nancy turned over the pile of turnips and cabbage and haggled with the stallholder for the best price before parting with her money and placing four turnips in her basket. 'Now, lass, let's go home and tell Theo the good news that he can take the sign down in the window advertising for a new barmaid. The Bluebell will soon be known for having one of the bonniest in Leeds and you'll soon have the drinkers flooding in. It was good luck on our part when Theo spotted you looking lost and weary, so just learn to smile a bit more and how to pour a good pint and all will be well in your life.' Nancy put her now-heavy basket onto her arm and marched off, leaving Eve to follow with the baby and wonder just what she had agreed to and what the next few days were to hold.

3

Before Eve knew it, two months had passed. It wasn't until Nancy suggested that she should take a Sunday off to visit her parents that Eve realised how long she had been working at the Bluebell. It felt as if the days had all merged into one, along with the names and faces that frequented the rowdy bar.

The last couple of months had certainly been eye-opening for her, with people from all walks of life visiting the inn: from the bank managers who did their business in the well-to-do area of King Street and stopped by to indulge in a quick brandy, to the washerwoman who made her living in one of the backstreet yards and came in every day for her mid-afternoon tot of gin. But it was the evening when things were liveliest. That was when the working men came in for drinks of porter and ale, leering at her over the bar as they drowned their sorrows, expecting her to listen or flirting with her in the hope of a quick grope or a kiss.

While Eve had only been there a short time, she had quickly learned the ropes, knowing how much water to add to a man's drink if she thought that he had drunk enough alcohol and what to say in return if his words were too suggestive. She'd grown up quickly and the country lass was now holding her own among the town folk of Leeds.

She looked around the empty room as she cleared stray tankards from the small wrought-iron tables that were positioned around the bar on the scrubbed oak floor. The air smelled of tobacco smoke and ale, and the curtains reeked of both as she tied them back, letting the early morning light shine into the room. On the wall behind the bar hung a large mirror, embellished with grapes and cherubs. When Eve saw her reflection, she noticed how pale she looked. Working inside all day was not doing her complexion any good, she thought, plus it had been a late night of drinking the previous evening, with some punters leaving in the early hours of the morning.

Perhaps her walk back to Woolford to see her parents would give her a bit of colour in her cheeks. She was dreading seeing them, but even though she knew that she would eventually have to tell them the truth, she had decided that, for now, all they needed to know was that she was safe and in employment. She'd decided to do as Nancy had suggested and not tell them the whole truth, only that she had been taken on as a housemaid to a decent family in the centre of Leeds so they need not worry about her. After all, it was nearly the truth — the Lamberts were a decent family although, of course, Theo was known to have his moments of swearing and bad temper and was all for making a shilling or two any way he could. Nancy concentrated on bringing her family up and running the kitchen as economically as possible, while giving cheek to any drunkard that caused any of them bother.

She also kept Theo in line when he became a little too familiar with some of the ladies who frequented the Bluebell. But on the whole, they were good folk and they had treated her well, respecting her privacy and teaching her their trade.

It had been a shock to her system, the first few weeks, when she realised just how drunken people could get and how much nonsense they talked when inebriated, but now she took it in her stride and looked to Theo for support if a bargeman or dock worker said something too crude to her. They'd soon be told to shut up, or drink up and get out. Another few weeks, she thought, and she'd be as tough as Nancy and Theo and would suffer no cheek from anyone.

The chiming of the clock told her the time was six thirty and if she was to walk home to Woolford and back in the day, she had better stir her shanks. She stopped clearing the bar and grabbed her shawl from the room behind the inn. Then she unbolted the heavy back door which led onto the inn's yard and stables. All was quiet as she closed the door behind her; the Lambert family were making the most of it being Sunday morning after hosting a late-night drinking session behind closed doors with some of their favourite customers. Even baby Albert seemed to know better than to wake up early — either that or Nancy had given him a few drops of laudanum before putting him down to sleep, giving his mother the peace she craved in the morning.

The midden in the yard smelt strong as she

stepped past the stable door, and the ageing bay draught horse snorted and watched her as she wrapped her shawl around her shoulders and made her way out of the yard onto Walker Street and down through the alleyways that were starting to feel familiar. It was cold in the shadow of the tall buildings that dominated the streets and the town was relatively quiet. The only people stirring were a milkman and his horse and cart and the homeless beggars down by the canal docks who always looked hungry and bedraggled.

As Eve walked over the sturdy metal structure of Crown Point Bridge, she remembered the young lad who had bumped into her when she'd first arrived in Leeds — and made out it was her fault. She was now certain that it had been him who had stolen her money, pickpocketing her chance of a decent life in Leeds. She shook her head. It was of little consequence now; she had a good life at the Bluebell, the only problem being that her parents would not understand or approve. How she wished that she could tell them the truth about her employment with the Lamberts.

* * *

Eve's heart was heavy and her stomach churned with every step taken in the direction of home. Her father would not have been happy about her leaving and he would have blamed her mother for letting her go. Now she would have to face him and lie to them both, something that she

40

had never done before in her life. Hopefully, once they knew that she was doing well, they would forgive her and realise that a quiet country life was not for her, that she had never wanted to go into service at the big house and end up marrying one of the local miners. She'd always dreamed of more, and working at the Bluebell was just the beginning. She would eventually find a better position, or perhaps she would catch the eye of a town gent; there were many even now who gave her the odd happence in tips just because she was pleasing to watch pulling their pint.

She'd watched and learned from the women who visited the Bluebell and had soon realised that pulling pints was not the only way a young woman with good looks and a nice figure could make a living. Not that she would ever sell herself on the streets as some women did, but if men were willing to wine and dine her without expecting anything in return, then she wouldn't say no. There was no harm in that, she thought, and plucked up her courage as her old home came into sight.

Her stomach churned as she opened the front gate. She knew exactly what her parents would be doing. Having attended chapel earlier that morning, her mother would be cooking dinner and her father would either be catching up on the news from his next-door neighbour or reading his Bible. Sunday at home was a day of rest, and Eve's mind went back to long, quiet days of not being able to do anything other than write to distant relations or help her mother

41

wash the dishes, to the feeling of being stifled by the Sunday Bible reading and the expectation that she would always toe the family line. She stood for a second in the ancient porch and calmed herself before knocking gently on the heavy oak door and pushing it open. It took a second or two for her eyes to adjust to the darkness within but there, just as she had expected, was her mother setting the dinner table while a pot of beef stew bubbled on the fire, and her father was reading his Bible by the fireside.

Her father looked up and scowled at her. 'So, you've decided to show your face. I wondered how long it would take.'

'I've just come to visit and let you know that I'm all right. I have safe lodgings and work with a good family in Leeds.' Eve felt tense at the lie but she really didn't want to tell them the whole story.

'Well, no matter where you are working, it's good to see you,' her mother said, crossing the room to her. 'I've missed you and we parted on such bad terms, so I'm just glad you're here. I worried about you every night after you left until James Fleet said he'd seen you and we knew you were safe.' Margaret Reynolds hugged her daughter tight and then stepped back and looked at her, scrutinising her deeply.

'James Fleet? Who is James Fleet and where did he see me at?' Eve was shocked that she had been spotted in Leeds and even more so that her whereabouts had been reported back to her parents.

'Aye, you should well look worried, bringing your wayward ways back under my roof on the Sabbath,' her father seethed, standing up next to the fireplace. 'James Fleet is the new coachman at the big house and he only saw you the once when you brought me my dinner there but he recognised you serving behind the bar at that place of sin. He told me you were making eyes at all the men and that you served him with a pint of bitter, just as though you'd be doing it all your life. So don't you dare tell me you've got a respectable job with a good family! You can turn and go back to that godforsaken spot he called the Bluebell. You are not welcome in my house any more, I'm done with trying to mend your ways. You're no daughter of mine.' Isaac shook his head, then stared at Eve. 'I want you to leave this house and not return. You are wilful and deceitful, a wicked daughter, so the devil can take care of you from now on.'

'Think about what you are saying, Isaac,' Eve's mother pleaded. 'Eve is our daughter, our own flesh and blood. Please, you cannot wash your hands of her just because she's working in a public house. She's our lass and I need her.' Margaret linked her hand with Eve's, holding back tears.

'It's all right, Mother,' Eve said. 'I knew what Father would say once he found out. I've always been a disappointment to him, never taking to the Bible and the preaching within it. I'd rather go than stay and be a hypocrite like him.' Eve pulled her shawl around her and kissed her mother on the cheek.

'Oh, stay, stay and have some dinner with us. Surely, Isaac, the lass can do that? You'd not cast her out on the Sabbath and send her back hungry?' Margaret pleaded with her husband.

'Let her be gone; she knew what she was doing when she decided to make her own way in the world. So hold your tongue, woman.' Isaac sat back down and stared into the fire, not looking at his wife or daughter.

'Don't worry, Mother, I'll write. I'll be all right — the folk at the Bluebell are good to me and I'm not going without anything.' Eve hugged her mother and then gave a final glance at her family home. She left her mother crumpled and crying at the kitchen table and her father dark and brooding, watching the simmering pot of stew. This was the last time she would visit home, she thought, as she fought back the tears and closed the door behind her. She had a new life now, a life that she was going to make the most of, whether the devil had her soul or not.

4

Five months later

'Come on, Eve, stir your arse and stop flirting with that bit of a lad. Me and Ma Huddleston are dying of thirst here!' Henry Twisleton, a regular at the Bluebell, yelled across the bar as he and the old woman who came in every lunchtime for a quick tot of gin watched as Eve giggled and laughed with the latest lad to catch her eye.

'Oh, hold your noise, Henry, you've not been standing there long,' Eve shouted back, winking at the young man she had been busy plying with drink as she went to serve the elderly man who always complained and who she knew would only drink half a pint of dark porter and then be on his way. The young man, however, if suitably entertained, might spend every penny he had in his pocket across the bar of the Bluebell. 'Half of porter, is it then, Henry, and a tot of Old Tom for you, Mrs Huddleston?'

Ma Huddleston nodded her head and held out payment in her mitted hand. Her face was weathered and her hair grey, while the clothes she had on had seen better days, but despite her appearance, it was rumoured that the old girl was worth a small fortune. She watched as Eve went about her business, eagerly awaiting her afternoon tipple from the white-striped pottery barrel behind the bar. Eve quickly measured out her usual, passing it to her with a smile and thanking her for her money, before the older woman went to sit in her usual corner; which she would leave in about an hour and then return to on exactly the same hour the following day.

Eve poured Henry's porter into a pewter mug and passed it to him across the bar. 'That will be a penny, Henry.' She looked at Henry as he fumbled in his waistcoat pocket for his change. He always did the same thing every time he came in. Paying in ha'pennys and farthings, drawing out paying for his drink as long as possible and making other customers wait for her service. Eventually, after counting his coins on the bar, he pushed them across for Eve to take.

'Is it right what I hear?' Henry leaned over and whispered to Eve, his stale breath nearly making her feel sick.

'It depends what you've heard, Henry; I'm not a mind reader.' Eve looked at him after placing the coin in the brass-plated till behind the bar.

'Theo's going to be holding dog baiting and cockerel fights in the yard behind. That'll bring him in a pretty penny or two, but it'll attract the wrong sort, never mind the peelers if they find out.' Henry grinned.

'Aye, that's right. Not that I'm for it. Who can be so callous as to watch two dogs tear one another apart? You'll not be getting me watching, Theo knows that, so he's taken on a new barmaid for this coming weekend — Jill Swinthwaite from the Cock and Bottle — she's used to rowdier drinkers because that place is crawling with them.' Eve shook her head, showing her disdain of the Lamberts' new moneymaking scheme.

'Aye, but he'll make money, especially if he runs a book at the same time for the bets. He'll get good crowds, but he'll have to keep it quiet.' Henry touched his nose with his finger and then moved off to join Ma Huddleston at her table in the corner, where Eve could hear them discussing the up-and-coming event that everyone seemed to know about, despite only a selected few customers being asked to watch the latest sporting attraction.

Eve stood back and sighed, looking around her at all the now-familiar faces. She knew everyone in the pub: what they drank, where they lived, who they were married to, what worries they had. It was her job, as a barmaid, to listen to their cares as they drowned their sorrows of a night and slobbered over the bar, perhaps trying to chat her up when the beer was talking. She enjoyed working here but life in the Bluebell was getting a bit repetitive. And now, with this new barmaid coming to work for a weekend, Eve felt a little threatened. Although it was of her own doing for refusing to have anything to do with the cruel sport, meaning they had no choice but to draft in Jill's help. But it didn't stop Eve from worrying that the drinkers might prefer her services.

'Another gill, darling, if you please?' The young man leaned over the bar and smiled at her. 'Have you always worked here?'

'For about eight months, now,' Eve replied while she pulled him a pint of the locally brewed ale.

'Then I should have been drinking in here

earlier.' The man passed her his payment for the pint and reached for Eve's hand as she took his money, holding her by the wrist and not letting her go, despite Eve protesting. 'How about a kiss with this, just to sweeten it?'

'You let me go, I'm not that sort of a girl!' Eve pulled on her arm but his grip got tighter. 'You were keen enough to talk to me before, winking and smiling. I know your sort, can't wait to lift your skirts for a penny or two.' The man pulled her towards him, scratching her bare arm on the edge of the bar.

'Theo! Theo, help!' Eve yelled through to the back room, hoping that either he or Nancy would come to her aid. 'You let me go, else it will be the worse for you. I'm not interested in you or what you have in your trousers.'

'We'll soon see about that.' The man tried to pull Eve over the bar, not caring that he was leaving welts on her skin. He just laughed at her complaints while the locals, who knew and respected Eve, yelled at the man to release her.

'Let go of her now, else you'll get the best hiding you've ever had in your life, boy!' Theo tapped the man on his shoulder and stood threateningly behind him. 'And then you can get yourself out of my public house.'

'Oh, I see how it is. You're first in line, are you?' The man smirked as he let go of Eve and turned towards Theo. 'We can look but we can't touch, eh?'

Theo lifted up his fist, threatening to smash the gobby upstart in the mouth.

'No, Theo, don't! We don't know who he is

48

and he might report you to the peelers.' Eve ran around to the other side of the bar and pulled on Theo's arm. 'Leave him be, perhaps I did lead him on a bit and he's had five pints. He's just the worse for drink.'

Theo's arm halted in mid-air as he held the man by the throat. 'You piss off and don't come back in! My barmaids demand respect. If you want the other sort, go and drink in the Black Swan — I'm sure Bonfire Nell will be able to accommodate you. Now, let me escort you to the door.' Theo grabbed the man by the scruff of the neck and, although he protested, the burly landlord was too strong for him, bustling him out onto busy Warwick Street.

'You owe me a pint, you bastard!' the man yelled.

Theo shouted back into the bar for Eve to bring him a pint as the angry lad continued swearing from outside.

'Here, have your pint, I'd hate to deprive you of it.' Theo threw the contents of the tankard over the young man's head and laughed as he stood drenched and swearing. 'Next time, learn to hold your liquor and your manners — now bugger off and leave me and mine alone,' Theo stood on the Bluebell's steps and watched as the young man staggered off down the street with folk looking at him. He shook his head and went back into the bar, where he saw Eve was nearly in tears. 'Go and have ten minutes on your own, lass, settle your nerves. The bastard won't be coming back, but perhaps you should learn to hold your own with such like or perhaps not flirt quite so much. Gentlemen are few and far between, my lass, especially in public houses. It's just as well I've taken on Jill from the Cock and Bottle for the weekend — she gives as good as she gets.'

'I'd have been all right; somebody would have helped me.' Eve wiped a tear away.

'What? One of these old codgers that we have in at this time of day? Go and compose yourself and come back down for the evening rush. Now, I don't doubt that the real trouble will begin this weekend. So you, my girl, stay behind that bar and let Jill serve on in the yard. It's a hard crowd that comes to watch the dog baiting I've been to and I'm not having the prettiest barmaid in Leeds sullied by rough hands.' Theo offered her a comforting smile before continuing, 'However, I need to make money to keep the wolf from the door and those sorts like to spend their brass and have entertainment, so I'm prepared to oblige. Especially now that the infantry is back in town; they've always more brass than sense.' Theo looked Eve up and down, knowing she still had no real idea of the ways of Leeds, which only made her more appealing to some of his drinkers.

Eve made her way up to her bedroom. She hadn't realised just how scared she had been until her legs started shaking on the last flight of stairs to her attic bedroom. Her arm was bruised, blues and purples beginning to show where the man's hands had been and the bottom of her ribs ached from being knocked against the wooden bar. She hadn't meant to flirt with him, she'd just wanted him to spend his money in the Bluebell and not anywhere else. But even Henry Twisleton had accused her of flirting as he yelled for her attention over the bar.

Eve closed her bedroom door behind her and went to lie down on her bed. Hugging her pillow, she thought about her life and what she could have done if she had not been so headstrong. Perhaps her parents had been right — she should have stayed at home and become a parlour maid at the big house. Even twelve months on, serving in one of the busiest public houses in Leeds, she knew she still didn't really fit in. And when she tried to, like now, it backfired on her. She couldn't return home, though, her father had made that quite clear. Her mother had not replied to her letters of late, and recently, Nancy had shown her little love. She shook her head sorrowfully, knowing she was trapped in a world of her own making. To make matters worse, the pub's clientele would alter for the worse once the abhorrent dog baiting took place. She would have to learn to toughen up or find the right man to take her away from all of it, one who was rich and kind and could offer her a good lifestyle. She wasn't stupid; she knew the chances of that were highly unlikely, given the trade she was in, but she could dream. She let the thought linger as she closed her eyes and slipped into sleep.

★ ★ ★

'I don't know why you took her on in the first place, Theo. You knew she came from Bible-reading stock and that she would be a sheep amongst wolves, as they would say.' Nancy shook her head at her husband as she folded her washing and watched her youngest two squabble over a kitten that they had been given. 'And don't think I've not noticed the way you look at her of late. I'll not be having you creeping up to her room at all hours of the night, thinking that this old bat is asleep. I know your tricks, Theodore Lambert, and I've put up with them before, but I'll not put up with them again.' She scowled across at her husband as he told her about the latest incident with Eve.

'She means well, Nancy, she just doesn't realise that men take her the wrong way. Some are perfect gentlemen with her and don't expect anything but a smile, but others like you say expect a little more than cheap flattery for their money, as happened this afternoon. As for me, you're reading it all wrong. Why would I go creeping up to that bag of bones when I've got a fine figure of a woman like you to satisfy me?' Theodore grabbed Nancy by the waist and fondled her breasts in order to quell her fears of him wandering.

'Give over, Theo, not in front of the children! We need to set a good example,' Nancy protested, blushing, and pushed him away. 'But I'm telling you, no matter what you think, unless she changes her ways, I say her time is limited here because she relies too much on you sorting her mistakes out for her. Jill Swinthwaite will show her how to handle men when she comes to work for us. They get no joy from her rough tongue but they still come back for more of it because they know it's all sauce and that she could put them in their place straight away if they stepped out of line. That's what we need behind the bar, not a soft country lass who doesn't swear or drink. Truly, she should never have left home so she must either learn or leave.' Nancy shook her head. 'It's your fault, you liked the look of her bonny face and you were smitten.'

'It's true, but folk do like her and she's good with the children and she never brings any men to her room. Now you would have something to complain about if her bedroom was used as a knocking shop, like the rooms above the Black Swan.' Theo grinned.

Nancy snorted. 'She would be out then — faster than any man could pull his breeches down and I'd be the one who would see to it! We might be rough and ready, but we will not have any whores in this house, not while I'm landlady here.'

5

Eve stared at the tall, dark-haired barmaid who stood tall and proud and full of confidence as she received her orders from Theo for the afternoon's dog fights out in the back yard of the Bluebell. Jill Swinthwaite's top was low-cut and her ears were pierced and adorned with glistening ear-bobs. Eve thought Jill looked the way a proper barmaid should look, making her feel inadequate in comparison. She noticed Theo put his hand around Jill's waist as he guided her through to the yard and showed her what he had planned for the day — a day that Eve was dreading. Although she had been warned that the customers that day would be more rough and ready than usual and was prepared for that, the thought of dogs ripping pieces off one another for the pleasure of people betting upon them still filled her with horror. She polished the few glasses that the Bluebell had and decided to make sure that there were plenty of tankards ready to be filled from the barrel of beer that Theo had placed outside on a table for Jill to serve from. And if she set everything up in advance, Eve thought, hopefully she would not have to deal with the new lass too much over the course of the day, so she arranged the tankards and glasses on trays for Jill to use outside. She'd heard both Theo and Nancy talking about Jill and knew that they admired her way with customers. She'd have to be careful lest Jill outshine her so much they were tempted to replace Eve with her and she made herself appear busy as she saw Jill walk back into the bar towards her.

'Your boss is a bit fond of himself, isn't he? Putting his arm around my waist! I nearly told him to keep his hands to himself, but thought better of it.' Jill stood with her back against the bar and talked over her shoulder to Eve. 'It's going to be bloody mad out there this afternoon and evening. All the punters from the Cock and Bottle are going to be here too, you know.' Jill turned to look at Eve and scrutinised her. 'I hope that you're quick behind that bar; there'll be no time for talk and niceties — that's not what they're coming for today.'

Eve felt herself getting annoyed that she was being told what to do in her own job by the temporary barmaid. 'You needn't worry about me; I'll keep you supplied with tankards and beer if you run out — I know my job and my place.'

'Just saying how it is. They can be rough buggers and don't like waiting for their drink. Besides, the more they drink, the more profit both public houses make, seeing as Theo and Max Baines, my boss, have come to an agreement to split the takings. Let's hope the peelers haven't cottoned on. Hope they don't show their faces today, the bastards!'

'I didn't know that the Cock and Bottle were part of Theo's new idea, although I wondered how the dog baiting had come about.'

'Aye, lass, do you not know that Theo Lambert is known as one of the hardest men in the district along with Max? Nobody gives them bother, not if they want to keep their lives and livelihood. The Cock and Bottle and the Bluebell just make them both look semi-respectable, but they have their fingers in more pies than you'd ever be able to imagine. The only thing they don't get involved with are ladies of the night — both of them keep their noses clean when it comes to running whorehouses.' Jill grinned as she looked at the shock on Eve's face. 'You're still wet behind the ears, aren't you? That's why Theo is fond of you, he likes his barmaids innocent — that is, until he gets the urge behind Nancy's back to take advantage of you working for him. You've been here a while now so you've been lucky; most barmaids only stay here for six months and then leave with a bun in the oven or with Nancy's boot up their arse. Or both . . . '

'He's not like that, he's always been a gentleman to me,' Eve protested.

'Aye, only because Nancy threatened to cut his balls off if he messed with anyone again after last time. But don't give him a chance, lass. I'd always keep your bedroom door locked anyway, just in case.' Jill smiled.

'How long have you worked at the Cock and Bottle?' Eve inquired to change the subject, feeling as if she had shown her ignorance once more and wanting to ignore what Jill had said about Theo.

'Since I was old enough to reach the bar. Me and Katie Dean know how to work the bar there like clockwork — we know every punter: who's got money, who's a waste of time and whose groping hands to stay clear of. Don't worry — another year in the trade and you'll be the same and I'll look after you today. They know better than to mess with me.' Jill looked up at the pottery casks that held the gin, rum and whisky at either side of the bar and studied them for a moment. 'Pour me a shot of Old Tom. I thought for a minute about the Pineapple Gin because it's not quite as harsh, but a shot of Old Tom will really help me survive the day.'

Eve picked up a glass from her newly set out tray and flicked up the tap on the gin cask, pouring the drink and setting it down on the bar before looking at Jill expectantly for payment.

'Now I *know* that you truly are as innocent as you look! You don't expect me to pay for it, do you? It's one of the perks of the job, it's how we barmaids get from one day to the next, and a drop of Geneva in you makes you less worried and more liked by the punters. Just as long as you don't get too big a liking for it and don't get caught helping yourself, else you'll get booted out.' Jill winked and quickly swigged the drop of gin back, closing her eyes. 'Oh, that's good! That lovely warm feeling you get when it trickles down your throat and then the numbing of your brain as it helps you feel better with yourself. You should try it; it would do you good.'

Eve shook her head. 'I was brought up being told that drink was evil so I've never drunk in my life.'

'And you work here, in this godforsaken place?

Lord, girl, you mustn't be right in the head! Everybody needs a quick sneck-lifter to get them through the day, especially on a day like today. Don't you show your pretty face out in that yard if you don't want to see the ugly side of life. Another hour and there will be every Tom, Dick and Harry out there, from all walks of life. Men who should know better than to bet on two defenceless animals tearing one another apart. It even makes *my* stomach churn and I've seen it more times than I care to mention.' Jill stood with her hands on her hips.

'I'm not that soft,' Eve protested. 'I'll be all right. Besides, it's you that's serving out there, not me.' Eve had heard enough lecturing from Jill, who was not that much older than herself.

'Aye, well, whatever you say. Just watch yourself with some of the customers, because they will want to come through to the bar if I'm slow serving them and they're cut from a different cloth to your usual's.' Jill looked at the disgruntled Eve and decided not to give her any more advice. She would have to learn from her own mistakes today. She'd find out what reality was when the crowd were baying for blood outside.

★ ★ ★

The yard behind the Bluebell was heaving with folk from every walk of life, from some well-to-do gentlemen who liked a wager, no matter what the odds, to gypsy folk with lurchers and terriers at their heels, wanting to hold their own dog fights in the shadows of the main event set up by Max

58

and Theo. Even soldiers from the newly built Carlton barracks, wearing their bright scarlet jackets with gleaming brass buttons, were there to enjoy the so-called sport.

In the centre of the cobbled yard was a clear area where the baiting was to take place, with Theo sitting at the side, dressed in his finest jacket, a new bowler hat on his head. His book for taking bets in was balanced on an upturned beer cask and filled with names and bets while his pockets were full of cash which he hoped not to lose too much of if the wrong dog won. It made no difference to him, really — his inn had never been so busy. Even if he made nothing on the dogfights, he would make it on the beer and spirit sales instead, he decided as he looked around at the crowds drummed up by himself and Max. He just hoped that the peelers would not hear the noise coming from his usually quiet yard as he watched men argue over which dog would win. The yard was full of ruffians and wrong'uns, but they came with money and that was all that mattered.

Theo watched as Jill smacked the face of a man who had tried to grab her breasts and shook his head; this yard was no place for his precious Eve, who was best behind the protection of the bar. He grinned as the crowd around Jill and the daring man made fun of him being put in his place, their dirty faces lined with laughter, their drink spilling over their tankards while Jill, unfazed, served the next man with his beer. She was a good barmaid but a bit too rough for his normal customers, whereas Eve was just right for the Bluebell. One day, in the future, he wanted it to be known as an establishment for the better-class gent, not a drinking hole like his friend Max was running. He wasn't getting any younger and he knew that before too long somebody harder than himself would come along and want a part of his world of betting and dealing. Besides, he also knew it was time he was more settled, for the sake of Nancy and his children.

A roar went up when two strongly built terriers both held back on sturdy chain leads with spiked collars around their necks appeared from either side of the crowd. Their owners yanked them back, making them hungry to fight one another as they growled and frothed at the mouth. One of the dogs was smaller than the other, but rippled with muscles, its jaws like traps as it barked at the taller bull mastiff whose lips snarled and eyes flashed at its rival. A mutter went around the crowd and Theo was drowned with a sea of last-minute bets from the gamblers at the sight of the two seemingly unevenly matched dogs. Theo quickly wrote down the bets and watched as the two dogs and their owners paraded around a ring made by the bodies of the betters, each one of them egging the dogs on and yelling for the fight to start. He glanced across at Jill as she made her way into the Bluebell for another tray of tankards and orders of spirits.

★ ★ ★

The yard and the Bluebell were full to overflowing with people and Theo smiled, knowing that even when Max had been given his share he would have made a nice amount of money to line his pockets with. Nancy was busy in the kitchen, cooking her usual batch of mutton stew to be served after the dog fight to those who could face it while his two barmaids were that busy, they didn't know which way to turn. Theo got to his feet and banged a gavel on the table and demanded everyone's attention.

'The bets are in, you've all been told the odds, now let's get to it, lads. To my left is Black Bob and I have yet to see a more ferocious animal.' Theo looked at the stoutly built terrier that was pulling on its lead and baying to be let off to get at the dog opposite it. 'And on my right is Gentleman Jim, a bit taller, but he's bred for killing. May the best dog win!' Theo slammed the gavel down and the owners of both dogs let their fervid animals off their leads while the crowd yelled and swore and moved in a united wave around the Bluebell's yard as the dogs set into one another, their jowls frothing and blood running from their mouths as they tore into one another.

Jill pushed her way through the crowds inside the Bluebell and looked at Eve. 'I'm dying for a pee. Can you hold the fort for me outside for five minutes and just take me two gins, a whisky and three tots of rum out to where my serving table is and then I'll follow with the tankards once I've relieved myself? There will be hell on if they don't have their drinks ready when the fight's finished.'

Jill didn't wait for an answer and quickly made

her way back out into the yard to the outside privy, leaving Eve apologising to her customers for a delay as she poured what Jill had requested and, balancing the lot on a tray, dodged the crowds, trying not to look at the warring dogs as she crossed the yard with her hands full. The noise and smell were stifling as great roars came out from the crowd while she tried to pick her way around the men who were baying for blood. Her heart was beating fast as she got to the table and put down the drinks. How could anyone enjoy such a cruel sport? she thought. As she made her way back across the yard, the crowd surged her way and knocked her off her feet. Before she knew it, she was down among the dirt of the stable yard and the two dogs were nearly upon her, the crowd jeering and yelling as Black Bob tore at Gentleman Jim, making him defenceless as he upturned the longer-legged dog onto its back and snatched at its soft underbelly, ripping the poor creature's belly open and then shaking the dying dog like a rag doll.

The blood flying around the ring splattered everybody's shoes but it covered Eve's dress, face and hair as she screamed at the sight of the death. She thought that she might be next when Black Bob dropped what was left of his opponent and stood, his tongue dripping with blood, glaring at her. Eve screamed again as the dog, with blood smeared around its jowls, bared its teeth. Before the dog could make another move, its owner lunged forward and grabbed it by the scruff of its neck. His dog was worth everything to him and the last thing he wanted was it biting a stupid, screaming barmaid. He hauled his exhausted dog back into the safety of the Bluebell's stables, where two fighting cocks were being kept for the next round.

Eve looked around her. Nobody showed any kindness to her; Theo was too busy settling bets while most of the men were more concerned about her spoiling the end of the kill than how she felt. Her eyes filled with tears as she tried to stand up, looking at her blood-splattered clothes and the tragic carcass of the defeated dog. She felt sick and her legs buckled and wobbled as she straightened her skirts.

'May I be of assistance? Here, take my hand.' One of the soldiers who had been standing at the back of the crowd came to her aid and held his hand out for her to take as she tried to walk back into the Bluebell.

'Thank you, I-I feel quite faint,' Eve whispered as she took the soldier's hand and tried not to glance backward at the carnage on the floor of the yard.

'It must be most distressing for you, for it's not a sport for the ladies, let alone you being so close to the kill. Us men can behave like animals ourselves, I fear. Perhaps a quick drink of something to replace the colour in your cheeks will help? You do look a little pale.' The soldier walked her back to the bar and went behind it, pouring a tot of brandy in a glass before passing it to her. 'And perhaps you would feel better if you freshen up before continuing to serve?'

'I thank you, sir, but I don't drink,' Eve said politely.

'Nonsense, this is for medicinal purposes and I'll pay for it, if that is what you are worried about. Now drink it back.' The caring soldier threw a silver threepence onto the bar and watched as Eve looked at the small amount of brandy and closed her eyes before swallowing it back. She shuddered as the warmth of the alcohol burned her throat while she gulped it down and then turned to smile at her saviour.

'There, you see? The colour has returned to your cheeks already. Forgive me, I should introduce myself — I'm Sergeant John Oates.' He smiled at the shaken young barmaid and thought how bonny she was.

Nancy came out from the kitchen and glared at Eve as she stood next to the sergeant she knew all too well to be from the new barracks at Carlton. 'Eve, go and get yourself tidy and don't take up any more of Sergeant Oates's precious time. Look at you, making a fool of yourself and getting covered with blood! Get gone and get changed and then come and serve these folks who deserve your attention. And they'll be wanting something to eat once the cockfighting finishes.'

'Yes, Nancy, I'm sorry. But I felt faint and this gentleman helped me.' Eve turned and smiled at her dashing helper.

'Aye, well, go and straighten yourself up and look lively, Jill's run off her feet and I have enough to do and all.' Nancy scowled at her and then turned to Sergeant Oates, a man whose reputation was well known to her. 'Thank you, sir, for coming to her aid — now, would you like a drink? And please take the payment for Eve's drink back, it is not for you to pay for it.' Nancy stretched a false smile on her face as she watched Eve glance backward before disappearing behind the curtain and making her way up to her room to change.

'She's always causing trouble, that one,' Nancy complained. 'Imagine walking across the yard just as the dog fight was coming to an end. I'm sorry if she spoilt the fight for you, sir.' Nancy held out the threepence for him to take back.

'She didn't. In fact, just the opposite, it was a grand fight and a pleasure to meet her. Eve, you say? Please keep the threepence; it was the least I could do for her.' John Oates smiled. It had been threepence well spent, he thought as he left Nancy to retrieve his plumed helmet from out of the yard. He'd had a most profitable day, even though he had bet on the wrong dog. He'd be back again to see the bonny, innocent lass behind the bar for she had really taken his fancy. He might not have won on the dog fight, but he'd definitely found a new sport to play.

6

Reflect, my friends, Gin is the noble cause
For which your swords should hew away the laws,
Wipe out the senate, drench in blood the nation,
And spread o'er the state wild desolation.

Timothy Scrubb

'Of all the people at that dog fight, you manage to attract that bastard Oates!' Nancy stood with her hands on her hips while she watched Eve sweep the wooden floorboards of the Bluebell after the previous busy but successful day of sport.

'Why, what's wrong with him? He was a real gentleman towards me.' Eve didn't stop sweeping. She had been in Nancy's bad books all morning, along with the Lambert children, who had been yelled at and sent out onto the streets as soon as they had been fed in order to get some peace in the house.

'He drinks, he gambles and he plays with every innocent young lass's affections, leaving them broken-hearted — or worse,' Nancy growled. 'You don't want to have anything to do with him, Eve. He and his army friends in their fine uniforms were stationed here last year and ran amok with the local lasses, leaving many of them wailing and crying when they got left behind. Him and his regiment must be back before they move on again. I'm warning you, lass, he gives his heart to no one, so don't be falling for his uniform and charm.' Nancy wiped her hands on her apron and shook her head as Eve leaned on her broom.

'He is dashing, though. I've never seen a man in uniform so close up before and he is so handsome.' Eve smiled, thinking about the few minutes they had spent together when he had come to her rescue and wishing that she had been able to thank him for his assistance.

'You can stop thinking that right now, my lass. He's a bad lot and you want nothing to do with him if you've any sense. I'd ban him and his mates if I could, but once they're in town, they drink like fishes, so it's not in my best interest to do so. But you listen to me, give him a wide berth if he comes back. And come back he will — because you just fell into his arms and are new blood to make sport with.' Nancy looked at Eve and knew her words were wasted. Sergeant Oates's looks and manners had already impressed her barmaid, who was just like a ripe cherry — ready for the picking.

Eve got on with the job of sweeping the floor and tidying the bar, ready for a more normal day of trade than the previous one. She'd put the horror of the dog's death behind her while she had lain awake in bed for most of the night, gazing at the ceiling and thinking about the handsome soldier, who she now knew to be Sergeant John Oates of the West Yorkshire staying at Carlton Barracks on the edge of Leeds. She just wished she'd not been covered with the dog's blood and had acted so feeble and stupid in his

67

presence. She had really shown herself up, she thought as she turned to unlock the front door onto Warwick Street.

Later, standing behind the bar waiting for her first customers, her mind wandered again and she smiled, thinking about the sergeant in his scarlet uniform with its high collar and shining brass buttons. His face was noble and with his blond hair and a stunning moustache, he was everything a dashing sergeant should be. She secretly hoped that he would return so that she could thank him for the help that he had given her, despite Nancy warning her that he was not to be trusted. Eve glanced up at the brandy barrel and the memory of the warm liquor slipping down her throat and the stare of John Oates made her blush. Her parents would truly condemn her soul now — not that they hadn't already done so. Not one of her letters had been replied to and no one had visited her since her visit home. She was on her own completely and, as such, was free now to do as she pleased, she thought defiantly.

She looked up at the cask of gin and thought of Jill telling her it was what got her through the day. It was not the first time she had heard that; she remembered seeing the old woman coming out of the gin shop and the letch who'd told her all about its properties. Perhaps she should try just a little tipple of the drink? It wouldn't hurt her that much, surely? She reached for one of her newly washed glasses and, with a quick glance around her, filled the glass a quarter full with the clear liquid. She looked at it for a

68

second or two, summoning up the courage to try the strange-smelling brew, which she had been told was made with juniper berries. She held her breath and then put the glass to her lips and sipped the drink that was the favourite of the nation — and, from what people said, was the downfall of many a good woman. She screwed her face up as the distinct flavour burst out in her mouth and the warmth slid down her throat. She swallowed the first mouthful quickly, not liking the taste, then took another drink, hoping that it would grow on her when she had become accustomed to the sharpness.

'And there was you, telling me that you were sweet and innocent and I was fool enough to believe you,' a voice she recognised said as she closed her eyes tight shut at the second gulp of gin, still not enjoying the drink. 'Next time try it with a drop of soda water; it's not as harsh.'

Eve turned and looked at the fine figure of a man that stood across the bar from her and blushed. 'I've never drunk it before and I thought I'd try it before anyone else was about.'

'I believe you — the look on your face told me that already. It's an acquired taste, but it's one that's all too easy to get fond of. Like I say, try it next time with a dash of soda; don't drink it straight as the old soaks do, they're hardened to it.' John Oates smiled at Eve as she quickly cleaned her glass and replaced it back behind the bar.

'I wish to thank you for your help yesterday, sir. I came back downstairs, hoping that you would still be here but you had gone.' Eve smiled across at the sergeant as he put his plumed helmet onto the bar and stood and looked at her.

'I had to return to barracks quickly because I'd already been gone longer than I intended and lost more money than I should have, gambling on that worthless long-legged hound. However, my day was not in vain because I met you and that's why I have returned here today, to see if you have recovered from your ordeal and perhaps entice you to have supper with me this evening?' John Oates smiled as Eve bowed her head and wondered what to say.

'I am indeed recovered, thank you once again for your assistance.' Eve paused, she remembered what Nancy had told her and thought that she would be going against everything that she had said if she was to accept John Oates's request. However, he was so handsome and so genteel, she felt her heart pounding as she gave her reply.

'I'm afraid I can't have supper with you this evening as I'm expected to work. However, my Sundays are free and I can come and go as I please. Could we agree to meet for supper then?' A mixture of the gin starting to work, her forwardness with the man she barely knew and the warning words of Nancy ringing in her ears made the colour rise to Eve's cheeks. She watched as John's cornflower blue eyes lit up with the suggestion of a Sunday with her on his arm.

'Sunday, it is. However, not just supper, we'll make a day of it. A stroll in the park, a luncheon and then perhaps a little tipple or two, now that

70

I can see you could get a liking for the demon drink.' John winked. 'I'll call for you here, at around ten?'

'Could I meet you elsewhere, not here? It's just that I don't . . . ' Eve hesitated.

'Stop, I know what you are going to say. You don't want anyone to know that you are walking out with a cad like me. You've been warned off by the good lady of the house, with her wicked tales of me,' John said, then he leaned over the bar and whispered, 'Every word is true; no self-respecting young woman would be seen on my arm. You can see for yourself what a wolf I am.'

Eve looked across at John and noticed the laughter lines around his eyes and lips. He was indeed a wolf — a nice tame wolf — one that she would dearly like to walk out with, no matter who warned her off him. 'I'd just like my private life to be kept just that. Until I see fit for anybody else to know my business.'

'Then how about we meet at Kirkstall Abbey on the far side of the town? It's private and secluded, but with a nice walk down by the River Aire. I'll bring a picnic, if you wish, and we can spend a pleasant afternoon getting to know each other. Shall we say eleven o'clock underneath the abbey's ruins? I'll be counting the minutes.' John grinned. 'And as for now, may I have a gill of your finest porter? And then, my pretty miss, I will leave you be, for fear of ruining your reputation.'

'You can indeed, sir, and that would be perfect.' Eve poured a gill into a tankard and passed it to him over the bar, her hand briefly touching his as he reached for his drink.

'Please, it's John — none of this 'sir' business if we are to walk out together,' he whispered.

'And I'm called Eve and it will be a pleasure to accompany you, come Sunday.' Eve looked bashfully at her suitor; she had never walked out with a man before and now she found herself being courted by one of the handsomest men she had ever set eyes upon, regardless of his reputation.

'To Sunday, Eve, my temptress,' he whispered, raising his glass to her as the curtain behind the bar moved and Nancy walked in on their conversation.

'Back so soon, sergeant? You'd think that something must have caught your eye in here,' Nancy said and glared at both of them.

'I was just in need of a gill to drown my sorrows after losing so much to your good husband and that bloody lame dog. But I'm on my way now, duty calls.' John Oates put his head back and downed his drink in one mouthful. 'Good day, ladies. Thank you for your time and welcoming smiles. I'm so glad that you have fully recovered from your ordeal, miss.'

Nancy watched as John picked up his helmet and placed it on his head before making for the door.

'Welcoming smiles!' she scoffed. 'I hope he didn't get too big a welcome from you, my girl. Remember what I told you. You want nothing to do with that one, he's rotten to the core. A real charmer on the outside, but rotten through and through.'

Eve said nothing. Even though John had joked about Nancy not liking him and had warned her that in Nancy's eyes he was a wolf, she had decided to judge him for herself. At this moment, nobody, not even the devil himself, could stop her from meeting her dashing sergeant on Sunday and she was counting down the minutes, just like he had said.

★　★　★

Eve looked at herself critically in her bedroom mirror. Her hair was not looking its best and her dress did nothing for her figure. She smoothed the striped skirts flat and reached for her best Sunday bonnet, adorned with forget-me-nots and a matching blue ribbon, which she fastened in a bow under her chin before giving herself one final check in the mirror and creeping down the stairs, trying not to wake the slumbering household. No matter what she wore for her meeting with John Oates, she could not match his handsome looks and sharp dressing, she thought, as she glanced around the empty kitchen and sneaked out the back door and through the cobbled yard with only the dray horse bearing witness to her escape.

It was a good walk to Kirkstall Abbey and its surrounding grounds and she set off in earnest through the stirring town, making for the outskirts and the wide, open farmland of Kirkstall, where newly built ironworks harnessed the force of the mighty River Aire. She now knew the streets of Leeds well, including which ones to avoid, where the smell of the open middens filled the air and the gutters ran with untreated waste. That was where the poor and desperate lived their lives. She might not have a lot, but at least she had a decent living and was warm and dry at night, she thought as she made her way past Hyde Park Corner, where the common man voiced his protests on occasion, and made her way out into the countryside.

With every footstep she took, her heart beat a little faster at the thought of the man she was about to meet. She passed the gatehouse and walked down to the looming gothic ruins of Kirkstall Abbey. The skeleton of the once-mighty abbey towered above her as she passed between the crumbling walls of the building. Like so many of the country's abbeys, it had been plundered and left desolate by Henry the Eighth, and the Cistercian monks who had once lived there peacefully had been forced to flee for their lives.

Eve shivered in the shadows of the ruin; although the sun was shining there was a slight nip in the air, a telling sign that though spring was here, winter could still make itself felt. She stood under the highest arch and looked around her; nearby, a man was sketching the scene and there were a number of people out for a Sunday stroll, most of them following the riverbank, where the fronds of the delicate willow trees moved quietly and gently in the breeze. It was a beautiful place. No wonder the monks had enjoyed living there, she thought as she spotted the scarlet jacket of John Oates astride his horse, cantering down the path to the abbey. Her heart felt like a trapped butterfly fluttering in her chest as he pulled on the horse's reins and dismounted next to her.

'I hope that you haven't been waiting long? I got held up with roll call and then the blasted cook had forgotten to make me up our picnic. I'd even given him a shilling too, the damned man. Anyway, here I am, with a picnic as promised and my mare will be quite happy to graze on the riverbank while we get to know one another.' John stood next to his horse and held its reins tightly while he looked Eve up and down.

'I've not been here long and besides, it is a lovely place. I've just been admiring the stonework; there are still some gargoyles left with their funny faces and it must have been so impressive before it became a ruin.' Eve looked around her and then smiled at John.

'It's a load of bloody old stones, but folk seem to admire it. It seems to be the place to walk out on a Sunday afternoon by the looks of the people down here. I was hoping that it would be quieter so that we could get to know one another a little more intimately.' John winked at Eve and then pulled on his horse's reins, leading it over to a seat that overlooked the wide-flowing river, which another courting couple had just vacated after sitting for a while, holding hands and whispering sweet nothings to one another, both dressed in their Sunday best.

'Your seat, madam? Will here be all right?' John dropped his horse's reins and let it roam freely after he lifted a wicker basket from the side of his saddle and placed it down on the ground.

'This is perfect,' Eve exclaimed. 'But you shouldn't have gone to so much trouble. Just look at how much you've brought!' She watched as John placed a checked rug on the seat and started to examine what the cook had packed in his basket of delights for them to share.

'It's amazing what the Queen's Army can rustle up when offered money. I rather think these apples and grapes would be bound for the Brigadier's table, but he's not going to be counting them. We've also got some oysters and some potted meat sandwiches, and since you now have a taste for gin, I sneaked a bottle out of cook's stores and poured it into a flask for us. I mean to make a day of it, my bashful one.' John reached for her hand as she sat down next to him and the open basket. 'I've been counting the days to seeing you again; I don't get many chances to be seen with such a beautiful woman on my arm and to have the pleasure of having lunch with her.'

Eve blushed as he held her hand tightly and patted it fondly. 'It is a pleasure, sir. I too have looked forward to this moment. Indeed, I have not stopped thinking about you since you saved me from the dog fight. You were a true gentleman among foul men.' Eve shook her head.

'That's not what Theo Lambert and his rough wife Nancy will have told you. I presume that they don't know that you are with me today?' John's face clouded over.

'No, nobody knows I'm here. I thought it best that I keep our meeting to myself. They seem to have a dislike of you for some reason.' Eve looked down at her feet.

'It was all a simple misunderstanding. One night I brought a guest into the Bluebell, and she and I both ended up a little worse for wear after the drink on that occasion. I'm afraid they found the two of us making the most of the stable to satisfy our natural desires. It was not a moment to be proud of, being caught by Theo and Nancy with my breeches down and astride a woman whose name I can scarcely remember. But it is better that you know the reason why my name is blackened and why they would not be happy with my courting you.' John looked at Eve, whose cheeks were flushed and her eyes downcast. 'I don't mean to embarrass you, but I want you to know why they do not have a good word to say about me.'

'I see . . . Now I understand. It doesn't matter to me, for I know men have urges. However, I hope that you will keep them at bay with me today: I'm not that sort of girl,' Eve said quietly as she raised her head and looked at John with just a hint of desire in her eyes.

'I promise I will, but you must promise me that this will not be our last meeting and that when we have enjoyed the day, you will go home and think of me every night until we meet again. You, my pretty Eve, make my head feel light and my heart beat fast when I just look at you and I'm not about to let you slip from my grasp.'

Eve smiled as she watched John Oates empty

the picnic basket and lay the goods on the bench between them. There was certainly enough lunch for the two of them, she thought, as John passed her one of the potted meat sandwiches and poured a generous measure of gin into the cup of the flask.

'I'm sorry, but you'll have to drink it neat this time; however, it's better quality than the one at the Bluebell. No turpentine in the army's gin, unlike that sold in public houses and by the street sellers!' John took the first sip and then passed it to Eve, watching her try not to pull a face as she sipped genteelly. 'Not that bad, is it? A little subtler than the gin at the Bluebell.'

Eve nodded her head; it was less sharp — either that or she was used to the taste now.

'I really didn't expect this many people down here, today. This place attracts a lot of visitors.' John scowled, knowing that he was not going to get his way with Eve with so many people walking around the abbey.

'Yes, it is indeed busy, but it is a beautiful place.' Eve bit into her sandwich and shook her head as another sip of the gin was offered to her.

'We've no privacy here, and I wanted so much to kiss you . . . ' John Oates looked at Eve and saw a look of shock on her face.

'Perhaps, after we have eaten, we could find somewhere more secluded? Somewhere we could get to know one another in private?' Eve suggested. She longed for her sergeant to kiss her, but like him, she didn't want to be seen doing it by the well-to-do people wandering around the abbey with their families. It was not

78

the done thing to kiss in public, she knew that.

'Then we will finish our lunch and have a wander along the riverbank. Perhaps there will be a secluded place where we will be undisturbed.' John passed the gin to Eve again and watched as she tipped the flask upwards, taking a larger drink this time. 'I need to get to know you and I can't with all these people listening and watching. I'm afraid my uniform attracts comments wherever I go,' he said loudly as a group of three young women smiled at the couple dining on the bench, giving John an extra glance as he opened a fresh oyster with his penknife.

'Perhaps it isn't the uniform that they are in awe of, but the man within it. You are extremely handsome,' Eve found herself saying. As the gin loosened some of her inhibitions she found herself looking at the soldier next to her with new feelings.

'Thank you for your kind words, but believe me, it is just the uniform, whereas your beauty shines out for all to see.' John moved the basket from between them and placed the opened oyster down on the top of it, moving closer to her. 'What the hell! We can do what we like, no matter what anyone thinks.' He closed the space between them and put his arms around her and then held her close to him before kissing her passionately on the lips.

Eve gasped and drawing back, looked at her lover. She had never imagined being kissed like that and as he held her face in his hands and looked into her eyes, she wanted more.

'I don't care who sees us, I'm proud of my soldier,' she whispered as he kissed her again. The three young women looked back at the couple and giggled and tittered at such an outward display of lust.

'Then I will not disappoint, my innocent Eve. We will make a pact to meet here or elsewhere most Sundays because we can't deny the feelings that we have for one another. I knew as soon as I saw you that there was a certain magic between us.' John put his arm around her and passed the gin flask yet again, smiling as she drank from it. Maybe not this time but definitely the next time they met he would have his way with her, now she trusted him and was besotted with him. She would be another conquest to brag about in the mess room with his brothers in arms, another notch on his bedhead and this one a virgin!

7

'What's got into you? This time last month you were a right shrinking violet and now you're strutting around the place like a prize peacock, flirting with all the men and carrying on. You just aren't the same lass.' Jill Swinthwaite shook her head as she watched Eve load up her tin tray with another round of tankards for the baying men out in the yard who had gathered once again for the dog baiting.

'I took your advice and decided that a tipple to get me through the day would benefit me, and it seems it does.' Eve grinned and lifted her tray of drinks up on one arm and looked at the dismay on Jill's face.

'You're not drinking too much, are you? You don't look drunk, so it's more than that, I think.' Jill watched as Eve shook her head and laughed before making her way through the crowds of men who teased her and reminded her of her previous month's escapade when she nearly ended up in the fight herself. Whatever it was, she thought to herself, it had made Eve come out of her shell, and if she was not careful, her services once a month at the Bluebell would no longer be needed.

Eve pushed her way through the betting men and served them their drinks, putting up with their comments and the occasional touch of her bottom, laughingly chastising them for being so forward. All the time she watched for a flash of scarlet jacket and the sight of her soldier. She'd met him at every opportunity and her heart had truly been given to him — but not yet her body, no matter how persuasive he had tried to be. She knew, however, that was her next step with him, and that if she wanted him to be true to her, she would have to let him have his way. But for now she would enjoy his caresses and sweet talk and try to keep his advances at bay. Her heart leapt as she caught sight of his jacket and the familiar blond hair and moustache as he entered through the gates of the Bluebell's yard and stood with a fellow soldier at the back of the crowd. She glanced across at Theo, making sure he was busy taking bets in his usual place by the upturned barrel at the edge of the dogfighting ring, before she made her way towards the two soldiers.

'You made it?' Eve whispered and touched John's arm gently.

'Of course — try and keep me away! Bill here has come to bet on the dogs as well and to make it look as though that is why I'm here so that Theo and the ever-interfering Nancy don't suspect that I'm here to see you. Can you meet me after the fighting, around the back in the cart house next to the stable?' John whispered, keeping a straight face as he took two full tankards and placed money in payment for them back on the tray.

'Yes, but I'll keep my distance this afternoon. Like you, I don't want the Lamberts to suspect a thing, and the barmaid from the Cock and Bottle is watching my every move. She's a nosy cow and has already accused me of having a drink in me,' Eve whispered back.

'And have you?' John grinned.

'Just a small one, just to get me through today,' Eve replied and then turned to smile at him as she made her way back into the Bluebell. She breathed in deeply, feeling excited and happy at the thought of meeting with John Oates later that day. All sense had left her, and as she walked back to the bar, all she could think about was his strong arms, his bright blue eyes and his kisses and whispers as he stroked her neck and caressed her breasts. Her body longed to be taken by him, but her head told her to be sensible and keep her virginity, which her mother had always told her was priceless. John might be handsome and he might even love her — she certainly hoped he did — but she was not ready to give herself totally to him, not without the promise of marriage . . .

'Is it busy out there?' Jill asked when she saw Eve's flushed face.

'Yes, it's the same crowd as last month. The soldier who rescued me from the dogs has just come into the yard with a friend,' Eve said casually as Jill loaded her tray with clean glasses and tankards ready to be refilled from the barrel out in the yard.

'That bastard! I hope he keeps his hands to himself. He's known for being a groper, thinking himself flash in that uniform of his. A gentleman he is not, no matter that he helped you up and made sure you were all right. John Oates has only got one thing on his mind, believe me. He must have been through every barmaid in Leeds — and that includes me. I wish someone had warned me about the bastard before I had my head turned by his looks.' Jill's eyes flashed when she caught the surprise on Eve's face. 'Don't you be giving your heart to him, lass, because he'll break it and think nowt about it.'

'N-no, I won't. I just thought that I'd tell you he was here,' Eve said dejectedly. 'He's not that handsome anyway.'

'No, he bloody isn't, the lying, cheating swine! Everyone knows him and his reputation,' Jill snorted and stepped out with her tray, making her way into the yard and leaving Eve to serve on behind the main bar and mull over her words. Was it true he had been with every barmaid in Leeds? Surely not. But anyway, he'd said that he had eyes only for her and that it was more than lust between them. Eve shook her head. Jill was just causing bother because she was jealous. She'd accused Eve of drinking and now she was jealous of her relationship with John Oates, it was as simple as that.

* * *

The clock struck midnight as Eve let herself out the back door of the Bluebell and made her way across the empty cobbled yard and into the cart house that was used to store the hay for the horse that pulled and the small donkey cart Theo and his family rode out in on occasion.

'John, are you there?' Eve whispered into the darkness. 'John?' she whispered again and wished

84

that she had brought the candle from her bedside table for light.

'I'm here. I thought that you were never going to come. I was just about to go back to the barracks before I'm missed.' John walked out of the darkness and to the front of the cart house and placed his arms around Eve tightly. He bent his head and kissed her gently and then stroked her long blonde hair while kissing her neck and whispering words of love to her.

'I had to wait until everyone was abed. Thank heavens Theo and Nancy were exhausted after the dogfighting, although I thought Theo was never going to go to bed — he was too busy counting the money he had made from his horrible idea of sport.' Eve's pulse quickened as John ran his hands down her body and felt her pert breasts.

'Never mind, you're here now, that's all that matters. I've thought of you all day and I must admit I felt jealous as you smiled and flirted with some of those wretched men that drink at the Bluebell. Am I just one of those men, Eve, or am I special to you?' he asked roughly as he held her tight and ran his hand up the inside of her leg, fumbling with her skirts. 'I can't contain myself any longer, damn it! I need to take you and make you mine.'

Eve tried to push him away. 'No, no, don't, please. I'm not like that. I'm not ready for this yet.'

'You've led me on and now I can't contain myself. Why are you here at midnight alone with me if this isn't what you want?' Oates pushed

Eve roughly onto the fresh-smelling hay and pinned her down, pulling her skirts up as she protested. He swore as he struggled with the buttons on his army breeches.

'Stop it, stop it now! Don't you do this to me!' Eve cried. 'I thought you loved me, that I was different!' she added as he held her hands down and entered her without care or concern that he was the first man ever to have touched her.

'You know you've wanted this since the first day you saw me.' John Oates said in a low, threatening voice as he concentrated on satisfying himself. 'Now hold your noise and let me plough up your furrow, damn you!' He dropped his head and bit her neck as Eve started to cry because of the brutality and the shame of finding herself in the sort of situation her mother had warned her about. Oh, she should have listened! It was like Jill and Nancy had told her — she was just another barmaid that John Oates thought he could use for sex. This was all he had wanted from her. She shut her eyes and tried to close her mind to the heaving man whose kind words and loving ways had disappeared as he thrust into her. Suddenly his grip on her hands tightened and, with a final push, John Oates finished the job that he had set out to do from the moment he met her.

Eve lay still for a second and said nothing as he climbed off her shaking body and lay next to her in the hay. She tried to stifle the sobs and pulled down her skirts, not talking or looking at the man she thought had loved her as she stood up, her weakened legs shaking. He pulled on her hand to come back and join him. Instead, she pulled her hand out of his grip and, with as much dignity as she could muster, walked out of the cart house, leaving him catching his breath. She walked back through the yard and climbed the stairs to her bedroom in the safety of the Bluebell's loft. There, she looked at herself in the mirror; tears were running down her face and there were red marks around her wrists where the strong soldier had pinned her down. There was a bite mark on her neck and running down her legs was his evil seed — seed that she immediately tried to wash away with her jug of cold water from the washstand — then she cried and sobbed as she sat on the edge of the bed; she had done many foolish things in her life but meeting John Oates in the very place she knew he had already sullied was the most stupid of all. How could she have been so gullible? But she had never dreamed that a man she cared for would rape her — because that was what it was, rape.

Eve undid her dress, casting it to one side, and then curled up into a ball, not even bothering to put her nightdress on as she pulled her bedclothes over her. There she lay, thinking about her life and wishing that she was back home, safe with her mother and father. They had obviously washed their hands of her, and who could blame them? A woman like her, who was headstrong and foolish, who had discovered that she enjoyed the demon drink and, worst of all, had lusted after a dangerous man outside of marriage. All because he was handsome and in uniform. Her father was right, she truly was a wicked piece of work and she could only blame herself for what had happened . . .

* * *

'You look white and washed-out. Are you all right?' Nancy asked Eve, who was sitting with the family at the kitchen table but had hardly touched the porridge in front of her.

Eve looked up and tried to smile, knowing that she must not let Nancy or Theo know what had happened in their cart house at midnight with John Oates.

'I'm just tired and missing home. I've not heard from my parents since that last visit I made and I'm regretting leaving on such bad terms.'

'Aye, you shouldn't fall out with your mother, she's your best friend in life if you did but know it.' Nancy looked around at her growing family and felt a little pity for her barmaid. 'Why don't you take today off and go and make up with them both? We'll not be busy today as folk spent their brass yesterday at the dogfighting. I'll make it right with Theo.' Nancy saw tears in Eve's eyes. 'You worked hard yesterday, lass, you deserve some time to yourself.'

Eve desperately wanted to tell Nancy the real reason why she was so subdued, but decided she really couldn't. Perhaps she ought to follow her employer's advice, though, and go and make amends with her parents if it wasn't too late to do so, and if her father would let her.

88

'That would be good, thank you. I miss talking to my mother,' Eve said, fighting back the tears. How she wished she could tell her mother about Sergeant John Oates and her mistaken feelings for him, how he had led her on. She wanted to tell her mother and father that they had been right in their guidance, that she should never have left home and ought to have been content with her lot.

'Then get yourself gone, else it will be dark by the time you return home.' Nancy watched as Eve pushed her chair back from the table and made for the door, leaving her breakfast untouched. Something was bothering the lass, she'd acted strange this last week or two, she thought. Perhaps it was as she said and she was just missing home, but Nancy suspected it was more than that. She'd seen her taking a quick nip of gin, which was completely out of character, but she hadn't mentioned it because it made Eve more sociable with customers. But now, judging by the look on her face, something was very wrong. She only hoped that it was nothing to do with Theo — and perhaps if she visited her old home she'd decide to stay there and not become the threat Nancy feared she was becoming.

* * *

Eve battled with her emotions with every footstep that she took towards her old home. She was thankful that Nancy had given her the day off — she needed to get away from Leeds and go

89

to a place with people she knew she could trust. She needed to seek her father's forgiveness and tell her mother of her heartbreak and how she had been deceived by John Oates, who, despite his misuse of her, she still had feelings for. She sniffed and held back the tears as she stepped out into the countryside and on to the village of Woolford with its coal pits and miners' cottages and straight-talking folk that made the rural village her home, a place that she had taken for granted, not realising how lucky she was to have been brought up in such a tight community.

She stood at the garden gate and wiped her nose and breathed in deeply. If she could reconcile with her family and earn their forgiveness, she would return home. She had seen and experienced enough of Leeds — although full of life and gaiety, there was a dark underside to the growing town, one that she was starting to be part of. Now, being used and abused by John Oates had made her realise just how far her morals had slipped and that it was time she took charge of her life.

As she stood outside the house she noticed that there was no smoke rising from the chimney and the garden looked unattended and although there were the usual rows of vegetables for the family's use, they looked neglected and unloved. It was not like her father to let the garden get in such a state, she thought, as she knocked gently on the familiar door that she had walked in and out of all her life. When no one answered, she lifted the latch and walked into her old home. There was no smell of cooking as she entered the kitchen, no flowers on the table, no loving smile and outstretched arm from her mother. Instead, sitting in the darkest corner of the kitchen, was her father, looking dishevelled and old and not even bothering to raise his head as she said his name.

'Father, where's Mother? Why is the fire not lit?' Eve looked around her. The usual spotless home was untidy, nothing was where it should be and her father looked as if he had not washed or shaved in months.

'Get your evil self out of this house!' Isaac shouted, raising his head and staring at Eve. 'I'll not have you standing there, looking at me. You've brought nothing but heartbreak to this house. I told you once that you were not welcome here anymore — and now you've killed your mother with your selfishness, you'll not get the better of me!'

'What do you mean? Where's Mother? What do you mean, I've killed her?' Eve wailed.

'She's where you put her with your selfishness, six foot under in the chapel yard, with her heart broken by her only child who lied and had no time for her and who turned her back on her family for the wickedness of Leeds.'

Isaac stood up and glared at his daughter as she sobbed openly in front of him. 'It's no good crying and seeking forgiveness now because she's dead and buried, all thanks to you, girl. Now, get gone! This is no longer your home and you are not my daughter. I always doubted that you were mine and since you have grown, I know my doubts were not without substance. Your mother's head must have been turned by the devil himself and you must be his spawn.'

'Father, think of what you are saying! I am your daughter. I loved both you and my mother. Oh, she can't be dead! Why didn't you tell me she was ill? I never heard from you, I didn't know,' Eve sobbed.

'Out! Get out of my house and take your false tears with you. She breathed her last breath with your name on her lips after worrying about you day and night. She's dead. Dead of a broken heart.' Isaac grabbed Eve's arm and pulled her out of the kitchen. 'Now go! Go back to Leeds, where you've made your bed and there you must lie in it. I never want to see your face again, you're no daughter of mine,' Isaac roared at Eve as she begged him to listen to her.

'Father, you need me! I'll look after you. Please, Father, don't do this. I didn't know Mother had died, I'm broken-hearted,' Eve cried, pulling on his jacket sleeve.

'Don't waste your breath, you trollop! Get gone! There's no need for you ever to come here again.' Isaac pulled her along the garden path and pushed her beyond it, slamming the gate shut behind her. 'Take yourself back to Leeds and let the devil have you, there's no home here for you!' Isaac turned and walked with his head down, back into his small cottage without even giving her a backward glance.

Eve choked on her tears and stared at the new world around her. Her mother was dead and her father never wanted to see her again. She had nobody now, unless John Oates returned once more to see her, and even if he did, she would be hesitant to give him any sign of her love. She'd lost her family, she'd lost her virginity and she'd lost any respect for herself, she thought, as she cried and walked through the outskirts of the village to the chapel and its graveyard. There, in the corner of the yard, with a simple cross marked with her name at its head and a bunch of orange chrysanthemums lying on it, was her mother's grave. Eve bent down and wept.

'Mam, I loved you, I didn't mean to break your heart. I loved you, I loved you!' she wailed as she spread herself across the grave, her skirts getting dirty and wet in the damp earth. 'Forgive me, Mam, I didn't mean to break your heart and hurt my father. I just wanted a different life, but you were both right, I should have stayed at home.' She hugged the cross and wept. She wept for her mother, she wept for the loss of her father's love — and she wept for herself most of all, for she was completely on her own now.

8

'What is wrong with you, girl?' Theo shook his head at Eve. For the second time that week she had left one of his best-paying drinkers standing unserved at the bar.

'I'm sorry, I needed the privy.' Eve didn't look up at Theo because she didn't want him to guess the predicament that she was in. Her world was falling apart and she didn't know what to do. For the last few months she had walked around like the undead and Nancy had caught her on more than one occasion helping herself to a tot of gin. And yet this wasn't the worst of her troubles — the baby she was carrying made her sick every morning and she couldn't think about anything else.

'Well, next time cross your bloody legs until you've served him! He'll be going to the Cock and Bottle if we're not careful and taking his money with him.' Theo growled and looked her up and down. 'And another thing — take more care with yourself. I know that you're still grieving over the death of your mother, but that's no excuse for not looking after yourself. Everybody has to die sometime, Eve, some, unfortunately, earlier than others, but you mustn't take her death or your old man's warped words to heart. You were not to blame, believe me.' Theo cursed under his breath. It was a shame to see the once innocent lass looking like any other downtrodden barmaid in Leeds. When she had first come to him, she had been fresh and bonny but now her complexion was pale and drawn and she was putting on weight around her hips.

'I'm sorry, I'll try and pull myself together. I just feel a little down at the moment.' Eve tried to smile and then turned to get on with the job at hand.

'Aye, well, I know you're hurting. But you'll be hurting more if I find you're no longer worth employing. For God's sake, smile at the customers! That's what they want to see when they come in, not the sort of miserable bloody face that they're used to seeing on their wives' faces.' Theo patted Eve on her back and then went about his business of checking stock. Whatever was troubling Eve was not making his life any easier, especially with Nancy nagging him about her every five minutes if they were in the same room together.

Eve looked at herself in the bar's mirror. Theo was right, she looked terrible; her hair was lank, her skin sallow and she had no pride in the clothes that she wore. In fact, pride was something that she felt she no longer deserved in the state that she was in. It would probably be better if Theo did sack her, because that would give her an excuse to throw herself into the freezing canal and end it all. She felt nausea rising up again as the smell of beer made her stomach churn. She must fight the urge to be sick, she thought, as a man ordered a gill of porter that she quickly pulled without making too much conversation and took his money in payment. Thank the Lord that it was her Sunday to herself in the morning. She could lie in her bed and not be at Theo and Nancy's beck and call, and then she would walk out of town to Carlton Barracks, where she would demand to see John Oates. She would tell him her news, tell him that she was now carrying his child and she expected him to stand by her. Surely he would be man enough to do that? He'd have to; she'd not lain with any other man and it was his baby she was carrying, he'd have to marry her.

Eve sighed. She knew she was deluding herself. She'd not seen a glimpse of *any* scarlet uniforms, let alone her dashing sergeant, since the night that he had forced himself upon her. She'd been used, just like the others before her that Jill Swinthwaite had told her of, only she had been left carrying an unwanted baby, and with nowhere to call her true home. Once the Lamberts knew of her condition she would be out on the streets with nowhere to go. John Oates was her only hope. She had to convince him to marry her — it was either that or throw herself into the cut, as many a desperate pregnant girl had done before. How stupid she had been and now her ignorance had come back to bite her, but perhaps all was not lost; if Sergeant John Oates would show an ounce of sympathy to her and at least pay for her lodgings until the baby was born, then she could leave it on the orphanage steps and go on to find work . . .

Every morning the same thoughts swam

around her head and she hadn't been able to think or concentrate since she realised she was with child. That, along with the loss of her mother and her father disowning her, had made life unbearable. Yet again she tried to convince herself that John Oates would not turn his back on her: he had said he loved her, so surely it was only the shame of him losing control of his feelings that was keeping him away from seeing her. Even though she somehow knew, deep in her heart, that she was only deluding herself, she would make the walk to the barracks and demand to see him. For she still felt something for him, despite what he'd done. The sight of him dressed in his uniform and his handsome face would make her heart miss a beat, she knew. She loved him even though he might not care a tinker's curse about her.

★ ★ ★

The wind was biting cold as she walked through the streets of Leeds. It was the run-up to Christmas and the shops were full of seasonal displays tempting people to spend their hard-earned money on a few luxuries to celebrate the one day of the year that most people had to themselves. With it being Sunday, all the shops were closed, which Eve was thankful for as she had no time to look at such frivolities when her mind was focused on the words she needed to say to John Oates. She turned away from the shop windows and the wide-eyed children who were gazing at the displays with wonder and hurriedly made her way out of town to the recently built army barracks. Her stomach churned as the austere red-brick building came into sight. She didn't know what to say and how she would get to see her baby's father but she had to confront him, no matter what.

'Good morning, miss.' The soldier guarding the entrance looked down at Eve as she stood in front of him, obviously needing his help.

'Good morning. I wish to speak to Sergeant John Oates. Could you let me into the barracks, or could you tell him that I am here and wish to speak to him?' Eve gazed up at the soldier dressed in the familiar uniform, the uniform that had captured her heart and made her forget her senses.

'I'm afraid I can't do that.' The guard looked down at her with an unsmiling face.

'But you must, it's urgent that I speak to him. Could I write a note for you to give him? I need to give him a message,' Eve pleaded.

'No, miss, it's not possible. His company is no longer here. They've been posted to Ireland, the poor buggers. Now, unless you're prepared to walk all the way to Dublin, you'll not be talking to him for a while.'

'Ireland!' Eve gasped.

'Aye, he's keeping those tattie eaters in their place and hates it over there, from what I hear. I'm just glad that I was lucky and got to stay here — you'll not get me sorting out the bloody Irish,' the soldier said. When he saw tears rising in Eve's eyes, he added more gently, 'It's best you forget him, miss, that's what I've told the others. You might never see him again.'

'The others!' Eve gasped.

'Aye, he was popular, was Sergeant Oates, he's left behind many a broken heart. Sorry, miss, but you're better off without him. You find yourself a reliable lad, not a soldier, for we are not the marrying kind.' Although the soldier didn't move from his post or change his expression, his voice was kind as Eve stood, shocked and dismayed at the news that John Oates was not only gone from Leeds, but was no longer in the country, and that it was highly unlikely that she would ever see him again.

The unrest in Ireland had been headline news in the papers for a few weeks now and Eve had read about how many of Her Majesty's troops had been deployed there. John Oates might be lucky to escape with his life, if what she had read was true, and the last thing on his mind would be her. In any case, it was obvious from the soldier's remarks that she was not the only young woman wishing to find the dashing sergeant. He would never marry her and the child that she was carrying was to be born a bastard.

'Thank you.' Eve looked up at the soldier and tried to stop the tears from falling. What was she to do now? She had meant nothing to him; his reputation had gone before him and she should have listened to Jill and Nancy's words of warning. She was stuck now — pregnant, nearly penniless and probably out on the streets once Theo and Nancy found out. She wrapped her shawl around her shoulders and retraced her steps back into Leeds, deciding to visit the gin shop on Briggate for a tipple to drown her sorrows and give her the courage to face up to the fact that her life — and the life growing inside her — were of little worth and that she was best off ending both. She'd been headstrong and foolish and had lost everybody that she loved because of her stupidity.

She walked through the streets, listening to the church bells of the mighty Saint Mary's summoning people to worship. They walked past her in their Sunday best, happy families with children at their sides, hard-working and righteous just like her family had been. She put her head down and made her way through the cobbled roads to the gin shop on the bottom of Briggate Street. A drink would give her the courage to either end it all or wrap her up in a blanket of comfort, depending on how much she drank. She realised now why the working classes enjoyed their gin so much: it was to escape the reality of the everyday drudgery of their lives. Lives like hers, full of hopes and ambitions that were thwarted by the reality of not being able to grasp that elusive step up in life. And she had ruined it all for herself. She stood outside the gin shop, the doors were closed and the shutters down on the windows. Even the old hag that brewed her own gin respected Sunday; she should have known that it wouldn't be open.

She stood outside the empty shop and looked around her, then made her decision. She'd walk down Briggate Street to Bridge End; there, she would follow the canal out to the countryside and, if there was a quiet spot with no one else around, she would throw herself in. It was the best all round, for she wasn't worth anything to anyone any more.

9

Eliza Wilson, known locally as Bonfire Nell, strutted along the causeway of Granary Wharf. Business was slow — it was Sunday and even those in need of her services thought twice about having their wicked way with her on the day of the Sabbath. Her only hope was them entering into the town on the canal or those with so much gin in them that they didn't care what day of the week it was. As long as they paid her for her services, she didn't care what colour, what creed or what their particular fancy was. Other than taking a beating, she was game for anything. She pushed her breasts up to the top of her bodice and swaggered her hips as she perused the tom puddings the tub boats that transported coal from the collieries, and the horse-drawn barges going up and down the canal wharf, hoping that someone would heckle her. She'd make enough money to have a decent bit of dinner back at the Black Swan, where she rented rooms which were her pride and joy.

'Hey, Nell, show us your leg! I've no brass, but I've got the urge. Go on, lass, make an old man happy,' a voice called from one of the moored tom puddings. The face that went with the voice was as black as the coal that it was carrying and Nell laughed and shouted back.

'No brass? Then there's no chance of a look, you old bastard! Go and play with yourself and come back to me when you've got paid.' She laughed as she swore. She knew he'd be straight to her once he had some money in his pocket. Old George Monroe was as regular as clockwork and Monday evening, when he'd got his pay and had drunk his fill, he'd be knocking on her bedroom door at the Swan. He could never manage sex but liked to watch Nell as she undressed before him, fondling and playing with himself as he got more and more excited, finally achieving climax without him even touching her. George was one of the easier ones and she only wished that most of her clients were the same.

She grinned to herself as she idled along the wharf side. It looked as if this Sunday morning was not going to be up to much . . . perhaps she should try her luck near Park Lane, where people stood on the corner shouting for more rights, more pay and whatever gripe they had with their world. None of them would last a minute in her shoes and they knew it. The women would look her up and down and the men would make sure their lovers and wives were ushered away from her, just in case she gave away their secrets and pleasures. No, Nell thought to herself, she'd do the wharf side for another hour and then try her luck up Briggate. The busy market streets attracted the well-to-do, so maybe there would be a gent there with an urge and a sixpence to spend.

Standing at the side of the canal underneath the Victoria Bridge, she spotted a young lass who looked as if she was touting for trade. Nell fumed as she walked quickly towards her, angered that the dolly mop was on her patch. Well, she would have to find somewhere else to do her trade; this was her patch and no one, unless she was one of Bert Bradshaw's harlots, was allowed on the patch between Granary Wharf and Bridge End.

'Hey, you bitch, what do you think you're doing? This is my patch! Unless that pimp Bradshaw has sent you down here, bugger off!' Nell stomped her way towards the young lass, holding her long skirts in her hands, showing her ankles to all the bargemen as she shouted and stood her ground. 'This is his patch through a night and mine of a day, now piss off!'

Eve looked up at her, her eyes red with tears and her body shaking as Nell took her by the arm and pushed her along the canal bank.

'Piss off and move on!' Nell shouted and watched as Eve stood precariously close to the canal edge. Nell sighed. 'I don't want to be hard because us girls should stick together, but just making a living is bad enough without the likes of you down here.'

Eve stood for a minute and then decided to do what she had planned and throw herself in the canal. She looked at Nell and said, 'Please don't try to save me. Tell those at the Bluebell Inn I'm sorry.'

'Stop, you silly cow! Wait, haven't I seen you before?' Nell suddenly realised what the young girl was going to do. 'Stop, things are never that bad, lass.' She reached out and grabbed Eve's arm just as she was about to jump into the dirty waters of the canal, yanking her back and scowling at her. 'And it's no good jumping in here, you'll only get fished out by one of the bargemen, half-dead or worse. Stand back and come and talk to me.' Nell grabbed Eve's waist and pulled her from the edge of the canal.

'Let me go, I'm no good to anyone, I'm better off dead and buried,' Eve wailed, pulling on Nell's restraining hands.

'What? Shunned by the Church and buried outside the graveyard in consecrated ground? You are worth more than that! I remember you now — I met you when you were fresh-faced and just arrived, and I told you to go back to your family. You should have listened to my advice.' Nell pulled Eve further back and made her stand with her back against the walls of the granary warehouse as she tried to make her realise that life was precious.

'I wasn't wanted back home and I'm not wanted here; I have nobody and nothing,' Eve cried and tried to break free of Nell's grip.

'And what do you think women like me have? There are hundreds of women in this town with nothing and nobody to love them. But you put your head up, walk tall and make the best of your life; as long as you are your own woman, that's all that matters. Us women can always make our way in the world, believe me, I know.' Nell pinned her to the wall and looked into her eyes and saw how much pain she was carrying.

'I could if it was just me, but I'm with child. Nobody will want a woman with a bastard baby in tow, so just walk away and let me end it,' Eve sobbed.

'I will not! Not if this what you're trying to take your life for.' Nell held her at arm's length and looked her up and down. 'You can't even tell. How far gone are you? It might not be too late to do something about it.'

'What do you mean?' Eve asked.

'You could always get rid of it. There's plenty of old crones that'll do the job or give you something to lose it, if that's what you want. Or is it yourself that you are worried about and not the child?' Nell said quietly.

Eve stared at Nell in horror. 'I can't bear to think of killing it! And for me to still carry on with my life? No, I couldn't live with myself. That's why we are both better off dead. Just let me go,' she cried.

'Has the father deserted you? Do you even know who the father is?' Nell asked sympathetically.

'He's a soldier, but he doesn't know that I'm pregnant. He's serving out in Ireland. I was a fool; I trusted him and now I'm in the state I am,' Eve sobbed and tried to get away from Nell.

'Oh, you never trust a soldier, lass. You love them and then they break your heart. I know, I've been there. It was a soldier who broke my heart too. He promised that he loved me, that he'd return and marry me, only for it to turn out that he'd said that to every girl in Wakefield.' Nell shook her head. 'Look, trade isn't up to much this morn, so walk back with me to mine — I'm Nell, known to all as Bonfire Nell — and we'll sit and talk. You'll feel better once you've cleared your head of thoughts. I suppose you've

106

found life hard in Leeds since your arrival — I told you then it was no place for a young lass on her own.' Nell felt sympathy for the weary-looking Eve. She was like so many young women who had been taken advantage of and, once left pregnant, could think only of taking their lives. So many young women were dragged out of the cut dead and with child — but she had saved this one for now.

'I couldn't do that; I couldn't go to your home. Besides, you don't know me. Just leave me be.' Eve shook Nell's hand off her arm. No matter how low she had sunk, to be walking with a prostitute, especially Bonfire Nell, whose name she knew from all the men with loose morals who talked about her when drunk in the Bluebell, made her stop and think.

'So I can save your life, but you are ashamed of me?' Nell stood back and looked at Eve. 'Yet you made the same actions as me and have ended up like you are. At least I make my living from it and play men at their own game. They don't get to ride rant pole with me unless they give me money. That's a lesson that you should learn from me, my dear stuck-up bitch.' Nell stood back and grinned. 'Aye, I'm a prostitute — and a bloody good one! I have my own rooms, no pimp owns me and many a man has left me with a smile on his face. I've even bedded the Prince of Wales, if folk did but know it. Although he was still wet behind the ears, only a lad. I'm the nearest thing to royalty that you'll ever get to see, although saying that, he was too busy tipping the velvet to care what I looked like.' Nell sniggered. 'Now, bury your bloody pride and walk home with me. I know how you feel because I've been there, and I left my baby on the workhouse steps in Wakefield on Bonfire Night. Aye, and when I get drunk, I start talking about that baby I lost on Bonfire Night and that's how I got my name: Bonfire Nell. Because I can never get over the regret of abandoning my child.' Nell's eyes almost filled with tears; she knew what Eve was going through and this time, perhaps unlike her, somebody could help this lass in need.

'I'm sorry, I didn't mean to show my feelings, it's just the way I was brought up. But I'm beginning to realise my upbringing was a sheltered one and that I should have been made more aware of life outside my family. My name is Eve Reynolds . . . Oh, Nell, you must relive leaving your baby at the workhouse steps every day. Did you ever find out what became of it?' Eve had stopped her sobbing and touched Nell's arm to show her pity.

'No, I don't know what happened to him. He could have died or he might have gone on to be a good man. He'll be eighteen now — I was only sixteen when I gave birth to him. My parents never knew and they wouldn't have cared anyway, for there was thirteen of us all living and sleeping head to toe in a house that you wouldn't keep a pig in, let alone a whole family. They were just glad to see the back of me when I left home and made my own way in the world. But anyway, enough of me. Walk with me to my rooms above the Black Swan — I promise they're not as bad

108

as you imagine. I might not be respectable but my home is all I've got, so I take pride in it.' Nell had never talked about her upbringing before, but she wanted Eve to know that she could have had it harder and that she was not the only one to have been left pregnant and heartbroken. 'Come on, come back with me and we will have a tipple together and you can tell me how you thought taking your life was going to mend your lot and who this dashing soldier is whose advances you obviously fell for.'

Eve hesitated for a moment. It had been a long time since she had been able to talk to someone freely about herself. Perhaps it would do her good and Nell seemed to be a kind person. She should bury her pride and take her hand of friendship despite the trade Nell was in and the clothes she wore. She nodded. 'Yes, I will. Thank you; nobody else would give me the time of day if they knew how foolish and wicked I'd been.'

'Foolish, yes, and everyone is occasionally — but wicked? I don't think you're that. Just a little gullible when it comes to men and every young lass is. The thing is to play them at their own game and make them pay — I learned that a long time ago.' Nell linked her arm through Eve's and smiled. 'There, sisters in arms and no more thinking daft thoughts of ending your life, not now you have Nell as a friend.'

*　*　*

'Who's that with you, Nell?' the inn's landlord shouted as he rolled a barrel of beer across the yard, stopping at the inn's doorway as he watched both Eve and Nell climb the rickety outside steps to the place she called home. 'I've never seen her with you before.' The grey-haired, red-cheeked man stood for a second and gazed up at his infamous tenant, who often had men visitors but never many female ones.

'This is my new friend, Eve Reynolds, and we're going to share a drink together. So if anyone asks for my services in the next hour, you can tell them I'm busy.' Nell looked down at her landlord. He was a good friend and never complained about the men who visited her and the hours they kept — why would he? Invariably they'd spend as much money drinking at his bar, plucking up courage before they went to see her, or drinking and boasting about their romps with her and the other girls and women that made their living around the Black Swan. If Leeds had a magazine like London had the infamous *The Swells Night Guide through the Metropolis*, then the Black Swan would take pride of place in being the best for a young man to gain satisfaction in Leeds.

Eve stood behind Nell, feeling unsteady as her hand grasped the worn wooden railing that led to Nell's home up and across the cobbled yard from the inn and above what looked to be an old wool spinning room. She'd told Nell about where she was living, what had happened to her mother and the guilt that she was feeling, as they had walked up from the canal basin. Nell had hardly commented, listening to her confessions without bias or opinion, making Eve feel guilty

110

about how fast she had been to judge her. After all, they were very much alike except that Nell was considerably older than her although she certainly didn't look her years. In fact, her being still able to attract trade at her age was unusual. Even Eve knew it was more of a young woman's game and that once a woman was over thirty, men looked for the younger and more attractive harlots.

'Well, abandon hope all ye who enter here!' Nell laughed as she opened the door to her home. She turned and looked at Eve. 'Don't worry, there's nothing in here that you wouldn't have in a normal house. The first room is where I do my entertaining and then the rest of the house is just my home. I don't usually let anyone past this next door and it's always locked.'

Eve looked around the room that they had just entered while Nell unlocked the door. This first room was of a good size, with a bed in the centre and a chair and washstand next to the far wall. At the window hung lace curtains tied back with a ruby-like jewelled sash that matched the rich red walls, which had two brass candleholders on them. Nothing was that different from a normal room, but Eve blushed when she noticed a horse crop down by the side of the bed.

Nell smiled. 'Some men enjoy playing games more than having a bit of how's your father. All they need is a good spanking and sending on their way after being told that they've been a naughty boy. Each to their own is what I say — and besides, I'd rather do that than have some of them heaving on top of me.' Nell winked and

111

opened the door into her living quarters, letting Eve pass into the room.

She gazed around the room and was surprised to see it was like any other living space. Nothing unusual. The walls were whitewashed and the floor was covered with a large, highly decorated rug with dark, varnished floorboards around the edges. The furniture was practical: a sofa and two chairs and a large sideboard with a glass mirror along the back of it on the wall. It was not what she expected, she thought, as she stood next to the fireplace with a carriage clock and two pottery spaniels upon the mantel.

'I'll light the fire; there's a nip in the air and I've given up on the day. I'll go back out later this evening. Trade is usually brisk when they all pile out from the music hall and want to continue their night of entertainment.' Nell bent down and struck a Lucifer on the edge of the match container and put it to the already laid newspaper and kindling, adding coal from the scuttle in the hearth as the flames took hold. 'There, pull up a chair and we'll share a gin and you can tell me more about yourself.'

Eve still kept her shawl wrapped tightly around her shoulders. Nell was right, it was cold, but it had not bothered her until now because she had been so consumed by her worries and now she felt herself shivering. She pulled one of the chairs nearer the fire and watched as Nell took two crystal-cut glasses along with a bottle of Old Tom out of the sideboard's end cupboard, pouring Eve a glass and thrusting it in her hands.

'Here, this will keep the cold out. The room

will soon warm through. I don't light the fire until I need to. I usually eat down in the Swan and I don't want my paying visitors to be too content when they visit me. It's best to get their needs seen to and send them on their way.' Nell filled her own glass and then clinked it to Eve's. 'Bottom's up! You look surprised — how did you think I lived? I still need a home, no matter what profession I'm in. Thankfully, I'm my own boss. I don't have a pimp on my back all the time, taking money which is rightfully mine, and I don't have a husband and children to drain me. I'm my own person and can live as I want, providing the men keep coming.' Nell drank deeply.

'You've got a good home; I don't know what I expected. It's the first time I've been in anywhere like this.' Eve glanced down.

'You mean a brothel? Don't hold back, I'm proud of what I am and at least I make a good living and I have a decent home. I have two more rooms, all well-furnished. And unlike half the houses in Leeds, my home is dry and the walls aren't running with damp. I use the privy and the water pump in the yard and I have good friends in the Swan. I have everything that I need and no man owns me, not like the poor buggers that are pimped out on the streets by that bastard Bert Bradshaw, who takes nearly all their takings and keeps them living in squalor.' Nell sipped her gin and poured herself another. She looked at Eve's still half-full glass before putting her own down on the small table next to her chair. 'Now, what are we to do about your life?

Do you think the Lamberts at the Bluebell will be understanding about your situation, once they realise that you are with child?'

Eve lifted her head and looked at Nell. For a brief moment she had forgotten about herself and had been enthralled by Nell's life. When she had first met her, she had thought of her as a wicked, lustful woman, the very worst in society. Now, in her company, she realised that she was just a woman making a living the best way she could. Albeit selling her body to the lustful men of Leeds, but beneath the hard exterior was a heart that had been broken, just like hers, and she couldn't help but feel they had a lot in common.

'Please, I shouldn't have burdened you with my troubles, Nell. It was just that for a brief time I lost my senses and wanted to end it all . . . ' Eve shook her head. 'I don't know what I'm going to do; as you say, I'm not the first woman to have a child and have no one to support them. It's just that I loved him and then he took advantage of me and now he's gone. I'll never forget Sergeant John Oates — and now that I'm carrying his child, I will never be able to.' Eve started to cry again.

'John Oates? You didn't fall for his lies, did you? He must have been with every young woman in Leeds that he could charm with his bonny blue eyes and handsome face. I'm afraid you have been just another innocent on his list of conquests, my dear.' Nell shook her head. 'He's got a reputation from hell.'

Eve sniffed. 'I know, I was warned, but I

114

thought I knew better. Like always, I didn't listen. Oh, sometimes I think myself stupid. Jill and Nancy did warn me but I took no heed and now look at me.' Eve patted her stomach, which she imagined to be larger than it actually was.

'Well, I can't see the Lamberts having sympathy with you then. Nancy won't like it. The last barmaid left pregnant, with rumours flying around that it was Theo's. She's not going to take at all kindly to your situation.' Nell looked across at the young lass who had suddenly taken a liking to her glass of gin as she refilled it and felt sympathy for her situation.

'Theo runs the inn,' Eve said, 'but it's Nancy that wears the breeches and she keeps him in order. She'll not have the time of day for me once she finds out that I'm with child. And to be honest, I don't enjoy working there anyway since they've got together with the Cock and Bottle and are holding dog baiting sessions in the yard. Their customers are changing for the worse.' She tipped her glass back.

'Well, lass, you'll have to think about what you and that baby you're carrying are going to do. My advice is to go back to your father and beg for his forgiveness; he'll hopefully think differently about you now there's a baby on the way.' Nell sighed.

'That I can't do. My father made it quite clear that he blames me for the death of my mother. Plus, we never did see eye to eye; he always called me wilful and stubborn. Carrying this baby will only make him even surer in his opinion of me, that I am wicked and sinful and

115

deserve all that I get.' Eve sat back as the gin relaxed her.

'You could always find another man to have you. Anything's better than living a life on your own when you have a child dependent on you and no support. There must be some desperate men drinking at the Bluebell, some that are in need of comfort of a night and wouldn't mind taking you on, despite that child growing in your belly,' Nell said as shock spread across Eve's face.

'I could never do that! I would only marry someone I loved, otherwise what is the point of marriage?' Eve closed her eyes. She was tired and the gin and the fire were making her sleepy.

'Well, I think you're going to be in for a rude awakening, my girl. If you think you've had it rough so far, I can assure you that there will be worse to come when you have another mouth to feed and nobody to look after it. All I can say is: if you get down on your luck, you know where I am. Now, by the looks of you, I think you're best off going home and going to bed — that last drink has gone straight to your head. And don't be thinking of doing anything stupid like throwing yourself into the cut again.' Nell stood up and watched as Eve slowly rose from her chair.

'Thank you, Nell, you've saved my life,' she whispered. Tears were still not far from erupting from her eyes as she gave Nell a quick hug and then made her way to the steps leading down into the Black Swan's yard. She teetered at the top and thanked Nell again, then gingerly walked down them and made her way back along the streets of Leeds, returning to her room, where she lay down and sobbed. She was well and truly lost. How she wished Nell had not been there to save her for then now she would be free of her life and worries. Instead, she was on her own, pregnant and unloved, and it was about to be Christmas, a time when family and friends were the most precious of blessings.

10

The streets of Leeds were busy with market sellers shouting out their wares and trying to attract the busy shoppers to their stalls. Children pressed their noses close to the glass of the shops selling toys and sweets, their eyes filled with wonder and hope that soon the stockings at the end of their beds would be full of the delights that Christmas brought. Eve wandered down the busy market street of Briggate, a basket on her arm and a shopping list in her hand. At the top were instructions to check that the good plump goose ordered for the Bluebell Inn, along with a decent joint of ham and some pork faggots, would be delivered on time by the butcher's boy. With that task complete, she moved on to other shopping, taking in the sights and sounds and smells. Even though she had the worries of the world on her shoulders, she couldn't help but feel the wonder and joy of Christmas Eve in the busy, thriving town, with the bustle of people buying gifts and food for their larders for the one day that every man celebrated, whether they were poor or wealthy. Her basket was full by the time she reached the end of the market. Turnips, potatoes, carrots and a bag of roasted chestnuts that had tempted her with the smell of them roasting — a temptation that she could barely afford in the condition she was in, but she had decided that if she couldn't afford a truepenny bag of roasted chestnuts she might as well be dead.

In her free hand she held a bunch of mistletoe to be hung up in the bar of the Bluebell, as Theo had requested, much to Nancy's disdain. Her argument was that no man — Theo especially — needed encouragement to take advantage of the season's goodwill and that folk would be merry enough without being encouraged to kiss under the mistletoe. Eve was thankful that she could perhaps forget about her situation for the next few days and busy herself at the Bluebell, but she couldn't help but think about how Christmas was celebrated at home, how she missed her mother and wondered what her father would be doing on his own this Christmas. Although he had washed his hands of her, she couldn't help but think that he would be lonely on his own. She shook her head; like Nell said, it was up to her to make the best of her life. Every morning she woke and worried if today was the day that her secret would be made public, that someone would notice her growing stomach and morning sickness.

After Nell had talked to her about whether or not she should get rid of her baby, Eve had given it serious thought. She knew that many babies were disposed of in such a way, but she also knew mothers lost their lives through that practice. No, she couldn't take its life without taking her own, so the notion of just getting rid of her unborn baby didn't even bear thinking about. She shouted 'Merry Christmas' to the flower seller on the corner of Vicar Lane and then made tracks back to Warwick Street and the Bluebell. At least this Christmas she had a roof over her head and on Christmas Day, she had been invited to join in the Lamberts' celebrations. She would try to forget the predicament that she was in for the next day or so and just enjoy Christmas.

'Lord, there's so much to do today!' Nancy puffed and swore and she gave her children the rough edge of her tongue as she cleaned the kitchen and made sure that Eve had brought back all that she had requested from the market. 'You'd think folk would want to stay at home and get themselves prepared for Christmas, but instead, they seem to want to sit in our bar and drink themselves silly. You'd better get in the bar and give Theo a hand; he's been run off his feet since we opened this morning. I don't know where folk get their money to spend on drink but I won't complain — it keeps the wolf from our door.' Nancy yelled again at her eldest as he pinched a spoonful of pudding mix from the spoon she had been stirring it with. 'I need twenty pairs of hands this morning, with all the baking, cleaning and Christmas planning to make sure the table is perfect tomorrow.'

'Everybody seems in a bustle in Leeds. The market stalls are heaving and I had to wait to be served everywhere, else I'd have been back earlier. I'll go and help Theo, the bar does sound really busy even though it's not even yet midday,' Eve said to Nancy, glad that she was needed in the bar and to get out of Nancy's way. Her employer's face looked flushed and it was clear

120

to see that her temper was bubbling nicely underneath her flustered appearance.

'Aye, take this mistletoe with you and hang it up on the central beam. It's always a good excuse for folk to flirt and get a quick kiss at this time of year, especially when they are well plied with drink. You'll be expected to stand under it and you'll know from last year that there will be plenty of groping hands as the day goes on.' Nancy passed Eve the mistletoe and looked her up and down. 'You look peaky; put some rouge on your cheeks before you go behind the bar, folk doesn't want to look at a washed-out drip. That's what they're leaving at home and expect to see something bonny behind our bar.'

Eve took the mistletoe and didn't reply; she knew she looked pale — she always did in the morning. She'd perk up in the afternoon and then she would feel more festive, although the thought of kissing some of the locals that frequented the Bluebell made her cringe. The idea of kissing old Joe, whose teeth were as black as the chimney with breath that stank like the sewers did not fill her with glee as she walked into the bar and was met with cheers and whoops of joy when she passed Theo the mistletoe to be hung over the Bluebell's customers' heads.

'Ah, the mystic mistletoe! Now, don't any of you take advantage of it too much.' Theo grinned and looked at the faces of his customers as he took the key-shaped leafed and white-berried bunch of greenery from Eve and winked at her. He walked from behind the bar and, balancing on a chair, tied the mistletoe to a nail in the centre beam that had been used yearly since Theo and Nancy had taken on the Bluebell. 'It's now truly Christmas,' Theo announced as he stood down from the chair, pulled his waistcoat straight and stood back to admire his work. A cheer went up and everyone raised their tankards and glasses and shouted: 'A Merry Christmas to one and all!'

As Theo went back behind the bar and stood with Eve, he whispered, 'I'll expect to get a kiss from you later on this evening. Perhaps when Nancy isn't looking.' He winked and then went on to serve the next customer, leaving Eve staring blankly at him. He had never said anything like that to her before. She overfilled a customer's tankard, making the beer froth and spill on the bar in her surprise. Theo reached over and patted her backside as she mopped the spillage up and whispered to her again, 'How about a Christmas bonus for us both tonight? Keep your door unlocked and I'll make sure that you get the present that I know that you've been after for some time.'

Theo winked and then grinned at his next customer, leaving Eve feeling shaken. She'd never encouraged him in the least, so why had he decided to show interest in her now? She decided not to reply to him and to get on with her day, giving Theo a wide berth. The last thing she wanted was for him to show her his attentions, especially in the condition that she was in — and she was certainly not prepared to suffer the wrath of Nancy. She smiled to hide her dislike of Theo's comments and joined in with the customers' singing of 'God Bless Ye, Merry Gentlemen' as old Joe stood up with his tankard in hand and his top hat still on his head to lead the Christmas carols.

Eve's stomach churned with the worry of Theo's words as the day went on. By evening, the Bluebell was as crowded as a mind, with customers pushing their way through to the bar to get served. The noise and the singing were cheerful and the air was filled with tobacco smoke and the smell of Nancy's mutton stew, the staple favourite of the Bluebell's customers. Eve had never seen the place so busy. Her feet hurt, her head hurt, and she'd been kissed so many times that she'd lost count and she felt exhausted as the last revellers made their way out of the doorway out onto a very wintry Walker Street, where the snow had been falling for well over an hour and everything was coated in a blanket of white.

It certainly made for the perfect Christmas as Eve listened to the church bells and renditions of various carols while late-night drinkers made their way home. She stood in the Bluebell's doorway and looked out into the street, her heart aching slightly as she remembered Christmases with her mother and father and how Christmas Eve had been so special to her. Now, she was uncertain about what life was to throw at her next; the baby growing in her stomach would change her life and she wondered what would become of her once the Lamberts knew about the child. She'd given Theo a wide berth all evening and she had every intention of locking her bedroom door, no matter what. There was no way she was about to compromise her job at the Bluebell — she had to save every penny she could before they discovered her secret. If Nancy even suspected her of being pregnant or encouraging Theo, she would throw her out — and she couldn't let that happen just yet. She bent down and pulled the heavy bolt along the bottom of the Bluebell's door and did the same again at the top, sighing as she did so. Tomorrow was Christmas Day, meaning no work except for the help in the kitchen that Nancy would expect of her when it came to Christmas dinner. She turned back into the bar to find Theo standing behind her.

'How about that kiss under the mistletoe? I think it's my turn now.' Theo caught her by the waist and looked into her eyes. 'Don't worry, Nancy's upstairs seeing to the children's presents. She won't catch us.' He grinned and looked down at Eve while she shook her head.

'No, Theo, it isn't right. Nancy wouldn't like it and you're my boss,' Eve protested and tried to pull away from his grip.

'All the more reason for you to keep me sweet, especially when I know you've been helping yourself to our gin on the quiet. I wondered what had made you come out of your shell and then I saw you having a sneaky tipple. Nancy can't abide thieving, especially when she's taken you in as one of her own.' Theo held her tighter and then kissed her hard upon the lips. 'Don't forget what I said: keep your bedroom door unlocked tonight. Father Christmas has a present he wants to give to you . . . ' Theo grinned. He'd been waiting patiently for his moment and now he thought it was here. 'Now, just one more kiss, under the mistletoe this time.' Theo pulled Eve towards him, holding her tightly as they ended up under the mistletoe together.

'No, please!' Eve tried to push him away but he was strong and held on, kissing her so hard that she could hardly breathe.

'You wanton hussy!' The screech could have been heard in the next street as Nancy made an unexpected appearance behind the bar. 'Is this what you get up to with my Theo when you think I'm abed? No wonder you look so ill at the moment, dancing with the devil under my roof with my husband!' Nancy strode over as Theo let go of Eve and pushed her to one side.

'It's not what it looks like, Nancy. In fact, it was a parting kiss because I was just telling her that I'd caught her drinking the gin on quite a few occasions lately, so I was giving her the boot. She was kissing me and offering herself to me to stop me from telling you,' Theo claimed virtuously, scowling at Eve.

'I did not! I might have helped myself to the odd gin or two, but I did not force myself upon you!' Eve shouted at Theo. 'It was you who grabbed me.'

'You thieving, lying little bitch! You get up those stairs and pack your bags and leave our home now!' Nancy yelled and grabbed Eve's arm, pushing towards the stairs. 'I never want to see your face again. I should have known you were trouble when your own parents disowned you.' She stood at the bottom of the stairs, her hands on her hips, glaring as Eve went up, sobbing.

Theo was appalled. He hadn't meant anything like this to happen. 'She perhaps meant no harm, Nancy. You can't throw her out on Christmas Eve. You know how these young women are attracted to me — they get the urge and just can't help themselves.' He looked at Nancy hopefully but from the look she gave him, he knew that once Eve was out of the Bluebell, then it would be his turn to receive her wrath.

'Shut up! I know what you are, all right. I know your game. Be thankful it isn't you that I'm throwing out tonight,' Nancy spat as she shouted for Eve to hurry up with her packing.

Eve sobbed and cried, pushing her few belongings into her carpetbag and looking around the room to make sure she had got everything that was hers. It was Christmas Eve, it was snowing and she had nowhere to go. How could Theo have put her in this situation? And how could Nancy be so cold-hearted? She put the purse with her meagre savings into the bottom of her bag — she wasn't going to lose them this time — and gave a final glance around the room that she had grown quite fond of. She had known that once they had found out she was pregnant, she'd have been thrown out anyway, but to be made homeless on Christmas Eve was cruel. The only doors that would be open to her at this hour would be those of the poorhouse — and once you were in there, you were lucky if you ever left.

'Come on, get your arse out of my pub!' Nancy stood at the unbolted doors of the Bluebell. 'I don't let women like you drink here, let alone work and stay here. Get yourself out on the streets where rabble like you belong.' She pushed Eve towards the doorway and the snow that was falling outside.

Theo stood back and said nothing as Eve clutched her bag, with tears running down her eyes, gathering her shawl around her.

'Please, Nancy, please show mercy! It's Christmas Eve and I have nowhere to go,' Eve wailed as she made for the inn's steps onto Warwick Street.

'Save your words, slut! I have no pity for you. I just hope that the bailiff of the poorhouse is not in his bed yet and that he has room for such a lost soul like you.' Nancy closed the door upon Eve and left her standing in the street, the snow falling down around her as the town hall clock struck twelve thirty. She was alone once more with no one to turn to as she walked, shivering, through the snow-covered streets of Leeds.

11

'Bugger off! I've told you all, no fucking for two days! Lord, even I deserve to celebrate Christmas and my idea of Christmas isn't romping in bed with the likes of you,' Nell shouted at the locked door of her home as someone knocked loudly on the wood. She put her glass of gin down on the sideboard and looked into the fire. Christmas to her was sacred — no matter that trade would be brisk; she still had some morals left and everyone knew that there was no entertainment as far as she was concerned for these two days — or so she'd thought. The knocking continued and she rose to her feet, to go and confront her late-night caller.

'Just bugger off, whoever you are! I'm bloody sick of wasting my breath,' Nell shouted as she went through her room of entertainment to open the door on the cold snowy night. She unlocked the door and prepared to give an ardent lover a piece of her mind. 'Bloody hell, what are you doing on my doorstep? Why are you not at the Bluebell? What's happened?' Nell looked at the shivering Eve with her mouth open wide.

'They've thrown me out and I've nowhere else to go except the workhouse. Please, can I stay with you this night, Nell? You're the only person I felt I could ask.' Eve looked up at the woman she had once thought the scum of the earth, only now truly realising just how easy it was to fall from grace — and that she herself was not far behind her. She shivered and shook, clinging onto her carpetbag, a snow-covered shawl around her head and shoulders, praying that she would not be turned away by the hard but kind-hearted prostitute.

Nell hesitated for a second. She was used to just having herself for company once her clients had gone and that was how she liked it — but she couldn't let the poor lass walk the streets on Christmas Eve and freeze to death. 'Of course, come in, come in and get yourself warm. After all, it's Christmas and even I'm not that heartless a bitch that I'd throw you out tonight!'

Nell stood back and watched as Eve walked into her home, leaving a trail of melting snow behind her. 'Here, give me your shawl and go and warm yourself by the fire. I'll pour you a tot of brandy to warm you through. You look half-frozen.' Nell took Eve's shawl and motioned her to sit in the chair that she had just left next to the dying embers of her fire. 'Here, I'll put some more coal on and poke the fire back into life; I was just about to go to bed once I'd finished my drink.' Nell picked up the poker and stirred the embers and added more coal from out of the brass coal scuttle that stood in the hearth and then she poured Eve a strong shot of brandy.

Eve cupped it in her hands. 'I'm so sorry, Nell, I shouldn't have come and disturbed you. It's just that I had nowhere else to go and the night is so cold.' She looked into the glass as tears ran down her cheeks.

'It's all right, lass, if you can't show a little Christianity on Christmas Eve, then when can you? Besides, we can't have you on the streets on a night like this; we've got to look after that baby you are carrying.' Nell sat down in the chair opposite Eve and held out her hands for her to hold. 'Drink your brandy, it'll warm you through,' she said, urging her to tip the drink back and then smiled at her late-night visitor. 'Have they fed you? Are you hungry?'

'No, I'm not hungry. I'm sorry, it isn't because they know I'm pregnant. I just can't believe what happened.' Eve shook her head. 'Theo decided to take his chances with me just before midnight when the Bluebell had closed its doors and kissed me under the mistletoe only for Nancy to catch us. I didn't encourage him in the least, but she wouldn't listen, and then, when Theo told her I'd been helping myself to the gin and that I'd offered myself to him to keep his silence, she demanded that I left. But it wasn't like that! It was him that had forced himself on me. Why would I want him touching me in my condition?' Eve sniffed.

'So they don't know you are with child? You should have told them then. Perhaps that would have shown Theo up for the rat that he is. I can tell you, he's known for getting familiar with his barmaids — you've done well to survive this long — and he's often got a woman pregnant, although Nancy would never listen to the girls. Yes, she knows his flaws but still sticks by him.'

'I didn't say anything. After all, it has nothing to do with him. It would only have made things worse anyway.' Eve's hands shook and she began to sob.

'Well, you'd better stay the night here. I have a spare bed which is always made up so at least you'll be off the streets tonight and then we will see what tomorrow brings. Stop your crying, lass — things are never as bad as they seem and we'll work something out.'

Nell looked at Eve, secretly wishing that she had never befriended the young lass. She was used to being self-sufficient and keeping herself to herself, but Eve reminded her so much of herself when she had first started in her profession as a lady of the night out of desperation. There was not much else for the vulnerable Eve to do if she insisted on keeping her baby and she worried that, once Eve was on the streets, the ruthless Bert Bradshaw would have her working for him as soon as the baby was born. No, she was too innocent to fall into his hands. If Nell could save her from that fate, she would. Meantime, the brandy would hopefully give her a good night's sleep and she herself was desperate for her bed.

★   ★   ★

It was the following morning and, despite her troubles, Nell decided to try and celebrate Christmas. 'I know you probably don't appreciate this but ... Happy Christmas,' she said, looking up at Eve and offering her a seat at her table, where she had laid a bowl of porridge. 'How are you feeling?'

'I don't know. I tossed and turned all night and I just don't know what to do. You shouldn't have stopped me from throwing myself into the cut, that time; it would have been the best place for us both.' Eve held her head in her hands and didn't dare look at her saviour again.

'Now, don't talk so soft. It's only a baby you're having. Once it's born, you can get back to work and get on with your life. You're only young,' Nell said and then sat down next to her. 'I think you should go back to your father; he'll have calmed down by now. Once he knows that you're having a baby, his heart will soften, and surely he won't turn his back on you now?' Nell knew she couldn't show weakness to Eve now. It would be all too easy for her to say, 'Stay with me' in sympathy for her situation but she must be strong and not show her emotions. That was how she had survived so long: being independent and keeping her head down. She'd made herself hard to the outside world and she knew that to show she cared looked as if it was a weakness to others.

'No, no, I couldn't go back to him, Nell! Truly, he wouldn't have me. A baby outside marriage would mean such shame to him and he'd hate me even more. I don't know what to do. I thought I might go back and face Nancy and tell her the truth, that it was Theo that demanded my attention and plead for my job back, at least until the baby starts to show. By then I could have saved a little more money and could perhaps rent somewhere until the baby comes.' Eve looked with desperation at her.

'And then what? What are you going to do once it has arrived? You can't just abandon it and go back to work,' Nell looked at her and saw sadness in her eyes.

'I'll have to do as you did, leave it on the orphanage steps or, if I've enough money, pay a baby farmer to look after it.' Eve bowed her head. She knew that neither option was healthy for her unborn: the orphanage would bring her child up half-hungered and badly clothed, while if she paid a baby farmer to take care of her child, the likelihood of the baby being killed by its so-called guardian was high once the first payment had been passed into their hands. She was at a loss what to do with her life and once again, suicide was looking more and more the preferred option.

'Well, for today and tonight, you are safe. It's Christmas Day and I aim to do nothing. I feel guilty when the good people of this town go to church and I turn my back on them — but they turned their back on me when I needed a hand. So, like you, I have no time for religion. Or should I say, most of the people who go to church who'd only look at me as if I'd got the plague if I went. So, I usually have a quiet morning and then I have an arrangement with Stanley, the landlord at the Swan. He gives me my Christmas dinner every year, has done ever since I landed in his yard without a penny to my name and in need of a job. A bit like you, except I had abandoned my baby and my heart was breaking. Oh, Eve, don't do the same as me; swallow your pride and beg your father for his forgiveness.' Nell put her hand on Eve's arm. She didn't want her to have heartache like hers.

'No,' Eve said firmly, 'I can't — I won't. He'd probably send me to the asylum rather than take me back in. He always said that I was too headstrong for my own good and that the devil drives me. Perhaps he was right,' she whispered and looked into the fire, leaving her bowl of porridge untouched as Nell closed the door behind her and went to arrange for another dinner to be served to the unwanted guest that she seemed to have attracted and now was beginning to worry about getting rid of.

* * *

'So, you've got yourself a lodger!' Stanley laughed and looked at Nell. 'Or are you expanding your business? I don't blame you — you're not getting any younger — but don't let Bert Bradshaw know, else he'll be down on you like a ton of bricks. You've only survived this long because you keep yourself to yourself and he doesn't think of you as that much of a threat.' Stanley looked at the worried Nell and shouted through to his wife that there was an extra mouth to feed for Christmas dinner.

'Don't even think it,' Nell said. 'She's only with me because she's with child and those at the Bluebell have thrown her out. That Theo was doing what he does best, trying to get his leg over and not pay for it, the bastard, and Nancy caught him.'

'Is the baby his? It's time he was caught out

and made to pay for all his lusting.' Stanley leaned on the bar and looked at Nell; she could stand up to almost anyone, but her heart was a good one and he knew that if she'd taken this lass in, she'd be in good hands, if only for Christmas Day.

'No, that's the stupid thing, it's a soldier's and it's really touched my heart. She's in the exact same boat as I was and I can't help but feel sorry for her.' Nell shook her head and sighed.

'You're getting soft in your old age. If it's the lass from the Bluebell that I think she is, they'll miss her. Folk have been coming in here and saying how bonny she is and that they didn't know what she was doing, working for a dump like the Bluebell. Hmm. I'm in two minds to offer her work until the baby shows its head, but I've nowhere for her to stay — that is, unless you're willing to share? You could do with the company, Nell. You keep yourself to yourself too much, you know — and I've said as much in the past. You could be really ill up there and we wouldn't know until it was too late, especially with the folk that come and go at yours at all times of the day and night.' Stanley shook his head.

Nell sighed and looked at Stanley. 'She's not a bad lass, but I wish I'd never got involved; I should have let her throw herself into the cut and have walked away. She'd just have been another nameless body that was found and nobody would have been any wiser. As it is, she's tugging on my heartstrings because she reminds me so much of myself.'

135

'You could put her up at yours just until the baby comes and then send her on her way. She can work for me until she feels unable to and I'll give her jobs that keep her out of view as her belly gets bigger — she can help the missus in the kitchen. Then, when the baby comes, she'll have to make her mind up what to do and she'll have had plenty of time to think about it.' Stanley put his head to one side like a curious cock robin and saw that Nell was considering his offer.

'I wish I'd never bloody said anything to you, Stanley Nelson, you've made the situation even worse!' she said. 'There's no excuse for me not to have her now, is there? I suppose she could stay; she could see to things for me while I'm out on the game. Bloody hell, Christmas Day and I'm showing a serious bit of Christian spirit; I'll be going to church before you know it!' Nell shook her head.

'Now, that would be a miracle. I'll come across with your two dinners and then I'll have a look at her for myself and ask her to work for me if I think she'll suit and you're willing for her to stay with you. Happen we'll both earn our wings in heaven, yet,' Stanley said, grinning.

'Nah, we're bound for the devil's lair, because I know exactly what you're thinking, Stanley. You've got your eye on her as my replacement! Well, I might be getting past my best, but I've not closed my doors yet. Still, perhaps she might be of use to both of us, depending on how fast she learns.'

'I'll tell you what I think when I come over

with your dinners — and then she'll have to agree, of course,' Stanley said. 'Now, seeing that it's my only day off, until my old lass tells me my dinner is ready, I'm going to have forty winks in front of the fire. It's bloody cold today, a proper Christmas Day, although I'd rather the Swan's doors were open and we were trading; money could be made if this government did but know it,' Stanley growled.

'Well, I'll go back and see what Eve has to say to the suggestion that she could perhaps stay with me for a short while. I just hope I don't live to regret it. I like my own company so she's definitely got to go once the baby is born. Especially if she thinks of keeping it, for I'll not be playing nanny to it, that's a certainty.'

Nell looked around the empty inn. The floorboards were in need of a wash, the plaster on the walls was in need of rendering, the brass bar around the bar had not been cleaned for some time and the spittoons needed emptying. She'd nearly laughed when Stanley had called the Bluebell a dump — it was a palace compared to the Swan. Even the locals called it the Mucky Duck. It wasn't the cleanliness that they went there for but the good company and the tarts that made you welcome. For all his faults, Stanley knew how to keep his ale fresh and his gin in stock; he also knew when to keep quiet about things and show a blind eye when needed. The old bugger was a wise one and perhaps he had a point when it came to Eve. After all, she herself wasn't getting any younger and no matter how prim and proper Eve would like to think herself, she'd already lifted her skirts for one man, and once the baby was born, if she decided to keep it, there was little else for an unmarried woman to do to make money. But she'd wait and see what Eve thought to the suggestion of working in the Swan and then introduce her to her world — and while she wouldn't be as ruthless as Bert Bradshaw, she would take a cut out of her payments if Eve was to live with her. Nell smiled; she could be a Madam, her own brothel, run by her. Perhaps Eve could be the first of many — now *that* was something to think about.

★ ★ ★

Eve looked down at the Christmas dinner that had been put in front of her. The goose looked greasy and fatty and the potatoes had been overcooked; as for the plum pudding and the lumpy sauce that had been poured over it, she'd never seen anything like it before. It was a good job she wasn't hungry, she thought, as she looked up at the man Nell had introduced as the landlord of the Swan and thanked him for presenting such a lovely meal to her.

'Now, before you tuck into your dinner, has Nell said anything about my suggestion? She told me of your plight and I wondered if you'd be interested in working for me at the Swan, just until the baby is born? Nell says she'll let you lodge with her — after all, she's plenty of bedrooms spare and this place could house a family of ten or more if it was rented out to somebody else.' Stanley looked at the young woman in front of him and knew that his drinkers would like to see her behind his bar and that men would pay to have their way with her.

'Yes, she has told me and I can't thank you both enough. I've nowhere else to go and nobody would want me in the state that I'm in. Not that you can tell yet,' Eve added quickly and looked across at Nell, who wasn't going to let her dinner go cold and she bit into a piece of the dark coloured meat and tore at the pimpled, greasy skin of the goose. 'I'll do anything that you want me to. I can cook, clean, pull a pint — just tell me what you want and I'll do it. I'm so grateful to be given a chance to work and be offered a place to lay my head.' Eve bowed her head and thought hard about her next words. She looked up, face determined. 'I'll not sell my body, though, not unless I really have to; it's the one bit of pride that I've got left.'

'Aye, well, Nell here wouldn't want the opposition and you are in no fit state at the minute. Right now, I've plenty of lasses offering themselves to anybody who will pay them, so I'll not be expecting that of you, not yet.' Stanley muffled the words 'not yet', knowing that once she was in a downward circle of life she'd certainly be drawn into the seedy world of prostitution. With her face and figure, she'd be popular, and she was young, just how some of his drinkers liked them. She'd be bedding men before she knew it, just to keep her baby fed and herself clothed. He'd seen it happen many times before; all the tarts that congregated in his pub had children at home waiting for them, going hungry and living in conditions that a dog wasn't fit to live in. Morals were a good thing, but they didn't keep a belly full or death from knocking on the door. Yes, Eve would be lifting her skirts — if not for him, it'd be for Nell. Because no matter how kind-hearted Nell was, she was a woman with a good head for figures and nobody's fool. That's how she'd survived under her own steam for so long.

'Then I'll expect to see you in the morning, Eve. Mrs Nelson can have a lie in bed for once if you can come across and see to the fires and give all a bit of a clean. We always have a full house on Boxing Day so it'll be very busy. The tradesfolk will be spending the brass that folk have given them in thanks for their services and it could get a bit rowdy.' Stanley grinned. 'Will you be back and trading, Nell, or are you having another day off?'

Nell wiped her chin free of goose grease. 'Nah, it's my best day of the year! My door will never be closed tomorrow. A girl's got to make money while she can.' She glanced at Eve and saw the shock on her face. 'Don't look so po-faced! You'll hardly be here so you'll not see me. And if you do walk in and catch me on the job, just walk past me. I'll not have time for you when I'm a beast with two backs. There's no place for blushes in this house, my love; you'll have to get used to that or, better still, join in. They pay more money for two of us.' Nell grinned at the shock on Eve's face. 'Don't worry, I only jest, but I must warn you, this is not the Bluebell.

140

Theo might have had a few dodges working but down here, near the canal, we get all sorts and you'll have to learn to go blind on occasion.'

'She's right,' Stanley said. 'We are tough down here, but we look after our own. So if you fit in, you'll always have someone to watch your back and look out for you. Now, seven in the morning, the door will be open; first job is light the fires and then we'll see how the day goes.' He winked at Nell as he left them sitting at the table, Nell with a nearly clean empty plate but Eve just looking at hers. The lass doesn't know what she's in for, he thought as he made his way gingerly down the snow-covered steps and back across the yard into his pub. But with Nell as her companion, she'd not be that innocent for very long, not if Nell had her way.

12

Eve dressed and washed from the jug of freezing water on her washstand. Nell had agreed that she could stay in the room right at the end of the building, which was over the top of the old spinning rooms. It was larger than the one she had left at the Bluebell, but also colder; one of the windowpanes that overlooked the yard was stuffed with a rag to keep the draught from blowing through and although Nell had whitewashed the walls and had it clean and tidy with some good pieces of furniture in it, the room was still a bit bleak.

She shivered and wrapped her shawl around her; it was still dark and the light of her tallow candle burned low as she made her way along the hallway that separated the bedrooms and then into Nell's living quarters. The coal fire was just in and so she stirred the embers and added a kindling stick to make it jump back into life before adding coal from the scuttle. She pulled her shawl tighter around her and picked up the iron kettle and unbolted the door into Nell's entertaining room, then made her way down the steps to the water pump.

In the yard, she filled the kettle, looking around her if there was any sign of movement in the Black Swan and if anybody had yet bothered to unlock the door for her to go in and start being busy. It all looked quiet, the pub's sign of a swimming black swan hanging above the doorway and the windows all shuttered from inside. Clearly, no one was awake yet and she climbed back up into the warmth of her new home. There she put the kettle on to boil and warmed her hands, thinking about the mess she was in and how grateful she was to have been offered work until her baby was born. Then, if it was born safely and she survived the birth, she'd have to move on and decide what to do with the life that she had brought into the world. Nell, she knew, was being truly kind to her and she couldn't expect to stay with her once the child was born. She would have to leave it at the orphanage or find employment where she could take the child with her; a brothel was no place for an innocent to be reared in and even she felt ill at ease with the situation, but beggars could not be choosers and she was just grateful for the kindness shown to her. She watched as the kettle started to boil and reached for the caddy from above the fireplace that Nell kept the tea in.

'Bye, this is grand to see, the fire stoked and the kettle boiling with tea nearly brewed.' Nell sat down in her chair and pulled her tight-laced ankle boots on, tying them and then grinning at Eve. 'It's a pity I haven't time to indulge. I've got to get down to the dockside for I've my usuals to satisfy — they like a bit of quim in the morning. They'll not be bothered that there's snow and frost on the ground and that it's Boxing Day. All they want is their usual knee-trembler before they set off for the next port of call.'

Nell walked over to the sideboard and poured

herself a quick gin. 'This will keep the cold at bay and get me more in the mood. Dock workers are a bit rough and ready, not like the upper-class gents that you get up near the music hall, but brass is brass and I don't attach myself to any of them. It's the best way if I have to survive in this life. You watch yourself at the Swan today; Stanley and his wife Maude will be right with you but some of the women like Rosie and Tilly that drink there are bitches. Don't let them talk down to you — most of them are just trollops anyway.'

Nell knocked her tipple back in one and then walked to the door. 'When you come back this evening, if the brush is outside the door it means I'm busy. I won't be long, so just wait in the Swan that is unless you want to join in? Harry Preston is my usual around eleven in the evening on a Monday night and he'd pay extra money for two of us; he's like clockwork, never fails — unlike his lovemaking, poor old bugger.' Nell winked. 'Take care of yourself, girl, and think about what I've told you.'

Eve watched as Nell, with her unkempt long dark hair, scarlet dress and high-laced boots winked at her and then left her. She had no intention of joining her in her romps and now that Nell had said the women who supped at the Swan were bitches she was not filled with excitement. However, whatever the customers were, she would have to deal with them if she was to earn money to pay her way but she now knew that living with Nell was not going to be the easiest of the homes that she had lived in.

Maude Nelson was still dressed in her nightgown and with eyes squinting, she looked up as the doors opened and Eve walked into the bar. She stared at the young lass who stood in front of her.

'So you're the one they call Eve that my Stanley has taken on? Well, I'll give you something in your favour: you're here on time. However, you've caught me in my night attire, a sight that's not right good at the best of times.' Maude grinned, her long grey hair hanging over her shoulders as she looked Eve up and down in the light of the inn's oil lamps. 'Don't just stand there, lass, you're here to work! Both fires need lighting, the kettle needs putting on and the shutters need drawing back, so there's plenty for you to be getting on with while Stanley and I are getting dressed.'

Eve looked around her and took her shawl off. Seeing that the fire grate needed completely emptying as a build-up of old ashes was spilling out, she decided to start on that and said, 'Where do you keep the coal and kindling sticks?' She watched Maude pull a face and make her way to the living quarters above the bar.

'Outside, in the shed. Mind you fill both scuttles up, I don't want you to be wasting time running back and forward across the yard when we have a full house — and make sure you riddle any cinders so that they can be used again. We aren't made of money here at the Swan,' she shouted as she left Eve looking around her in the dim light.

Eve sighed and then made her way to open the wooden shutters that kept any chink of daylight from entering into the bar and the snug that was at the far side of the none-too-clean bar, trying to put her finger on the peculiar smell of the place and likening it to cooked cabbage mixed with wine that had gone off. It was certainly no palace and not a patch on the Bluebell. She unbolted the wooden shutters at each window and then went to sort out the two fires, one in the main bar and one in the snug. Down on her knees, she started to clean and clear the ashes from the main fire, filling the bucket that was by the side easily as she swept and riddled the coals that could be used again. She then took the full bucket out into the yard and emptied the ashes into the ash pit next to where the coal shed stood, filling both the bucket and the brass coal scuttle up to the brim with coal and kindling before returning to light the fire. Her hands were filthy by the time she had finished both fires, so she went out to the water pump in the yard and washed her hands under the freezing water, taking the large black kettle to fill and hang on the crook above the main fire.

She felt cold, dirty and miserable; her new place of work was getting worse by the second as the early morning light came in through the windows. The windows had not been cleaned since the glass had been put in them, she thought as she stood behind the bar and looked at the scene around her. The place was a mess!

The tables and chairs had all seen better days, the tankards and glasses looked as if they had never been washed — and as for the floors and walls, there was so much dirt on them she doubted that they had ever been washed. With the kettle boiling on the hearth, she started to make some sense of it all. Picking up a brush that she found, she began to sweep the dirt and muck from off the flagged floor, opening the doors to brush it out into the yard. She then took the metal mop bucket which, along with the mop, looked as if it had never been used for a while, filling it with boiling water from the kettle and starting to mop the floor, cleaning around the metal stands of the tables and chairs.

The doors flew open and two young women came in and looked Eve up and down. 'Bloody hell, that's a novelty for sure!' one said. 'I've never seen that being done in the Mucky Duck at this time of a morning — or at any other time, come to think of it. You must be new, else you'd know doing that was a waste of time.' They grinned at one another.

'He's got himself a right Cinderella here, Tilly,' the mouthy one said, nudging and winking at her friend, and then they both went and stood at the bar.

'Maude not about?' Tilly asked. 'Is she still having a bit of how's your father with Stan? I thought they'd be past it at their ages, didn't you, Rose?'

Eve looked at the two, who were obviously the women that Nell had warned her about. 'She'll be here shortly. I'm Eve and I've come to work here. Do you want serving?'

'Do we want bloody serving? Too true, it's been perishing down by the docks last night! These fellas don't seem to understand that a girl's got to make a living whether it's bloody Christmas or not. It's the only time I've known them to want to go home to their missus, to make do with her when they decide they need home comforts and forget about us poor buggers. Two gins and make them large'uns.'

Eve put her mop down and walked behind the bar, going to the cream-coloured ceramic barrel that had Gin written on it and about to pour it into two of the glasses.

'No, not that! That's used if any excise men walk in. You'll find the harder stuff under the bar, in an unmarked bottle. It's Stan's brewing and probably all turpentine, but it hits the spot and that's all we're bothered about.' Rose leaned over the bar and pointed to the clear bottle that held their usual and watched as Eve poured it. 'So, you're Eve, then, are you? Where's your Adam and never mind about Nip-me-tight, less said about him the better.' Rose winked at Tilly as she took a long sip of her gin.

'I don't have an Adam — and what are you on about with nip-me-tight?' Eve held her hand out to be paid.

'We'll make it right with Stan, we have an understanding,' Rose said as she waved her hand away. 'Nip-me-tight — surely you've heard of Nip-me-tight? Tilly, you tell her the tale.'

Tilly grinned and then went into verse:

'Adam and Eve and Nip-me-tight
Went down to the river to bathe.
Adam and Eve were drowned
Now who do you think was saved?'

'Nip-me-tight,' Eve said, realising too late what was going to happen just as Rose reached across the bar and nipped her arm tightly between two fingers, making her yell.

'Well, you did ask for it, lass! You'll have to be quicker than that if you are to work in the Mucky Duck,' Rose said and grinned.

'Nell warned me about you two, she said I'd have to be on my toes.' Eve looked at the two prostitutes. Both had clearly been pretty in their day but a lifetime of doing trade on the streets was beginning to take its toll and Eve noticed that Tilly had sores on her neck and that her lips had scabs on them.

'Bonfire Nell? Do you know her? The old cow, she'd fellas down on the quayside just waiting for her. They think she's a bit classier than us, but she still spreads her legs for money, so she's really no better,' Rose snarled.

'I'm staying with her; she's putting me up and she got me my job here. I know what she is, but she's been good to me and I've got a lot to thank her for,' Eve said firmly, defending her new-found friend.

'She'll be doing it for a reason, it'll not be anything else other than you're of benefit to her, so don't you be fooled. She's not been her own woman for this long without being a hard bitch. Bert Bradshaw or Stan here would have had her working for them if she wasn't as hard as nails. She's seen something in you.' Rose leaned over and looked again at Eve. 'Mind, she's getting to an age where she'll soon be past her best, so perhaps she'll be learning you the tricks of the trade — that is, if you don't know them already. Bert Bradshaw won't like that if he finds out; she's on borrowed time with him as it is, so I've heard.'

Eve shook her head in protest. 'No, it's not like that, she took pity on me. I'm expecting and the father has gone to fight overseas, so I've no one to take care of me. She got me this job and I'll be staying until the baby is born.' She didn't like to confess that she was pregnant but in her mind it was better than them thinking that she was joining Nell on the game.

'A bun in the oven? Now that's bad news for you, lass. Nobody wants a woman with a baby in tow and unmarried, I suppose. Well, you've come to the right spot; there will always be some kind of work for you at the Swan, but you'll not have to be choosy if you want your baby to be fed.' Rose looked at Tilly. 'Ours are in the workhouse. We left them on the steps because it's no good raising a child in the game that we're in.'

Tilly nodded sadly. 'I lost one last year. I can't carry them anymore because of this disease that I have, caught from the men I've bedded. Later on it'll make me lose my mind and then eventually it will kill me, I know it will. Lass, you need to get away from here once the baby is born and go back to where you've come from. Don't end up on the streets like me and Rose.'

150

Tilly hung her head and swallowed down a long drink.

'Hold your noise, Tilly, things aren't that bad,' Rose protested. 'We don't go without much and Bert Bradshaw leaves us alone. You'll be right, you'll see. Hey up, here comes some punters, so stop your blubbering else they'll not look twice at us.' Rose elbowed Tilly as a gang of men from the wharf walked into the pub.

'Hey, we've got a new face behind the bar, a bonny one and all! Now *that* makes working on Boxing Day worthwhile,' the first man through the doors shouted to the group of men behind him, then leaned on the bar, grinning at Eve. His face was covered with coal dust from unloading the tom puddings that brought coal from the southern side of Leeds up the canal and his hands were pitted with dirt as he opened his palm up to reveal his money. 'A gill, if you would . . . and anything else you fancy giving me.' He turned around and winked at his colleagues and they cheered and egged him on.

'It'll just be a gill, then, nothing else,' Eve said curtly as she pulled the cocky fellow a drink.

'Leave her alone, Jack, she's not for you. Besides, she's already up the duff. She's been with your sort before, more's the pity,' Rose yelled at the forward dock worker and pulled on his arm. 'You're better with me and Tilly, so leave the lass alone.' She smiled at Eve as she beckoned the docker to join her and Tilly.

'Pity, that, lads. I could have taught her a thing or two,' Jack boasted as he followed Rose to his usual corner in the pub while the rest of his workmates got served by Eve. She poured each one of them what they needed and was left with just one quiet man standing at the bar.

'Don't worry about that rowdy lot, their bark is worse than their bite. Especially Jack Middleton. He likes to think he's a great one with the ladies and he might be, for all I know, but it's funny how he always has to pay for it.' The clean-shaven man smiled at Eve and passed her his money as she poured him his drink. 'So, you've come to work at the Mucky Duck and you are with child. Does your husband approve of you working here? It's got a reputation from hell!'

'I have come to work here, sir, and unfortunately, I have no husband, that's why I am here because I need money and a roof over my head,' Eve said, blushing. She didn't like confessing that the child she was carrying was to be born out of wedlock but Rosie had left her with no option but to let it be common knowledge that she was not wed.

'I see. And your lover, does he know you are with child?' Ivor Standish looked at the bonny lass as he drank his gill and tried to blank out the noise and the taunts coming from the corner of the room where the quayside workers were sitting with Rosie and Tilly, plying them for trade.

'No, sir. He's a soldier and he's gone with his regiment to Ireland. I had nobody until Nell across the yard took me in out of pity and got me a job here. It's just until the baby arrives and then I will move on.' Eve looked at the man showing interest in her and tried to smile.

'That's a shame, but it is all too common a tale that you tell me. I hope things progress well for you. Unfortunately, I lost my wife in childbirth last year and she left me with two children to raise on my own. So, I too have got my problems. Let me introduce myself. I'm Ivor Standish, and unlike that rowdy lot in the corner, I work in the pay offices down on Granary Wharf; however, for my sins, I drink with this unruly lot once in a while.' Ivor smiled and ignored the yells of his workmates.

'I'm Eve, Eve Reynolds, sir.' Eve looked at the man who was obviously interested in her for reasons other than the rest of them were as she noted that he kept himself clean and tidy and that his clothes were of better quality than the dock workers. She judged that he must be in a better-paid job than them.

'Please, call me Ivor — none of this 'sir', not here in the Mucky Duck,' Ivor said, grinning.

'Aye, his name's Ivor, Ivor big eon,' shouted the mouthy Jack Middleton as he eavesdropped into the conversation and made the corner of the room laugh at his joke.

'Close your foul mouth, Jack Middleton, there's no need to embarrass the young woman,' Ivor shook his head and shouted. 'Sorry, they are always like this until they've drunk as much as they can and have squandered their money on Rose and Tilly — and it's not even mid-morning yet. They've worked through the night and now, after drinking here, they'll go back to their wives and homes and sleep until work again in the evening. It's their wives I feel sorry for; it's no life for them, so no wonder some turn to other means to make ends meet. I only work through the day and when I do join this gang, I just have the one drink and then return home to my children.

With it being Boxing Day, I'm returning home early. I promised the children a treat once I was home and I just hope my eldest, Katherine, who is now ten, has watched carefully over her young brother for the hours that I've been away.' He shook his head. 'They miss their mother and I really should get someone to look after them while I work, but our rent is so high that I can't afford to.' Ivor looked at the new maid behind the bar and thought that, even though she looked weary, she was still too good to be working at the Mucky Duck.

'I'm sorry for your loss,' Eve said. 'I lost my mother last spring and, even at my age, my heart aches with her loss. You don't appreciate the love that they give you until they've gone . . . ' She looked up at the handsome man who seemed interested in her and she smiled at him. 'Your daughter is young to be left with such a responsibility; she must be mature for her age.'

'She's had to grow up fast and she's always been a clever lass, so I know that she'll be all right. She knows where I work and besides, we only live on The Calls, so she's not got so far to run and find me if anything is wrong.' Ivor smiled. 'Are you looking forward to your baby being born? Will you be keeping it? It'll be a hard decision but you don't look or sound the sort to be hard-hearted.'

'That's the trouble, I'm too soft to have got rid of it and I don't think I will be able to abandon a baby on the orphanage or workhouse steps. I don't know what I'm going to do . . .' Eve's eyes filled with tears and she tried to fight them back.

'I'm sorry, I didn't mean to upset you. Look, Stan and Maude may lack some manners, and their cleanliness is something to be questioned, but Stan does look after his girls. I can see he will be keeping you behind the bar for now, given your condition, but he doesn't take his girls' savings as Bert Bradshaw does, and they usually drink for free, so . . .' Ivor rested his arm on the bar and drank his drink.

Eve looked shocked. 'Oh, I'm not like Rosie and Tilly! I'm not putting myself on the streets. That's not what we agreed to. No, no, I couldn't — I just couldn't sell myself. Once this baby is born, I'll leave Leeds and find a house that, hopefully, will take me into service.' Nell had never told her that Stanley made part of his living from the girls that flirted with his customers. She watched as Rose pulled on one of the dock worker's hands and urged him outside, obviously to satisfy his needs and take some money from him.

'Well, I wish you luck. But don't be staying here too long, else you will get drawn into his trade. The Nelsons might be charming, but they take advantage of innocent young women like yourself. This corner of the world is not for the likes of you if you want to keep your pride.' Ivor went quiet as Maude came into the bar.

'Well, I see you've all in hand and I needn't

have worried,' Maude said as she looked Ivor up and down and then spotted the mop and bucket by the doorway, still full of water. 'You could have found time to empty that and put it away. Folk don't want to look at a mucky mop bucket when they're drinking.'

'I'll put it back where I found it straight away,' Eve said, thinking to herself there were a lot muskier things here than the mop bucket and, pulling a face, she threw the dirty water down the outside drain, aware that Rosie was going about her business up the side of the inn's sheltered wall. Had she really stooped this low in life? The sooner the baby was born, the sooner she could move on. She didn't belong in a place like this — even the Bluebell had been head and shoulders above this corner of Leeds. The only person, so far, who had been anything near normal in her eyes was Ivor and even he had looked her up and down and made her feel uncomfortable. Perhaps he wasn't all that he seemed, even though he did seem genuinely broken-hearted over the death of his wife.

Eve looked up towards the stairs and doorway to where Nell and now she lived. Her mother must be turning in her grave; her daughter was working in one of the dirtiest inns in Leeds and living with a prostitute. How low had she sunk? Not to mention the baby she was carrying, the baby that she sometimes wished she had had the strength to destroy. But no, her religious upbringing was still telling her that would have been totally wrong. It was not the baby's fault, after all, it was hers for being so stupid and ignorant of men's ways. Though that was something she was learning about quickly, she thought, as she watched Rosie's quayside worker grin at her and button his trousers up before entering the Swan to re-join his mates.

'Fastest threepence I've made for a while!' Rosie grinned and jangled the money in her palm. 'A woman need never go hungry while there are men like him in the world. His mates will have something to say about him being so quick on the job, but that's what you want.'

'I don't know how you can.' Eve shook her head.

'Needs must, lass. Don't look so judgemental. Nobody's perfect and you should know, seeing you are carrying that baby, Miss Prim,' Rosie spat as she opened the door to yells from the corner of rough quay men, with Eve following her, carrying the mop bucket.

'I see Rosie's been bringing in the trade; she knows how to keep the men happy,' Maude said when Eve came and stood beside her. 'When you've had that baby, you could do worse, young Eve. Rose and Tilly want for nothing.'

'I don't think so,' Eve said quietly, looking over at the laughing, flirting women she knew were just putting on an act for the men who would pay them for their services.

'Don't you look down your nose at them, my lass, they're good women. Besides, you're living with Bonfire Nell — and who do you think she is?' Maude looked annoyed at her new barmaid's judgemental attitude.

'I'm only there until I get on my feet,' Eve said

and held her head up high.

'Aye, and I'm a monkey's uncle! You can dream, but this is real life, lass, and you'll sink a lot lower yet, especially when that baby is born and you can't afford the clothes upon your back. But for now, that long-faced Ivor Standish is waiting for a drink. I could do without his sort, standing at the bar the way he does, looking miserable and hardly spending any brass. Go and serve him and then you can get yourself into the kitchen, where there are some potatoes needing peeling,' Maude growled. Then she smiled at Ivor, who was watching them talking together . . . and showing interest in Eve. Stanley was right, men liked this latest employee. She'd be a good asset to the Swan once the stuck-up mare had been talked around to their way of thinking. Nell must have thought that, else she wouldn't have taken her in, no matter how much she said she had pity for the lass.

'Maude's a hard woman,' Ivor whispered. 'Old Stan is the kinder person, even though he can be a bit ruthless if anyone harms his girls.'

'I didn't know that the Nelsons were like that. Nell never told me,' Eve said quietly.

'Bonfire Nell? Aye, you've been sheltered, lass. You really don't belong here, so don't listen to Maude, she's only out for herself.' Ivor sipped his newly pulled gill and looked after Eve as she went into the Swan's kitchen. It was true she didn't belong here; she was a cut above the rabble that frequented the Swan but no doubt it would drag her down like it had done everyone else over the years.

158

13

'So, you had the sense to stay away while Councillor Hargreaves satisfied himself?' Nell looked at Eve as she came into her living room, looking tired and worn.

'Yes, Stanley told me what he was up to. I can't believe he'd pay you for letting him do that.' Eve slumped down in the chair next to the newly stoked fire and yawned.

'He's an old devil, but he pays well. Besides, it's no hardship to me that he likes to watch me taking my clothes off through the keyhole of the door. If that's his pleasure, then so be it. I'd rather that than rolling about in bed with him. I've had a quiet evening, really, because after he'd gone I had an unexpected visit from Sergeant Jones, bless him. He brought me a bottle of gin and all he wanted was someone to listen to him and his worries.' Nell smiled. 'How was your first day? The Swan's not like the Bluebell, but Stan and Maude will look after you.'

'It was a hard one and I'm tired. Those women you warned me of, Rosie and Tilly? They are so brazen! They don't bat an eyelid at what they get up to. I could never do that — and I didn't realise that Stanley takes some of the money they earn while doing trade in the Swan. He's really not much better than this Bert Bradshaw you all keep talking about.' Eve yawned again. She had taken advantage of the glass of gin offered to her by Stanley as she waited for Nell's two late callers to make their way down the steps and back home to their wives after their secret meetings with her.

'Believe me, if you ever met Bert Bradshaw, you'd know the difference. Stanley looks after those girls, feeds them, makes sure they get a drink or two and just expects a little payment for letting them trade in his public house. Bert Bradshaw would take the clothes you stood up in if you weren't making him money. He's completely ruthless, uses women worse than dogs — and so do the monkeys that work for him. Don't ever cross him, else it will be the worse for you. I keep out of his way and keep to my clients and my patch when I can. I go out of my way not to cross that man.'

Nell cursed under her breath; Eve wasn't the only one who had endured a long day and all she wanted was her own company and her bed. Every day was getting harder and harder, she was fed up walking the streets and then lying on her back, pretending to enjoy the sexual fantasies that some men enjoyed. 'Here, join me in a gin and then I'm away to my bed. We've both got work again in the morning and neither of us can enjoy a late morning lie-in when there's money to be made. A drop of the mother's ruin helps to ease the head, although I've had more than my fair share of it today, just to keep body and soul going.' Nell teetered across in her stocking feet to the sideboard and poured two large gins, passing one to Eve. 'Did Stan give you his special brew of gin from under the counter? It's as coarse and rough as his arse, but it doesn't half hit the spot.' Nell sat heavily down in the chair next to her and raised her glass: 'Cheers to us independent women!'

'Cheers!' Eve looked across at Nell; she could see she was drunk. 'Yes, it is rough stuff, but he only gave me a drop.'

'Oh, he'll wean you onto it before you know it; another month and you'll not be able to do a day without it, especially with *that* growing in your belly,' Nell slurred and pointed at Eve's stomach.

'Do you know an Ivor Standish who comes into the Swan, Nell? He's different from the other men that drink there,' Eve said, hoping that she would get a sensible answer out of the drunken Nell.

'Aye, he's a miserable bugger, tight as a duck's arse! Doesn't spend any money on anything, that's why his wife ran off with another man, leaving him to look after their two young ones! It serves him right.' Nell grinned.

'He told me she died,' Eve said and looked at Nell.

'Oh, he would, he can't stand to hear the truth. He'll have more money than the Bank of England, because he doesn't spend any of it, living in that good house down by The Calls. I don't know why he drinks in the Swan, because he's management, not one of the workers.' Nell looked at her glass of gin and tipped it back as she thought of Ivor.

'He seems all right, but as you say, I don't know why he drinks there. He didn't stay long, though, he was worried about his children being on their own.' Eve felt the warmth of the gin slip down her throat and the cares of the day start to gently ease away.

'He should get them a nanny; he can afford one. There you go, lass, that's a job for you, nanny to the Standish children, which would be much better than any job at the Mucky Duck. The only trouble is you'll have a baby of your own before long and he'll not want that. Why don't you get rid of it, Eve? It's not too late by the looks of you.' Nell drawled. 'I know it's hard, but it'll ruin your life; no man wants a woman with a child.'

'I couldn't, Nell. I'm beginning to show, I think I'm at least seven months on and it would be like committing murder.' Eve ran her hand over her loose-fitting skirts and showed Nell the rounded belly that was developing there.

'Then your other option is to make him think he loves you. You are bonny enough, so flirt with him; he'll fall for it because he'll like to be singled out from the rest of the rabble that drinks there by you. Like you say, he's desperately in need of somebody to look after his children — and perhaps give him some satisfaction in bed. It would work in both your favours, both of you would get the security you need — and don't forget, he's worth a bob or two.' Nell yawned and looked across at Eve, seeing her words start to hit home.

Yes, Nell's words did make sense. He was a good-looking man, he wasn't a big drinker and he had money. Nell was right, perhaps he *was*

162

the answer to her problem. Two children as well as her own to bring up wouldn't be that much work, not if she had a stable home to bring them up in. Oh, she would have liked to have married for love, but in her desperate plight she couldn't be so fussy. Eve smiled. Nell had sown a seed of thought and, in her gin-soaked haze, it seemed a solid plan. She'd put it into action the next time Ivor Standish stood at the bar.

★　★　★

It was still dark as Eve lay in her bed, looking up at the ceiling. She'd gone there the worse for wear and had thought of nothing else but of Nell's plan to get her married off to Ivor Standish. It had all made sense to her last night with gin inside her, but in the bleak hour before dawn she knew it would never happen. If he'd any sense he'd set his sights higher than the barmaid at the Mucky Duck, especially if he had the money that Nell said he had. She raised herself out of bed and her mouth was dry and her head fuzzy as she made her way to the washstand to try and revive herself and get dressed before going to her work at the Swan. At least today would not be such a shock to the system because she knew what she was in for.

Rose and Tilly had seemed to take her presence in their stride and accept that she was no threat to their seedy world and Stanley had said she'd done a good first day's work when he had given her the gin before she returned to Nell's. It was only Maude she was not keen on;

163

the woman spoke her mind and could be curt with her words.

Quickly, she dressed in the frosty air of her bedroom, the fern patterns on her bedroom window telling her that it must have frozen hard through the night and that she must wrap up well for the day. The frost-patterned windows glistened and shone in the light from the gas lamp outside in the yard and Eve shivered as she closed her bedroom door and walked along the landing past Nell's bedroom, thinking that she would still be in her bed and that she shouldn't make much noise.

Instead, Nell's bedroom door was open, the bedsheets thrown back and the room empty. The fire had been lit and the kettle was still warm as Eve entered the main living room. Nell must have gone out early or she was entertaining in her other room. The girl listened with her ear to the door, hoping that it wouldn't be the latter, else she would be late to go to the Swan, for she'd no intention of walking into a room with Nell busy on the job. There was no noise, Nell had obviously gone out early that morning and left her to herself.

Eve pulled the blackened kettle onto the red coals and waited for it to boil as she sat back in the Windsor chair next to the fire. She closed her eyes and rested her hands on her belly and contemplated the mess she was in. Although Nell had been kind to her, had shown sympathy towards her plight after being in the same situation herself, she knew she couldn't stay with her forever. Then, when she had been drinking,

Nell, showing the hard woman that she had turned into, had kept advising Eve to do away with the child that was growing within her. Now her hand felt the growing life inside her kick and Eve smiled and looked down at her stomach.

'I'll not harm you, my little one. It isn't your fault that I'm in this mess,' she whispered. 'We'll come through it somehow.'

Eve wiped away a tear and looked at the gin bottle and the glasses still on the table from the night before. She idly picked up the bottle and glanced at the liquid within it and then went on to pour herself a measure in one of the used glasses. That would give her the courage to take on the day, she thought as she swigged it back and took the kettle from off the heat. If that's how Nell took on the day, then she would do the same thing; it would be the only way to make sense of her days at the Mucky Duck. She closed her eyes and thought of the day ahead, of the stench of the place, the swearing and leering and the two women who had lost their moral sense a long time ago. How had she come to this, a young woman that had been brought up properly in a loving home that she had turned her back on. Oh, perhaps she deserved all that she got, it was the result of her own headstrong ways and stupidity, after all. She sipped the gin and put the fireguard around the fire. Like it or not, it was her life for now and there was nothing she could do.

* * *

'So, you're back with us again? You haven't thought better of slumming it with the likes of us?' Rosie leaned over the bar and pointed to the gin bottle beneath the shelf.

'No, I've nowhere else to go; besides, it's not too bad,' Eve lied as she poured Rosie and Tilly two large gins.

'You know, when you've had that baby, you could make a good bob or two if you buried your pride. The fellas yesterday was eyeing you over, but they'll not want to know until the baby's born.' Rosie took a quick drink and then looked over to where Tilly sat. 'She's not so good this morning. I doubt she'll be with me for much longer, for the syphilis is affecting her thinking; she'll be in the workhouse before long, poor cow.' Rosie leaned across and whispered, 'You could make up for the loss of her. I reckon me and you could pull plenty of men between us.'

'No, never! I told you yesterday.' Eve glared at Rosie.

'Suit yourself, snotty cow! It was just a thought.' Rosie walked back to her usual corner and glanced back at the barmaid she thought had more pride than sense as she handed Tilly her drink.

Even with a drink of gin in her, Eve found the morning hard going, Maude decided that perhaps her kitchen, if nowhere else, needed a tidy and set her about it while she and Stanley ran the bar. The kitchen of the Swan was not much cleaner than the main bar; every wall had shelves on it, all of them covered with dust and baking tins and pots that had never had a good clean in years. Eve made a start by scrubbing the pine

166

table with a block of carbolic soap and a scrubbing brush, removing layers and layers of grime that had built up on its surface, then she swept and scrubbed the stone-flagged floor. By the time she came around to opening the pantry door to tidy the shelves within, the sleeves of her dress were grey with dirt and her skirts were covered in filth. Gritting her teeth, she set about emptying the cluttered shelves ready to wash them down. She screamed as she picked up a bag of flour off the floor and disturbed a rats' nest. The grown rats fled from her path while the blind young lay there, defenceless, as she screamed again in shock as they fell down out of their nest and around her feet.

'For God's sake, what's up with you woman?' Stanley came running into the kitchen and looked at the panic-faced Eve and the nest of rats that squirmed and writhed around her.

'Rats! You had rats in the flour!' Eve looked down at the pink, bare-skinned babies with bulbous blue eyes that couldn't see and tiny ears that couldn't hear as they squirmed in what was left of their nest.

'They are only kittens! Here, I'll throw them onto the fire, that'll soon get rid of them.' Stanley bent down and gathered up the newly born rats in one hand and threw them onto the back of the kitchen fire. Eve listened to their squeals in horror. 'That's got rid of the little bastards,' he said. 'But look at you, you look as black as the fire back. You'd better get yourself cleaned up if you're to serve behind that bar later on in the day.'

Eve stood in front of him, tears running down

her cheeks. The creatures may have been rats, but to put them to death by throwing them on the fire was terrible in her eyes. Life, it seemed, was cheap in the Swan, whether human or animal. Dear God, what else lurked in the food supplies of the Swan? If there were rats, there were bound to be weevils in the oats and bugs in the upstairs beds. She had to find some way out of the place, no matter how good Nell's intentions were. She didn't belong in such a slum of a place. Pulling herself together, she nodded her head at Stanley and made her way out of the kitchen and out into the freezing-cold air of the yard to cross back to Nell's. He followed her into the bar, laughing.

'She was screaming because she'd seen a rat, lads. A bloody rat!' Stan shouted as the men from the wharf jeered.

She heard a voice yell after her as she crossed the yard and was about to climb up the stairs to the safety of her own room, 'We've rats as big as dogs down at quay. Come and see them with me, love, and I'll give you something to scream about!' And she had to stop. Nell had the brush outside the door; she was busy with a client and that meant Eve she couldn't go in, not until she had finished her trick.

Eve sat on the bottom step and cried. She was cold and wet and hungry — and now she knew not to eat again at the Swan. She shivered in the bitter air and listened to the raucous taunts of the men within the Swan, hating the place. She couldn't stay much longer with Nell — a brothel was not the right place for the likes of her . . .

168

'You look in a right state,' Nell said, looking at Eve as she pushed her way past the man who had just paid her and was now on his way.

'I don't think I can work there any longer, Nell,' Eve sobbed. 'It's filthy, the folk are crude and vulgar and I don't fit into this — this hellhole!'

'This hellhole is what most ordinary folks know. Especially ones in your condition. What's brought this on all of a sudden? You seemed to be taking it all in your stride yesterday.' Nell looked at Eve as she sobbed.

'Rats! I picked up a bag of flour and it was full of rats — and then Stanley picked up the newly born ones and threw them on the fire and they screamed as they burned to death. And everything is that mucky and no one cares. Just look at me, I'm filthy!' Eve cried.

'That's where you're wrong — everyone cares. It's just they care about people and things in a different way to what you're used to. Now, stop your bawling, get changed and go back and get on with it. There's nowhere else that will take you, lass, so unless a knight in shining armour comes along and sweeps you off your feet, then this is your lot. Swallow your pride and get on with it — or failing that, turn to Stanley's gin to get you through the day,' Nell growled at her, knowing all too well that Eve was lucky that she had somewhere to stay, unlike the many homeless beggars in Leeds.

'I'm s-sorry, I just don't know what to do.' Eve hung her head.

'I'll tell you what you do: you make the best of a bad job, you bury your pride — and you look after the job that you're in until that baby is born. Then we'll see how you feel. Now get changed; Maude will be after your blood if you're not back soon.' Nell stood and looked at Eve, shaking her head. The lass wasn't going to last at the Swan, but Lord knew what she was going to do. Other than the workhouse, nobody would want her.

* * *

'So, you're back! Screaming over some rats, indeed, we thought the place must be on fire!' Maude stood behind the bar with her arms crossed, a look of contempt on her face.

'Sorry, they took me by surprise,' Eve said quietly.

'Aye, well, they've gone now and one of the lads from the quay is going to bring his dog around; he's a champion ratter so that'll soon catch any more that we've got. Where there's food and warmth, there's always rats — you should know that. I'll give you your due, though, my table and floor through there shine like new pennies, so you're certainly a good worker.' Maude smiled. 'You can stop behind the bar for the rest of the day: the only rats there are the two-legged kind that like a drink. But I can see we're going to have to toughen you up.'

Eve suddenly felt better and smiled. Perhaps, underneath the grime and dirt, it was just like anywhere else. She'd never been praised by

Nancy when she worked at the Bluebell, but at least the hard-faced Maude had shown her some appreciation. 'I'm sorry for making a scene,' she said and pulled her shawl tightly around her; she was still cold from sitting outside waiting for Nell and she shivered.

'Go and warm yourself in front of the fire for a minute, we've got a lull in trade at the moment and it'll be quiet until later on. Nell, I see, is as busy as ever! The number of men that walk up those stairs is nobody's business.' Maude shook her head. 'She wants to be careful else Bert Bradshaw will be giving her a call; she's still more popular than any of his molls.' And with that, she went back into her newly cleaned kitchen, leaving Eve warming her hands in a near-empty bar.

This Bert Bradshaw, Eve thought, must be feared by everyone; even at the Bluebell, where they didn't run whores, they had breathed his name with fear and loathing. Surely he couldn't be that bad? And if he was, why wasn't somebody doing something about him? She rubbed her hands together and stood with her back to the fire, watching her skirts did not catch the flames. The few words said by Maude had made her feel more appreciated and warmed. She went behind the bar and leaned upon it, waiting for her next customer. As it was, she didn't have to wait long and she smiled as a known face entered and made his way towards her.

'I was going to go home and then I thought, no, I'll just go and have an odd one in the Swan and see how the new lass behind the bar is

171

doing.' Ivor Standish smiled and stood at the bar, kicking one of the spittoons on the floor out of his way. 'My neighbour is looking after the children today, so I know that they are in good hands and not up to any mischief. And you look as if you are surviving the traumas of work in the Swan very well.

'You wouldn't have thought that an hour ago! I was absolutely filthy from scrubbing the kitchen out, so much so that I had to go and change. A gill of bitter, is it?' Eve looked across at the man Nell had told her was a miserable soul.

'You know my habits already. You were brave enough to tackle the Swan's kitchen? If it's anything like the rest of the place, it will certainly be the worse for wear. I've never once seen anything here polished or cleaned.' Ivor passed Eve his money and then wiped his top lip free of the white froth of his drink.

'Remind me, please, what are your children called?' Eve asked with interest, recalling the drunken conversation between her and Nell and wondering if the man in front of her might just be a way out of her plight if she showed enough interest in him and his family.

'Katherine and Peter. They make me strong enough to carry on with this life; without them, I'd have nothing. I know I have a position of responsibility down at the quay but my children are everything to me, as was my poor dear wife.' Ivor cast his eyes downward and didn't look at the young woman he thought extremely pretty and too good for the Swan. 'I only wish she hadn't departed life so soon; I worry that with no mother to tend to their needs, my children will grow up neglected.'

'I'm sure that as long as they know their father loves them and cares for them, they will be all right. However, daughters, I feel, do need the care of their mother or an older female they can discuss their troubles with.' Eve smiled.

'Yes, I must admit I'm at a loss sometimes with Katherine. And the house is in need of the loving touches that my dear wife did — and I was too busy to notice at the time. I do have a woman who comes in and cleans for me once a week and makes a meal for us twice a week, but she will never replace my wife.' Ivor sipped his gill and looked across at Eve and wondered whether he dare mention to her what he was thinking.

'They sound well-loved and I'm sure that they will take no harm under your watch.' Eve smiled and picked up a cloth and decided to clean the glasses under the bar that looked dusty.

'I don't suppose you would like to meet them, would you? Perhaps come to tea at our home? I wouldn't normally ask, but you seem to be a decent young woman who's just fallen on hard times and you've been kind enough to listen to me and my woes. Please feel free to reject my offer if you would feel uneasy visiting a widowed man and his family.' Ivor looked at the expression of surprise on Eve's face.

'Oh, I wouldn't feel in the least uneasy. If you think that your children would benefit from my company, of course I would be only too pleased to call and see your family. It would be a pleasure to do so. Although I'm not looking forward to giving birth to this baby I'm carrying, I do love children. It will be a real treat to have tea and to meet Katherine and Peter, not to mention the time spent with you, Mr Standish.' Eve smiled and looked at Ivor coyly.

'Would Sunday at two be to your liking? I'm sure the children will be excited about receiving a visitor. The day after will be New Year's Day — maybe you can usher in 1867 with a feeling of hope for both them and myself,' Ivor said quietly, not daring to make eye contact with Eve.

'Sunday at two it is; it will be a delight. I will look forward to it, yours is the first true hand of friendship that I have been shown since I came to Leeds.' Eve looked across at Ivor and noticed the smile on his face.

'Indeed, it is a hand of friendship that I offer you. I promise I will not take advantage of you, for I am not cut from the same cloth as some of my less reputable workmates.' Ivor looked around him as he watched those that were listening in to their conversation.

'I know, I can tell you are a man of honour, else I would not accept your invite. I will indeed look forward to my visit.' Eve blushed and then went to serve one of his so-called mates, who was rattling his tankard on the bar, wanting attention.

★ ★ ★

'Bloody hell, Eve, take some of that rouge from off your face! He's asked you because you are a simple lass; he doesn't want you going looking like a tart.' Nell perused Eve with a keen eye as the girl wrapped her shawl around her before setting off to see Ivor Standish and his young family.

Eve quickly rubbed at the rouge she had put on her cheeks to give them a bit of colour with the back of her hand. 'I looked pale and I wanted to look a little healthier. What do I say to his children? What if they don't like me? If they don't like me, he'll not ask me back again. I still can't believe that he has asked me, what with me being in child,' Eve said anxiously.

'Will you shut up and just go and enjoy your day? You know what girls of ten like and the boy's only young, so just humour him. Have you got that bag of sweets that I bought for you and have you borrowed some of my cologne?' Nell looked closely at Eve for a final time and decided that she was fit enough to go and see Ivor Standish and impress him with her maternal feelings for his children in the hope that he saw in her a future wife.

'I didn't bother with your cologne. I decided to eat a Parma violet sweet instead, so at least my breath will smell sweet.' Eve didn't want to offend Nell, but her cologne smelt cheap and nasty and she had thought better than to wear it.

'Well, go on then! Go and make a fuss of the Standish family! Worm your way in and try to make a better life for yourself, because it's the only chance you'll get, so grab it with both hands. He's a boring sod, that Ivor Standish, but that's better than a drunkard. And when that baby comes he'll think twice about looking at you, so catch him while you can.' Nell stood back with her hands on her hips and shook her head as she watched Eve leave. She knew it was only a social visit but she hoped that it would kindle a love match. Eve could do worse — and besides, she was in need of having her privacy back. She really didn't like her home not being her own any more.

★ ★ ★

Eve walked quickly down the relatively quiet streets that led to the canal basin and the part of Leeds known as The Calls, quickening her pace as she heard St Peter's clock strike two as she turned onto the street where she knew Ivor lived. It was a respectable-looking street of red-brick terraced houses with steps leading up to the front doors, the windows on either side adorned with lace curtains to stop nosy neighbours from looking in and letting the prying inhabitants look out onto the street without being noticed. She noticed the curtains at number two twitch as she stood on the doorstep and tugged the black cast-iron ring pull, breathing in deeply and pulling her stomach in as she heard the door handle being turned moments later.

'I'm so glad you are here. I thought maybe you'd change your mind, thinking that I'd been a little forward in my invitation to you.' Ivor stood in the hallway in his waistcoat and striped shirt, a gold watch on an Albert chain hanging from his pocket. His hair and moustache were immaculately groomed and he opened his arm wide to invite Eve into his home.

'I'm sorry, I'm slightly late,' Eve said as she walked into the tiled hallway and looked around her at the floral wallpaper on the walls and a painting of highland cattle. 'I've not been down this street before. At least you're near your work.'

'Nonsense, you are very punctual. Now, come and meet Katherine and Peter — they are in the sitting room, waiting for you.' Ivor put his hand on Eve's waist and guided her into the very lushly furnished room, where two very nervous children stood as instructed by their father. 'Katherine, Peter, say hello to Miss Reynolds, who has come to join us for tea today.' Ivor smiled at the two children, who had obviously been told to stand to attention and welcome her.

'Good afternoon, Miss Reynolds, I'm Katherine and this is my brother Peter — but he's a little shy.' Katherine put her arm around her brother as he tried to hide behind her skirts and peep around his older sister.

'Good afternoon, Katherine; your father has told me a lot about you and Peter.' Eve looked at the little blonde-haired girl who was dressed immaculately, with a red ribbon in her long ringlet hair to match the red tartan dress that she wore. 'And Peter . . . ' Eve said softly and knelt down to the little boy's level. 'Are you the shy one? I bet you are not too shy to take one of these chocolate drops that I have brought for you and Katherine.' Eve opened her posy bag and took out a small paper cone filled with chocolate drops, offering it to Katherine and Peter as she smiled at them both.

'Thank you, Miss Reynolds.' Katherine looked up at her father for permission and placed her hand in the bag to take one when Ivor smiled and nodded his head. 'May I take one for Peter as well? He will come and get his own once he is used to you,' Katherine said politely.

'Yes, of course — and I'll be leaving them here for you to eat after I've gone, so he need not be shy then.' Eve watched as both children put the chocolate in their mouths and then went back to a pile of building bricks that they had been playing with before her appearance. 'They are beautiful children, Ivor, and so well-mannered; no wonder you are proud of them.'

'Yes, they are my pride and joy. I just wish their mother was still here and could see how they grow.' Ivor sighed. 'Anyway, they seem to be happy in your company. Look, even Peter is not that concerned about your presence now he knows that your bag contains chocolate.' He looked across at the blond, curly-headed lad who was now grinning at Eve. 'You really shouldn't have spent your hard-earned money on my two children; you must need every penny you earn — not that it will be a great deal, knowing Stanley and Maude.' He shook his head and looked at Eve. 'That place gets worse every day. Maude has never kept a clean hostelry, but at least the place looks a little cleaner since you showed your face behind the bar — although you are far too good to work there, of that I'm sure.'

Ivor pulled a chair out from the table that was covered with a green chenille tablecloth which was already laid out with the best pink-rosebud decorated china in readiness for the tea promised to her. He offered the seat to Eve and watched as she removed her shawl.

'I'm afraid beggars cannot be choosers, Ivor, and with me being in the condition that I am, I can only be grateful for the chance of work and for the pittance that they pay me. Also, although I must confess that I am not happy with her trade, Nell has been a godsend, letting me stay there with her. My parents always brought me up in God's word and told me not to have anything to do with women who sell their bodies for money. But who am I to criticise? I was led astray by the first man that set on eyes on me, so I am in no position to judge.' Eve dropped her head for a second, remembering all her worries, then shook her head determinedly. 'But still, I am here today, having tea with you and your lovely children, for which I am truly thankful.'

'No, it is I who am thankful. Not many people give me the time of day because I'm afraid to say they find me a little boring. I work long and hard, I save my money and I raise my children the best I can and I thank the Lord of a Sunday morning for what he gives me each day. That is how I run my life; I expect nothing from any man — and if someone gives me a kind word then I will do likewise. Just like you did, Eve, when I came into the Swan, and your company was so refreshing in that dowdy place,' Ivor said as he stood up and looked down upon his children playing together.

'It's kind of you to say so, Ivor. I feel I don't quite fit in there but I will stay until my child is born and will then decide what to do with both our lives.' Eve watched and laughed as the tower of bricks that Katherine and Peter were building together collapsed and Peter lost patience with his attempt at building. 'Here, little man, let me help.' Eve got up from her chair and squatted down with the children and started to build another tower. Katherine passed Eve the bricks while Peter stood and watched for a second and then decided to join in. The tower was soon built and both children laughed as they all stepped away from it.

'It's where a princess lives, Peter, and she is about to be rescued by a valiant knight,' Katherine said as she reached for a peg doll that her father had made and put her on the top of the tower.

'Yes, we all need a valiant knight to save us, Katherine,' Eve said, smiling as she turned to look at Ivor. 'I'm sure Peter will grow up to be just that when he is older and you are a beautiful princess with a kingdom all of your own.'

Ivor shook his head, smiling. 'I'll put the kettle on, ready for our tea. It looks like you have won my two over with your tales of chivalry.' He glanced at the three of them together and couldn't help but think how at home the Swan's barmaid looked and how, perhaps, it would not be a bad thing to see more of Eve Reynolds if she was willing.

14

Eve leaned back against the bar and poured herself a glass of Stanley's special brewed gin; she understood now why it was so popular with Rosie and Tilly: it dulled the senses and made the days at the Swan more palatable. There wasn't much joy in her life at the moment, apart from the fact that Ivor was taking interest in her and had actually asked her to visit him at his home again at the weekend. She'd enjoyed her time with him and his family and had bent over backwards to impress that she was good with children. He was perhaps her only hope out of the hell she found herself in and he had seemed to accept that, even if she was with child, she was worth more than a life at the Swan.

'I hope that you are not drinking us dry,' Maude said sharply. 'Two tipples a day free, and then you pay for the rest out of your wages. So don't think I'm not watching you. No other landlord is that understanding, but my Stanley knows it takes Dutch courage to serve some of our customers down in this neck of the woods.' She looked at Eve and noticed her cheeks red with the effect of drink on her. 'Besides, it'll not be good for that baby that you are carrying.'

'This is my first sip of the day and I need it before the evening rush. I've found that it makes me more sociable.' Eve smiled at Maude. She'd got used to her now and she quite admired the hard but fair woman who ran the Swan, even though she looked as wild as an old witch.

'Aye, they are a rough lot that you've to deal with, that's why we know a nip of gin helps. Just don't get to drinking too much for it gets a hold of you before you know it, especially our Stanley's concoction.' Maude leaned on the bar next to her and looked around the room. 'The lasses must be out on the streets this afternoon; I've not seen either of them. Lord, Tilly looks like death warmed up at the moment! I doubt she's long for this world; once she takes to her bed, she'll not get up again. It's best you don't go that way, Eve, so don't get led astray by them or Nell, especially after that baby of yours is born. Respect yourself and do right by yourself. Put the baby in the workhouse and get a job more suitable for the likes of you and stop serving behind a bar, seeing to the dregs of the world, for I think you are better than that. No wonder that Theodore Lambert took you on until Nancy got jealous — he saw that you were a cut above the rest.' Maude sighed and looked at Eve; she was beginning to show and the men who drank there wouldn't want reminding of what awaited them at home, wailing babies and nagging wives.

'I'll not be deserting my baby. I couldn't do that,' Eve said abruptly.

'Oh, and Nell is all right with you having a baby bawling and crying at all times of the night, upsetting her callers? The men she attracts will not want to hear a baby crying when they are about their business with her.' Maude put her hands on her hips and looked across the room as the door swung open. 'Talk of the devil and she appears,' she said as Nell made her way over to the bar.

'Are you gossiping about me again, Maude Nelson? Still, if you are talking about me, at least you're leaving some other poor soul alone.'

'I was only saying that you'll not want a baby crying and screeching at all times of the day and night when you are entertaining. I was trying to tell this one that she'd be better off abandoning it at the workhouse, then at least she could get on with her life.' Maude looked at Eve and then glanced back at Nell. 'She's not having any of it anyway, so it's up to you what you do with it.'

'I've said the same to her myself. But I can understand her not wanting to part with it. You never can forgive yourself and you are always looking for a face in the crowd which you hope is that of the child you abandoned. I should know, I was in the same situation myself and my lad will be nineteen now — a grown man, if he survived.' Nell closed her eyes, propping herself up at the bar and sweeping a tear away as it fell down her cheek.

'You've been on the pop, Nell; you always do this when you've had one too many. Eve, take her home and then come back. Nell gets like this once in a while and then she's no good to anyone, let alone any fella.' Maude looked at Nell, who was usually a hard woman but once in a while her memories came back to haunt her so badly that she usually took to her bed for a day or two.

Eve had never seen Nell look as drunk and she put her arm around her and walked her out of the Swan and across the yard, negotiating the stairs up to their rooms. She smelt mightily of cheap cologne and tobacco and she had bad scratches on her neck; every few steps she stopped and looked at Eve.

'You keep that baby, we'll manage. You'll break your heart if not,' Nell slurred.

'I'm going to keep it, don't worry,' Eve said as she helped her up the steps.

'We'll bring it up between us and it'll want for nothing,' Nell said, holding the top banister rail as she opened the door to their home. 'Don't listen to what folk says, I'll do the streets again when I have to — bloody Bert Bradshaw can't stop me. I'm Bonfire Nell, the best trick in Leeds, and he bloody well knows it!' Nell stumbled to her chair and reached for the bottle of gin that was stood on the table next to her and sipped from the bottleneck before attempting to unlace her boots.

'Here, I'll undo those.' Eve bent down and unlaced her boots and then added some coal from the scuttle to the dying embers of the fire. 'You look frozen, Nell. And why are you in such a state today? You don't usually get like this.' Eve looked at her drunken friend and shook her head as she watched her try and concentrate on her reply.

'That bastard Bradshaw says he's going to kill me if he sees me up near Lands Lane. He says I belong down here near the canal, where the filth belongs. I told him *he* was the filth and oh, he

184

didn't like that! Look, he tried to strangle me.' Nell stretched her neck to show Eve the scratches and bruises that circled it. 'But I had to go there, because it was where I last saw my boy . . . I swear it was my darling boy, I'm sure it was him,' she sobbed.

'Oh, Nell, you stay out of Bert Bradshaw's way! You've always said he was a bad lot, so don't antagonise him. Now leave that gin be and let's get you into bed. I'm afeard that you will fall into the fire if I leave you here.' Eve put her arm around Nell and took her weight as she walked her to her bedroom and laid her on the bed, covering her with a patchwork quilt.

'I miss my boy, my baby boy,' Nell whispered as she closed her eyes.

Eve stood in the doorway for a second, looking back at Nell. The sight of her in such a state made her realise that she could never give the baby she was carrying away. She would have to find some way of keeping it — and with God's help, that's just what she would do.

* * *

'You've not been in the Swan all week and I've missed you,' Eve said genuinely to Ivor as she stood on his doorstep, waiting to be invited in. 'I thought perhaps you had thought better of seeing me. Am I still right in thinking that we were to meet again today?'

'Oh yes, yes. I'm sorry that I've not had a chance to see you but we have had a busy week down at the wharf and I've rushed home each

185

evening to make sure my children are all right. Mrs Whappit next door keeps an eye on them, but she's in her seventies, and the woman who comes and does our laundry helps as well when she has time. Since my wife sadly left me, I've been relying on other people's kindness, but I can see that my reliance on them is beginning to wear thin. However, that's not your concern, so please, stand no longer on the street and come in and join us in our home. I'm afraid it is a little untidy — I'm finding life hard on my own.' Ivor swept his hair back and looked stressed as he bade Eve enter.

'Is there anything I can do?' Eve said, hearing the sound of running feet above her head as Katherine and Peter chased one another around their bedrooms and called to one another in a game of hide-and-seek.

'You can make the sunshine and warm the days up so that those two upstairs can go out and play and stop driving me mad,' Ivor sighed as he led Eve through to his living room.

Eve looked back at the table that was cluttered with unwashed plates and the shelves of the kitchen that were in need of a good dust, which was just as bad in his main living room. A woman's caring touch was definitely missing and Ivor apologised and balanced some of the discarded dirty plates on one of his hands before taking them into the kitchen and scullery.

'Here, let me help.' Eve took her shawl off and placed it on the back of a nearby chair.

'No, you are our visitor, you've come for tea and company,' Ivor said as he looked up at the

186

airing rack above the kitchen range, which was full of Katherine's petticoats and his shirts, all needing to be put away upstairs.

'Ivor, you are struggling and I can always have a drink of tea when we have finished and all is tidy. Now, where is your brush and shovel? Let's start with the floors and work our way through your house. It won't take long and then you will be tidy for the week.' Eve smiled as a look of relief came upon his face.

'I can usually keep on top of things but I've been so busy. It's been work, something to eat and then bed. I fear the children have been neglected,' Ivor said as he got Eve the brush and shovel from the scullery.

'Well, they sound healthy enough on the neglect, the noise that they are making now!' Eve smiled as she heard the squeals of Peter as he was found in his hiding place by his older sister.

'They're going to grow up wild if I don't do something soon. Six months without a mother's supervision is too long and I'm never here. I wish my sister over at Beverley would take them both in, but she's got seven of her own and her husband is a bully of a man.' Ivor watched as Eve rolled her sleeves up and picked up the pegged rug from near the range and took it outside to the back door to shake before sweeping the stone floor free of crumbs. 'You shouldn't; you are my guest and friend. I must pay you for your help before you go.'

'Ivor, as you say, I'm your friend, so stop it! Your home is like a palace compared to the Swan so it will only take a short time to get you nice and tidy. Now, why don't you take Katherine and Peter for a walk? It may be cold, but at least it's fine and then they can let off steam,' Eve said as she heard two sets of footsteps come running down the stairs to see who their father was talking to.

'Oh, hello, I'm glad that you have come back to see my father,' Katherine blurted out as she came to a halt next to Eve. 'He smiled all last Sunday evening after you had gone home. I think he likes you.'

'Katherine, remember what I said? Children should be seen and not heard. Now go and get your coats on, we are going for a walk to quieten you both down.' The children vanished and Ivor shook his head, blushing slightly. 'Children, they say things they really shouldn't . . . '

Eve smiled. 'Yes, they have a tendency to say what they think they see or embroider the truth a little. Now, go and leave me for a little while and enjoy their company while I make your home tidy. I promise I won't pry, just give things a quick tidy and clean where needed and I'll make you a drink of tea for your return.'

'I can't thank you enough, Eve. I still feel bad leaving you cleaning on your day off,' Ivor said, smiling. 'Don't bother cleaning upstairs, though, we keep relatively tidy up there.' He turned and looked at his children as they came back into the room. 'Now, let's leave Eve to it and then we can come back to the scones that Mrs Whappit left us the other day. Bless her, she's a dear soul.'

Eve watched as Ivor put his arms around his two children and took them out of the front

188

door, leaving her alone in a house that she was not familiar with. She had not thought that she would be working at cleaning Ivor's house when she had walked down the street and knocked on his door, but he had looked so lost and ashamed that his home was not as tidy as the previous week. Besides, if she made herself useful, he might realise just how seriously he was in need of her help . . .

Eve leaned on the broom and looked around her; the house was of a good size and well built, a proper family home, and Ivor would not be short of a bob or two. His wife must have been desperate to have left him, if what Nell had said was true. Or was she dead as Ivor had told her? Surely she wouldn't leave two young children with their father if she hadn't needed to. Well, whatever the reason Ivor's wife wasn't there, she, Eve, was going to make the most of it and try to get herself well in with Ivor and his family. He needed a woman to run his house and family and she needed to get out of the Swan and Nell's care — if she could call it that. At the very least, housekeeper to the Standish family would be an ideal position, for now and when the baby arrived — better still, he might grow that fond of her he'd propose marriage. Ivor Standish might just be her ticket out of poverty, she thought, as she swept the floor and replaced the rug before finding a duster in the scullery and wiping all the furniture down before moving into the parlour where she had been entertained the previous Sunday. She stood with her hands on her growing stomach and looked around her; yes, she thought, she could be quite happy here as either housekeeper or wife. It could be the perfect home with a good steady man who would be there for her when needed and who would probably bring her baby up as his own.

★   ★   ★

'Here, love, are you working for Ivor Standish?' An elderly woman leaned over the garden wall as Eve visited the outside privy in the back yard.

'No, just visiting, I said I'd give him a quick clean while he spends time with his children,' Eve replied. 'The poor man is working all hours and since he lost his wife he seems a bit lost and doesn't have much time with his children. Are you Mrs Whappit? He says that you look after him and the children?'

'Aye, that's me. But I only keep an eye out for those children of his — poor little buggers are left on their own for hours on end. And let me put you right: he didn't lose his wife, she left. And I don't blame her. Ivor Standish is a strange man; he's got a terrible temper and he treated his wife something terrible. The shouting and carrying on was nobody's business when she lived here.' Mrs Whappit folded her arms and looked at Eve.

'I don't really know what happened to her — and I don't listen to gossip,' Eve answered.

'Well, she jiggered off, just disappeared from one day to the next and I can't say I blame her. But she could have taken those little 'uns with her — I wouldn't have left them with *him*. He's got a good house, though, I'll give him that, although I think she was the one with the money — he's only a jumped-up pay clerk down at the wharf. The fellas down there don't mix with him because he's a sod with them and all.' Mrs Whappit shook her head. 'Are you carrying his baby? He'll not like that, not another mouth to feed, cos he's a right tight arse!'

'No, it's not his. Like I say, I'm only visiting. Now, if you don't mind, I'll go back in and wait for their return.' Eve turned her back on the gossiping neighbour and closed the scullery door behind her.

She frowned. The old woman had surely got him wrong, for he had shown nothing but kindness to her and the children seemed happy enough. Mrs Whappit was just an old gossip; all couples rowed and in Ivor's case it had been probably easier to say that his wife had died than to admit the shame of her leaving him. He was a hard-working man who had been left with children to bring up on his own. It must have been her that was the selfish one, from what she could see.

Eve carried on happily with the cleaning. The house was well decorated and the furniture was of a good standard — and despite Ivor telling her not to go upstairs, she thought that she would do him a service and just quickly tidy the rooms, knowing children could be untidy at the best of times, especially in their own rooms. She walked up the stairs slowly and tried the first door at the end of a long corridor, but found it locked. Having no option but to leave that room, she decided to ignore it but it was a pity, because there was a strange smell coming from it, a smell that was really foul and she decided that she had better mention it to Ivor on his return.

When she entered what was obviously his bedroom, she saw there was no sign of a woman ever being there — no feminine decorations such as roses on the wallpaper or a pin tray on the dressing table; indeed, she thought, no sign of his wife, whether alive or dead, remained in the house. He must have decided to really get rid of any sign of her she'd hurt him so badly, one way or another, Eve thought. The children's bedroom was stark also, with little to show in the way of toys, but she put that down to Ivor being as frugal with his money as everyone had said, because it was clear that he loved his children, no matter how neglected the next-door neighbour thought they were. She quickly finished dusting in the children's bedroom when she heard Ivor and his family return, the front door closing loudly behind them.

'Eve, where are you?' he shouted, standing in the hall. 'We're back early because it's too cold to stay out, but we have enjoyed our walk together — '

He broke off abruptly, hearing her moving at the top of the stairs. 'I thought I told you not to bother with the bedrooms?' he shouted as the children hurriedly took their coats off and hung them on the hall stand, before running into the kitchen.

'That was good timing, because I was just finishing. And I thought I'd help by just dusting upstairs. Although I don't know why you were so worried about the state of your house, it really took no time at all to tidy.' Eve smiled at both children as she went into the kitchen and put the filled kettle onto the fire. 'Did you have a good walk with your father?' she asked.

'Yes, we fed the ducks down by the canal and then watched the torn puds and barges sail up and down the canal. Father says that one day soon, we will be sailing on one of those to a new life in Liverpool,' Katherine said and looked at her father, hoping that she had not spoken out of turn.

'Now, Katherine, I said perhaps one day we should leave Leeds for a new life in Liverpool, but it'll not be quite yet. We would have to find a new home and new work and besides, we would be perhaps leaving the things we love behind us. I have many things to settle before I put any plans into action. Now you go and get those scones and some butter from the pantry and let us all enjoy some tea and thank Miss Reynolds for making our home so tidy. Peter, are you all right sitting there or do you want to go and play?' Ivor looked at his young son, who had placed his head down on his folded arms on the table and looked bored.

'Can I really go and play, Father?' Peter raised his head, surprised that he was being allowed to escape the gaze of the man that sometimes was too strict with him.

'Yes, go into your bedroom and Katherine can join you once she has buttered the scones.' Ivor watched as his son climbed down from the table and his daughter placed three scones on the table with a ceramic butter dish in the shape of a cow next to it and diligently buttered the scones, putting them on a plate that she took from the dresser on the back wall of the kitchen. Eve put four teaspoons of tea from the tea caddy into the teapot.

'Not too much tea, Miss Reynolds, we like our tea weak in this house — and besides, it costs money. We are careful with the pennies, aren't we, Katherine?' Ivor said as the girl thought twice about the amount of butter she had spread on her scone and scrapped some of the excess off before putting the cover back on the butter dish and taking it back into the pantry. Her father would only chastise her later when Eve had gone if he thought that she had spread too much.

'Father, I'll take mine and Peter's half scone upstairs with me.' Katherine looked shyly at her father and hoped that she had not said anything wrong.

'Yes, you go and leave Miss Reynolds and I to our tea. And be sure not to make too much noise. We don't want Mrs Whappit coming around and complaining.' Ivor watched as his daughter balanced the halved scone on her plate and made her way up the stairs to join her brother.

'I met Mrs Whappit when I used your privy. She seems a decent soul — and her scones are delicious,' Eve said as she bit a mouthful and smiled across at Ivor.

'She serves a purpose. I know it's good she's there to keep an eye on my children, but at the same time, she can be an interfering old devil.

What did she say to you? She'd want to know who you were and why you were here, I bet?' Ivor said and looked across at her darkly.

'Yes, she did. And she asked if the baby I am carrying was yours. Don't worry, I put her straight, although she had the cheek to ask me in the first place.' Eve blushed and looked across at Ivor.

'She never has a good word for me. I'm sure she thinks I'm the devil himself, the nosy old witch!' Ivor sipped his tea. 'Thank you for getting my home a little tidier; I do miss a woman's touch around the home. It sometimes gets the better of me, that and the children. I really would have preferred you had not bothered with dusting upstairs, there really was no need.' He glanced up at Eve, his look making her feel slightly uncomfortable but giving her a chance to offer her services to him.

'You can ask me for help any time, Ivor. I don't mind. I'd like to get to know you and your family a lot better if you don't mind me being so forward.' Eve looked across at him and hoped that he would take up her offer.

'Thank you, Eve. You are too kind and I am glad that you have joined us today. I sometimes get quite withdrawn and imagine the worst of people. My wife used to lecture me about my moods and said that I should be more understanding of people.' Ivor put his head down and looked at his empty teacup.

'You sound as if you miss your wife. It is sad that you've lost her . . . ' Eve was desperate to quiz him.

'Yes, I have my regrets when it comes to my

195

wife, but she really did not understand me sometimes; she should have listened to me more, then she would still be with me,' He mumbled.

Eve frowned, not knowing what Ivor meant by that statement and suddenly decided to change the subject because his mood seemed to be darkening. 'I couldn't help but notice when I was cleaning that there's a smell coming from the locked room upstairs. Perhaps there is a dead mouse in there — they can make quite a smell for such small creatures. Or it could be something else or happen my nose is too sensitive.' Eve smiled and then, looking at his face, realised that it had not been the right moment to mention the offensive smell.

'I told you not to go upstairs! I don't know what's behind that door because it's not been open all the years we have been here. It probably is a mouse, as you say, or something that next door is brewing up. There are always offensive smells coming from the Whappits,' Ivor said, looking agitated.

'I'm sorry, I shouldn't have mentioned it,' Eve said quietly.

'No, perhaps not . . . Look, I'm sorry, Eve, but I seem to have developed a headache and my mood is not what it should be. Would you think the worse of me if I asked you to leave and perhaps visit another day?' he looked across at Eve with a steely gaze, making her feel totally unwelcome, and she quickly put her teacup down in its saucer and realised that Ivor was perhaps not the straightforward person she had thought him to be.

'No, of course not. Ivor, I'm sorry if I've offended, I was just trying to help.' Eve stood up and reached for her shawl from behind the kitchen door.

'You haven't offended, it's just I have a lot on my mind; another day and you will be more than welcome in our home.' Ivor shook his head slightly and walked over to Eve, putting his hand into the middle of her back and guiding her out of the kitchen and down the hallway. 'I appreciate your friendship, Eve, so please forgive me for being such a terrible host, especially after all your hard work for me.' He stood with the front door open and looked unsmilingly at Eve. He had thought she would be perfect company, but yet again a woman had not listened to him and had seen fit to do what *she* wanted to do. He could not ask her back, certainly not just yet, not until his mind was more settled.

'Good afternoon, Ivor, perhaps I will see you in the Swan this week?' Eve said with a little less warmth than she had first shown him. He was indeed a moody soul and she now understood why the men down at the quay did not like him. Perhaps working for him would not be right, let alone plotting to marry him. No wonder his wife left him, she thought, now believing that that was the real story as she picked her skirts up and walked back up the cobbled streets of Leeds.

She sighed. What dealings that she'd been involved in so far with men had been nothing but worry on her part and disdain on theirs. She'd be better off without them, she thought, as she walked into the yard of the Swan and made her way up the steps back to the rooms she shared with Nell. Either that or use them the same as Nell did, drinking gin and taking them for what she could get out of them, performing the oldest trade in the world. Then, as she entered the room that Nell entertained in and found herself face to face with Nell, legs outstretched and a man on the job, his trousers around his ankles and making the most awful grunts, she shuddered, making herself scarce as Nell glowered at her before burying the man's head in her heaving breasts. A police uniform and truncheon had been cast to one side and she realised that Nell was entertaining the lustful sergeant she's heard about — she'd never noticed the brush was out on the doorstep, so lost in her thoughts of the moody Ivor. Now Nell would have something to say to her.

15

It had been over a month since Eve had last seen Ivor; his visits to the Black Swan had come to a halt since her visit to him and gone, also, was any hope of her finding employment with him. Even if he came in and asked her to work for him she doubted that she would accept, for his mood had reminded her too much of her father's — and after all, if he couldn't abide using too much tea and butter at teatime, would his purse strings ever be anything but tight? Perhaps Mrs Whappit next door had been right about him and the face he put on when visiting the Swan was one of convenience and the real man was not a nice one at all.

'I think it's time, Eve, that you helped more in the kitchen rather than serving at the bar — that stomach of yours is getting bigger by the day and you must not be far off from your time.' Maude looked at the young lass who looked tired and wan from standing all day on her feet. Her stomach was extended and the knowing eye of seeing many a pregnancy had noted that her baby had dropped lower in her stomach in preparation for its birth.

'I'm all right, thank you, Maude,' Eve said, smiling gratefully. 'I just wish my mother was still alive to talk to. I'm scared, more than anything, I don't know if I can manage to bring this baby into the world and then what will become of us when I do?' Eve ran her hand over her stomach and, looking down, felt tears welling up in her eyes.

'Aye, lass, it'll come out whether you want it to or not. It's not very pleasant but hopefully you'll both survive. I've told Nell, I'll be there for you. I've helped bring many a baby into the world and you'll not need to be paying for a midwife, for you'll be all right in my hands.' Maude looked at the young lass she had become fond of. She'd never had children of her own, but if she had, she would have hoped for a daughter as placid as the lass who served well behind her and Stanley's bar; she'd been a real boon to the Swan since she'd arrived. The only thing that she did have concerns about was the tots of gin that Eve helped herself to most days, but she realised it was just a prop to help the girl through the day. Serving the ruffians from the canal docks was a skill that was better honed with a drink or two inside you, to return the cheek given and make yourself oblivious to the comments made between the rough dock workers. 'Have you got a few bits ready for the baby? You'll need them any time now,' Maude asked as she scowled across at a crowd making a din in the corner of the bar after coming off their early morning shift at the docks.

'Yes, I've managed to save enough money to buy the basics and I've got a drawer full of stuff. Even Nell has been knitting for me and has made a lovely layette for the baby.' Eve smiled.

'Nell knitting! Well, I've heard everything now.' Maude chuckled.

'Yes, she seems more excited than I am. I just don't know how I feel because our future is so uncertain.' Eve sighed. The reality was, she was frightened beyond belief but felt that she could not confide her true feelings in anybody.

'It'll be all right, lass; something will come along. We'll see how you are after the bairn is born and perhaps you'll manage to still work here if it's a good one and sleeps all day.' Maude smiled, although the last thing she wanted was a bawling baby behind the bar. The men who supped there did so to forget their wives and babies at home and certainly didn't want to be reminded of the commitments that bled them dry of their wages. Their conversation came to an abrupt end as the Swan's doors were flung open and a dock worker ran in and yelled at his colleagues who were drinking in the corner.

'Lads, lads, you are missing the fun! The peelers are down at the quay and they are going through Standish's office and have arrested him. They put him in a Black Maria and handcuffed him. He's only gone and killed his bloody wife! The bastard!'

Eve looked at Maude and they both watched with their mouths wide open as the Swan emptied in a few seconds, all the dock workers jostling to get out of the doors to see what was going on and jeer at the man that they had not liked and find out the juiciest gossip to take home to their wives.

'Lord, I didn't see that coming!' Maude exclaimed. 'I always thought he was a strange bugger, but I never thought that he'd kill his wife. It's his children I feel sorry for. Poor little devils, what will they think when they realise that he's killed their mother? What will become of them?'

Eve felt her body begin to shiver. She had set her sights for a short while on a man who had murdered his wife! Why on earth was she such a bad judge of men? Every one that she had known was wicked to the core. But Maude was right — what was going to become of Ivor Standish's children and what had they seen while they lived with him? She had only been involved with them twice but she felt she had to know what was to become of them. She breathed in deeply and felt for the bar, feeling suddenly faint at the thought that she could have been his next victim if she had continued setting her sights on him.

'You've gone as white as a ghost, lass. Are you all right? Get yourself home and come back when you feel more up to it; you've looked peaky all morning and this must be a shock to you. We've both served the bastard and he seemed to take a liking to you,' Maude said.

'Oh, Maude, I can't believe that he's killed his wife. But I'm all right, just a bit tired. I might go and lie down for a while and then come back before we get busy if that's all right with you?'

'You are eating enough, aren't you?' said the older woman. 'You've got to eat for two, you know. And don't worry about Ivor Standish, he'll be in the best place if he has indeed murdered his wife. To think we've served him many a time, a murderer in our pub, and now he's made a right mess of trade this morning! I'll have to go and tell Stanley, and yes, you go and have a lie-down,' Maude said, shaking her head and walking off to the kitchen to tell Stanley the news. Eve made for the door; she had no intention of going to lie down, but she did have a walk to The Calls planned, to see if Ivor Standish's children were all right . . .

★ ★ ★

Eve could hear the noise before she got anywhere near Ivor's house. There were crowds of people gathered outside the red-bricked terraced house, all talking and muttering about the killer who had lived there. Occasionally the word 'Murderer' was yelled out and the crowd booed in response. She pushed her way through the many bodies, men from the docks dressed in their work clothes, those from the nearby offices in suits, while women in their long skirts and blouses yelled and jeered as the line of peelers held the crowds back and went back and forth into Ivor's house.

'What — what's going on?' Eve asked the woman next to her.

'That bastard Standish, he's killed her! They found her body inside the wardrobe in the spare bedroom this morning.' The woman turned and looked at Eve. 'We're waiting for what remains of her to be brought out, pay our last respects. And look — there's the matron from the orphanage!'

Eve felt sick as she looked at the horse and flat cart that was waiting for the body of Ivor's wife to be placed on it and watched as the matron, in her long black skirts and white mob cap, went through the front door of the house, accompanied by a policeman.

'She'll have come for the children. Poor little buggers, he'll have been bad with them and all. Imagine living in the same house as your murdered mother? And God, she must have smelt. If it hadn't been for their neighbour, Mrs Whappit, complaining about the stink to their landlord, she'd never have been found,' the excited woman next to her said as the crowd surged forward, only to be pushed back by the rank of peelers linking arms.

Eve gasped, realising it was the body of Mary Standish that she had smelled that day when she had cleaned for Ivor. No wonder his mood had changed and that he had not wanted her to go upstairs. She'd been in there, dead, as she had cleaned and made tea for her murderer. Thank God she had stayed away from him! It could have been her as well, lying dead in the spare room if he had decided to get rid of *her*. The crowd went quiet as the matron, along with Katherine and Peter, came out of the front door, both children crying as she took hold of their hands and led them away from the house of death.

'Poor little buggers, nobody will want them. He's ruined their lives, that's for sure,' the woman whispered to Eve. 'Some of their father will be in them and you don't want to think that you'll be bringing up a murderer. Besides, just think what they might have seen.'

Eve thought of the afternoon when both children played happily with the bricks as she and Ivor had supped tea and exchanged pleasantries. Now they were both fatherless and motherless and would have a hard life being brought up without love and care in the orphanage.

The crowd held its breath as a stretcher covered with a white sheet was carried out of the house and placed on the cart with reverence. The woman beside Eve crossed herself and whispered a silent prayer as the body was made safe, then the door of the house on The Calls was closed behind the last peeler to come out of it and, with a line of them following the cart and remains of Mary Standish, they set off to the mortuary, where her body would rest until she was laid to rest.

'Nothing more to see here, get on your way!' a peeler yelled and ordered the crowd to disperse, others in the line moving people on.

Eve looked back at the house she once wanted to be employed at. She noticed Mrs Whappit talking to a reporter from the *Leeds Mercury*. She would be giving her story and would no doubt revel in the fame of living next door to a murderer. Eve walked back along the street with her head hung down, walking along with people who were boasting that they had known Ivor, that he always had been a funny devil. They too wanted some of the fame that Mrs Whappit was achieving at the price of another's misfortune. It was a ghoulish world that she lived in, where folk revelled in death. There would be crowds going to see where the murderer of Mary Standish had lived for weeks now, fascinated by the dark side of folk's lives.

'Hey, what are you doing down here? Have you come to leer like the rest of the buggers? You should be thankful that you are not in there, dead as a Dodo as well! He could have slit your throat before you knew it.' Nell linked her arm through hers. 'I saw him being dragged out of his office, the bastard! He's spoiled any business that I was going to get this morning. Fellas are too busy talking and gossiping about him,' she moaned. 'Still, I've just got enough for a gin or two, so come on, we'll go up Briggate and have a drink or two. Celebrate your escape from out of the murderous arms of Ivor Standish. And I really need a drink. First thing that happened this morning was that Tilly admitted herself to the poorhouse. She knows she's had it, poor cow. The syphilis is eating her alive and it's coddled her brain. Rosie couldn't look after her any longer.' Nell sighed.

'Poor Tilly, I feel sorry for her,' Eve said quietly. When she had first come across Rosie and Tilly, she had scorned their coarseness but now she realised they were only like that because it was the only way to survive in the darker side of Leeds.

'Aye, well it comes to all of us ladies of the night if we are not careful. It's the price you have to pay for selling your body to live. Thank the Lord, up to now I've been lucky! I don't know how because I've shagged most men on that dockside — and one or two gentry, who are usually the more pox-ridden of the two.' Nell looked at Eve and grinned, noticing her blushing. 'When are you going to stop being so coy about sex? Everyone does it. It's no good being shy about it. It wasn't a fairy that put that baby in your belly and well you know it.'

'I'm just not used to talking about it so openly, Nell. I still find it strange,' Eve whispered as she followed her into the small gin shop at the end of Briggate.

'You live and work with prostitutes and yet you are still ashamed of us. But if it wasn't for women like Rosie, Tilly and me, there would be a lot deader women like Mary Standish when their husbands couldn't get what they demand. We do society a favour — and the same folk that scorns us through a day will be visiting us the next evening and revealing their innermost desires and expecting satisfaction. They are hypocrites, much like yourself, Eve Reynolds. I thought that you would have known better by now.' Nell looked up at the shelves of the gin shop and stood for a moment, waiting for a reply from Eve. 'What's up? Cat got your tongue?'

'No, I just thought I'd felt a twinge but I'm all right now.' Eve breathed in deeply; she had felt a sharp pain as Nell had lectured her, but it had now subsided.

'Right then, we'll have two shots of Old Tom and then we'll head home because you look a bit peaky. It'll be because of the news of Ivor — but he'll soon be dangling from a gibbet, and serve him right for killing the fairer sex. Two Old Tom's, if you would.' Nell shoved her hard-earned money across the bar top and watched as two shots of gin were poured into glasses for her and Eve.

Unlike Nell, Eve couldn't drink the gin back in one mouthful so while Nell ordered herself another, she sipped it and looked around the gin shop, which was the busiest shop in Leeds. The shelves were lined with glasses and bottles of nothing but gin and folk came in and out after buying a bottle or drinking their tot straight back before going out onto the streets again. Suddenly Eve was gripped with pain again.

'Ahh, that hurt!' she gasped as she bent double and quickly put her glass back down on the bar as another pain gripped her.

'Bloody hell, we'd better get you home! I bet the baby is on its way so let's just hope that we make it. Do you think you can get yourself back home? The workhouse is nearer if you can't.' Nell looked at Eve with worry in her eyes.

'No! My baby is not going to be born in the workhouse! I'll get myself home,' Eve said between bouts of pain. 'Get me home, Nell, please get me home!'

16

'I can't do anything more for her, Nell, she needs a doctor else she and the baby are both going to die. The baby might already be dead for all I know, because the awkward little bugger is coming backside first and it can't get out.' Maude Nelson stood at the end of Eve's bed and looked around her at the bloodied bedclothes and then urged Nell to step outside the room with her. 'Nell, she'll die if we don't do something for her soon,' she whispered once they were out of Eve's earshot.

'But I've no money for a doctor, Maude. Besides, a doctor wouldn't come here and dirty his hands bringing a whore's baby into the world, because that's what he'd think he was doing. God, I just don't know what to do — but we can't lose her.' Nell covered her ears to cut off the cries and wails coming from Eve's bedroom.

Maude shuddered. 'There's a doctor on Water Lane, at number two, I think. He used to come in and drink himself blind after he got struck off from practicing. He might be our only hope. He's a good man and got struck off for performing abortions for women who really needed them. He'll expect payment, but not as much as other doctors; he might be happy with a bottle or two of gin if you're lucky. He should certainly be able to do something and I daren't do any more. The baby might be small but it's not for coming and Eve will bleed to death if we're not careful.' Maude wiped her bloodied hands across her brow and looked at Nell.

'Help! Please help!' Eve yelled from behind the bedroom door.

'You've got to go for him, Nell, and go now. For pity's sake, we'll manage to pay him somehow,' Maude pleaded with Nell as she hesitated.

'Right, I'll go. Number two, you say? What's his name? Can you remember?' Nell reached for her shawl and made for the door.

'Butterworth. Tell him it's me who's sent for him and don't take no for an answer. He's her only hope.' Maude watched Nell run down the stairs and across the yard in the direction of Water Lane. She said a silent prayer, hoping that the old quack would be at home and sober enough to know what he was doing if Nell could convince him to attend.

★ ★ ★

Nell ran through the streets, ignoring the calls and taunts of her usual customers, her mind focused on making the old soak Butterworth listen to her plea. She couldn't let young Eve and her baby die, she just couldn't; she'd saved her once before and she'd do it again, providing the old bugger would come with her.

She ran down the rundown street known as Water Lane and looked for number two, noticing as she knocked and hammered on the peeling front door the unscrubbed steps and the weeds growing out of the guttering of the house.

From deep within its walls came a voice: 'I hear you! Bugger off and go and find somebody else to plague, you little bastards or I'll come out and tan your backsides!' Nell stood her ground as she heard a bolt being pulled back from behind the door and held her breath as it slowly opened to reveal a man, small in stature with long grey hair and glasses perched on the end of his nose. He looked shocked at the sight of her standing on his doorstep. 'I thought you were the children that take great pleasure in knocking on my door and then running away.' He turned to go back into his house. 'You must have the wrong door.'

'No, no! Please, we need you. Maude Nelson from the Black Swan sent me because we have a friend who's struggling to give birth. Maude hoped that you would be able to help, else Eve and the baby will die.' Nell stood up on the step and put her hand on the old doctor's arm, turning him back again.

'I don't practice any more. I was struck off, and she knows that. You're wasting your time,' he growled.

'Please, she'll die without your help and she doesn't deserve to die. She's had such a hard life already, without leaving this earth so soon. Please, I beg you. Maude said you were a good man and that you were misunderstood, that you were helping women in trouble when you were struck off. Please, we'll pay you no matter what the consequences are, we just want to give Eve a chance.'

211

'She's a prostitute, I bet, if she's anything to do with the Black Swan — like yourself, I presume?' The doctor looked judgementally at Nell and breathed in.

'No, she's not, she was taken advantage of and so has fallen on hard times. Please, sir, she deserves to live.' Nell pulled on his sleeve as he stood hesitantly on the step.

'I'll get my bag — but you've not been here or even seen me if she or the baby dies. They'd hang me if I was linked with another death.'

Nell sighed and breathed in, glad that she had convinced him to come and try to save Eve, if not the baby.

★ ★ ★

Butterworth shook his head, looking at the blood-soaked bedclothes and Eve writhing in pain. 'How long has she been like this?' he asked Maude.

'Two days now; the baby is stuck because it's coming out the wrong way around.' Maude looked at the old doctor and watched as he felt Eve's stomach and listened for a heartbeat from the baby with his stethoscope.

'Close the door and leave me to it. Hopefully, I'll save both, but if not, you've not seen me here.' He reached inside his bag and pulled out some forceps, then swore at both hesitating women to leave him to the job in hand.

Minutes later, Maude and Nell looked at one another as they sat next to the fire which had brass pans full of warm water on the flames in readiness for the birth. Both hung their heads in worry, both wondered if they had done the right thing in getting the aged doctor to help.

'Do you think we've done right? He's a bit past his best, isn't he? God help her, please let him save her,' Nell whispered just as the room was filled with an almighty scream from Eve's bedroom.

'Oh, Lord, she must have died!' Maude held her apron up to her eyes and sobbed. 'God have mercy on us, we should have got her a proper doctor.'

'Listen . . . no, listen! That's a baby crying, Maude. It's been born and it's alive!' Nell stood up with a beaming smile on her face. 'The baby's alive, now let's hope Eve is.'

Both women cast their eyes to the opening bedroom door and the ageing doctor who held the newborn in his arms, wrapped in the blanket that had been in the makeshift cot waiting for the newborn to venture into the world.

'We have a baby girl, ladies. She's a bit blue and has perhaps come before her time, but she is alive, as is her mother. Now, they both could do with your attention — a good wash and some peace and quiet, especially in the mother's case, for the birth has left her weak and she will need some care over the next few weeks.' Butterworth passed the wrinkled, blue-faced baby to Nell and looked at the shock on her face. 'Not a bonny picture, is she? That comes with it being a breech birth, but once she gets her mother's milk in her, she'll soon be pink and bonny. She's a fighter, I'll give her that.'

'I'm so grateful that you saved them both. I thought they were going to die.' Nell clutched the baby tightly to her and walked back into Eve's bedroom, Maude following with a bowl of warm water and a flannel to help wash mother and baby down. 'Oh, Eve, look at your little girl! She's so small and looks so angry at being brought into the world.'

Eve tried to sit up and look at her offspring, smiling weakly as she took the bundle from Nell. 'You nearly killed me, my darling — and that's the second time I nearly gave up on life because of you.' She bent her head and kissed the little wrinkled brow as the baby pushed its hands out of its cover and started to wail. 'You look like a newly born kitten with your eyes hardly open and all those wrinkles . . . Shush now, it will be all right, I promise. We have one another now, Mary, and I'll always be there for you, no matter what life throws at us.' Eve closed her eyes and held the baby to her breast.

'Mary? Why Mary?' Nell looked down at Eve.

'It was Ivor Standish's wife's name; I thought it would always remind me never to trust men and to play them at their own game,' Eve whispered.

Maude tutted. 'Enough of this talking — save your strength! Let me give you and Mary a quick wash and tidy and then you can both sleep.' Maude looked down on the nursing pair and washed Eve's face gently, motioning Nell to leave and deal with the old doctor, who was standing in the doorway.

'She'll be weak for some time,' he said, 'and she will need your help. The baby is underweight but seems to have a healthy pair of lungs on her and it was a blessing that she was small — I'm afraid it might have been a different outcome otherwise.' He picked up his Gladstone bag and looked at Eve.

'Thank you,' Nell said. 'We are so grateful for your help and will be forever in your debt for what you have done for Eve today. And saying that, how can we pay you? What would you like for saving our dear friend's life?' Nell held her breath, she had little enough savings without giving what she had away.

'I don't think a demand of two shillings would be out of order; if I was still registered, I would be charging twice that, and as you pointed out, I did save two lives today.' The doctor looked at the disappointment on Nell's face.

'I think I can just manage that,' she said. 'Excuse me while I get you your money. It is indeed a fair price to pay for the lives of my dear friend Eve and her daughter.'

Nell walked to her bedroom and knelt down and got her savings box out from under her bed. She counted two shillings into her hand, which left two silver threepenny pieces in the bottom of the box. Not a lot to live on in the next coming days; she would have to hope that trade improved in the coming week, she thought as she smiled and put the money into the old doctor's outstretched hand.

'I thank you, madam. If you need me again, you know where I am.' Butterworth pocketed his pay, picked up his bag and Maude escorted him down to the yard, leaving Nell standing at the door, feeling tired and dreary after fighting for Eve's life and spending almost every penny on her and the baby. And she had even more responsibilities towards them now, she knew, for both mother and baby were dependent on her and she would have to go back on the streets tomorrow, no matter what. There were three mouths to feed now and hardly any money to do it with.

★ ★ ★

Eve looked down at her newborn; she was exhausted and hurting. Baby Mary was now contentedly asleep, wrapped up clean and dry in a blanket, and she too was clean and comfortable in her newly made-up bed, cosseted and seen to by both Maude and Nell. She closed her eyes, feeling the weight of the world upon her shoulders. She had thought that she would feel differently once her baby was born but now, with the small body lying in her arms, all she felt was despair. How was she supposed to raise this child that was totally dependent on her? She had no money, no husband — and no place to call her own. Many had told her to leave her baby on the orphanage or workhouse steps and at least Mary would be fed there or perhaps she might be lucky and be adopted by a childless wealthy couple and given the kind of life that Eve knew she could never give her. She looked at the little creature now fast asleep, her hands clenched tightly, a few wisps of hair just visible on her head, and struggled to make sense of her feelings. Oh, she did feel an attachment to the babe, but not the overwhelming feeling of love and protection that everyone had said that she would have once her baby was born. What she knew was that the baby was responsible for changing her life and bringing about her downfall, so how could she love it?

Tears filled her eyes and started to fall as Mary moved and her translucent lids fluttered and she looked up at her mother. 'I don't know what we are going to do,' Eve said. 'I can't even promise that I will grow to love you because you are the biggest mistake of my life — but I'm going to have to make the best of it for both of our sakes.' She closed her eyes and rested her head back into the pillow. Right now, she wished both her and her newborn dead and free of earthly worries, for there was nothing but hardship to look forward to, as far as she could see, and the old doctor should not have saved her.

★   ★   ★

'They always say one in and one out.' Nell sat on the edge of Eve's bed, nursing Mary and making gurgling noises at her as she held her delicately small fingers while she told Eve of Tilly's demise.

'At least she's free of worry. Mine's just starting. I think you're right, I should take her to the orphanage and leave her there — at least I could get on with my life then.' Eve's mood had not mended and even after a week in bed with Mary by her side, she still did not feel a bond towards her child.

217

'You can't do that,' Nell protested. 'No, she can't leave you on those orphanage steps.' Nell tickled the side of Mary's face and shook her head. 'Your mother is feeling sorry for herself and she needs to get out of that bed and stir her shanks.' She looked up at Eve. 'Move your arse, Eve, a week in bed is long enough for anybody! Stop moping and help me around the house if nothing else because it could do with a good clean. I've hardly been at home since this one's been born — and if I have, I've been running after you. Somebody has to make some money for us all to live on, especially as your doctor bled us dry. Although it was worth every penny of it, wasn't it, darling?' Nell looked down again at Mary, who seemed to have taken more to Nell than her mother.

'I don't feel up to it,' Eve groaned.

'You've had a baby, a small bit of a thing, come to that. Working women are back on their feet the next day, they haven't got time to roll around in bed and feel sorry for themselves. Now, today I'm going up The Headrow and Briggate and when I get back, I expect you up and going and some dinner on the table. I know you can manage that. This one will sleep once she's had her feed and you can take your time; it'll do you good to focus your mind on something instead of languishing, feeling sorry for yourself.' Nell passed Mary back into Eve's arms and stood at the end of the bed.

'You are going up Briggate and The Headrow through the day? That's Bert Bradshaw's patch, you'll have to take care. What's wrong with the

218

Quayside? He knows to leave you alone down there through the daytime.' Eve was shocked at Nell's choice of place to do trade; she was risking a good beating — or even worse — if she was found to be taking trade from Bert Bradshaw's prostitutes.

Nell shook her head. 'Not much choice. Since Ivor Standish's death, the place is swarming with peelers. Besides, it's better money up in the town centre, especially if I can catch the eye of a gent in need of a little light relief.' She grinned. 'I need to get money back in — you and this little one cost a pretty penny to save. Not that I regret it; how could anyone, looking down at that bonny little face?' Nell walked up to baby Mary again and pulled back the blanket from around her now pink and plump face.

'I'm sorry, Nell, I must sound so ungrateful,' Eve said. 'It's just I feel so low . . . You will take care of yourself up in the centre of town? Are you sure that you shouldn't stay down by the docks and wharf? After all, Sergeant Jones is a regular of yours — and he's been coming a lot more of late — so he's hardly going to charge you or haul you in.' Sergeant Robert Jones was one of Nell's favourite customers; she kept him satisfied while he turned a blind eye to her touting for trade down by the docks.

'No, he's had a bit of misfortune. His wife died a couple of months back and he's been left with a young son to raise on his own so he's too busy to look after my neck down at the docks at the moment, although I expect he'll not be too busy for his Friday night appointment.' Nell grinned. 'The fool told me that he loved me last week and I told him he was in shock after losing his wife. How could a respectable sergeant be in love with a whore like me?'

'Well, he does seem to be here a lot and I've seen him bringing you flowers — that's not usual behaviour from a client, is it? You could do worse than to take him on his word. Besides, the amount of time you've told me to be careful and you're putting yourself at risk, going up into the town?' Eve frowned at Nell and decided that perhaps her friend was right, she *did* need to pull herself together and help, at least with the running of the house, and then see if she would be accepted back at the Swan with her baby in tow. However, *she* was right when it came to Sergeant Robert Jones: he had been visiting a lot of late, perhaps just to talk about the death of his wife and find comfort in Nell's body.

'Nah, he's just grieving and being sentimental because of it. Right, I'm off; Bert Bradshaw doesn't frighten me. Now, your clothes are over there and the fire's lit, the kettle's filled and there are some potatoes that need peeling which will do us today with some tripe and onions that I begged off Blackwell the butcher in return for a favour.' Nell winked. 'Where there's a will, there's a way. We'll not go hungry, lass.'

After Nell had gone, Eve looked at the baby by her side and sighed. It *was* time she moved, no matter how battered and tired her body felt. She wasn't gaining anything lying there, letting everyone run after her. She lowered her legs over the side of the bed and looked at the bloody patch that had been made over the days she had been in bed despite cloths being placed to catch her flow. Although her bleeding was subsiding, she was still weak and her head felt light as she walked across to the washstand and started to clean herself, leaving Mary wrapped in her blanket at the side of the bed.

She stared at herself in the wardrobe mirror and saw that she looked pale and too thin. Gone was the healthy-looking country lass who had come into Leeds full of hope and ideas for a better life. Now she was just like all the rest of the backstreet women, who looked hard and talked hard, and hard was what she was going to have to be if she was to survive.

17

Eve sat on the bottom of the steps that led up to her and Nell's home; baby Mary was in her arms and she was enjoying the warmth of the early spring sunshine as she looked out across the yard in the direction of the Swan. She waved when she noticed Rosie coming out through the doors on her own. She'd not spoken to her since hearing that Tilly had died and wanted to give her condolences.

'So, you're up and about and not looking so bad considering what they say you went through to get this one into the world.' Rosie sat down beside Eve, a bottle of gin in one hand, a copy of the *Leeds Intelligencer* in the other. She passed Eve the bottle and urged her to take a sip. 'Go on, it's just what you need, a pick-me-up after giving birth.' Rosie watched as Eve drank deeply and then passed her back the bottle.

'That was good! It's the first drink since I had her.' Eve looked down at her baby.

'You'll need more than that little sip if you're to survive to bring her up.' Rosie took a mouthful of gin and then passed it back to Eve, who sipped quickly again, feeling a sense of contentment for the first time since Mary had been born as the gin dulled her senses.

'I'm sorry to hear about Tilly,' Eve said as she looked down on the sleeping Mary. 'I hope she didn't suffer too badly.'

'It's one of those things, lass. Syphilis gets all of us tarts eventually, the dirty bloody disease. Nell and I have been lucky so far, but it'll get us, I know all too well that it will. Have you seen the front page of the *Intelligencer*? Ivor bloody Standish is staring right at you. I don't know why they wasted space doing a sketch of him and he's not exactly handsome. Or he won't be, when he's shitting his trousers, dancing on the hangman's noose.'

Rosie passed Eve the paper to look at, folding the front page so that she could read it while holding the baby. Eve read about the trial that had found him guilty and she shook her head as she read that he was to be hung at Armley Prison at seven o'clock the next morning. Looking at the artist's sketch of Ivor, she thought that it made him look more glamorous than he was, satisfying the public's fascination with murder and the dark affairs of Victorian society. 'He wasn't such a bad man,' she said. 'He loved his children. And there are always two sides to every story.' Eve passed the paper back to Rosie and sighed.

'Not a bad man? He murdered his bloody wife, Eve! He always was a moody bastard, nobody liked him.' Rosie looked at her, shocked.

'You don't know what his wife was like — it might be her that drove him to kill her,' Eve said quietly.

'Nah, he was a bad 'un. I always steered clear of him. You seemed to have taken his eye, though. In fact, you'll catch many a man's eyes now you've got your figure back. Why don't you bury your pride and join Nell and me in our upstanding profession?' Rosie laughed. 'At least, it's upstanding when it's a threepenny quick one!'

Eve shook her head. 'No, Rosie, I don't think I could ever do that. Although I feel guilty at the moment because Nell is paying for the three of us and I'm just sitting about with this one on my lap. I went to ask Maude if I could start back at the Swan but she'd watched me walking across the yard and said I looked too weak to be of any use to her at the moment and that I should get my strength back.' Eve sighed and jiggled Mary as she started to stir. 'I don't think she was keen on having the baby in the back room while I worked.'

'Aye, she can be a funny one, can Maude, when it comes to babies. She and Stanley have never been blessed and although she's good at bringing them into the world, she's no time for them when they're here.' Rosie put the paper down to one side and took another swig of her gin. 'What if you started with those men who don't demand much, like the dirty old bugger who just likes to watch Nell undress through the keyhole? And then she's got another that just wants you to stroke his head and listen to his woes of married life. You'd be earning some money while Nell is working on the street and down at the quay.'

'Lord, I don't know if I could do that! But I suppose it is one way of making money without letting them touch me. I don't think I could bear a man's hands — far less anything else, come to that — on me that I didn't have feelings for. And besides, I have my pride.' Eve hung her head.

'We all have that, lass, but we need to keep a roof over our heads and our bellies full. You should be thankful that you've got Nell, else you'd be living on the street, making ends meet however you could, no matter how much pride you've got. And she needs to take care, does that one. I hear she's been going off her patch and touting along The Headrow and that'll not go down well with Bert Bradshaw if he catches her. I think it's time you buried that bloody pride of yours and joined us, for you're no different or better than any of us, and now that you've got that babe and you aim to keep it, you've not much choice.' Rosie looked angrily at her and Eve knew full well that she could not just stay with Nell and expect her to look after the three of them and do nothing. Besides, she could do with someone to work the Swan and surrounding streets with because it was safer when there were two of you touting for business in that part of Leeds; you knew somebody was there to cover your back.

'I couldn't do it,' Eve said firmly but she knew Rosie was speaking the truth and that there was no other way out for her at present. Her dream of meeting a respectable young man and him looking twice at her now she had a child was just that, a dream. She looked down at Mary, who was about to start crying, and she swore. The baby that she vowed she would never give up to the orphanage was going to be her downfall, and no matter how much she had dreamed of loving her and making a way in the world for the both of them, at that moment she could see no future but one of darkness and despair.

'She's hungry, is the little thing.' Rosie looked at Eve. 'You'll have to feed her.'

'She's always hungry, I'll go upstairs and feed her,' Eve said quietly, nearly in tears.

'Sit here and feed her, nobody will mind and nobody will give you a second glance; besides, there's only me here at the moment.' Rosie gently put her hand on Eve's arm. She'd been there, had felt the same feelings as Eve and knew well the despair after having her first baby without a husband's support.

'I couldn't, folk will see my . . . ' Eve disclaimed as Mary started to cry, wrinkling her face and making fists of her small hands as she cried to be fed.

'Oh, for Lord's sake! Nobody down here is bothered. You are feeding your baby, that's all that matters.' Rosie looked at Eve. 'Go on, get on with it and shut her up from bawling.'

Eve hesitantly untied the ribbon of her blouse and let Mary catch on to her full breasts. The baby suckled contentedly as Rosie watched on and the little body instantly became quiet.

'And once she's filled her belly, give her a small drop of gin to settle her down to sleep. That always does the trick. She'll not always be a baby and you'll have to make the most of it until she can fend for herself. Poor little bugger, none of 'em asked to be brought into this world! We have them and then we regret it.' Rosie swigged back another mouthful of gin and then swept

226

away a tear and glared at the fairly well-dressed man who entered the yard and looked at the three of them. 'What you looking at? Never seen a nursing mother before, you bastard?'

He stood and looked at her and shook his head. The town was going to the dogs, with women having children they couldn't afford and surviving off gin, as clearly the two women in front of him were.

'I'm looking at two women who should have more respect for themselves and a child that doesn't stand a hope in hell,' the gentleman replied and then walked back out of the yard after looking disgustedly at the two women he believed to be harlots.

'That's right, piss off! I bet you wouldn't say no to a quick how's your father? Just don't like to see the consequences of your deeds.' Rosie stood up and nearly toppled backwards.

'Snotty bastard!'

'Rosie, shush, stop it! I knew I shouldn't have fed her here.' Eve looked down at the contented baby, who now looked up at her with open blue eyes, and closed her blouse up. 'He thought I was a prostitute and you made me sound like one.'

'Well, you might as well be, because there's no other way of making a living in this neck of the woods. Bury your pride, close your eyes, open your legs and think of bloody England, because that's what we all have had to do!'

★　★　★

227

'Oh, Lord, I'm tired! Every bone in my body aches and I'm sore in places that no decent woman would talk about.' Nell sat down in her chair when she came in from working her patch on the quayside a few days later. 'And I'm not finished yet; that bloody weird Councillor Hargreaves, him with his fat belly and podgy hands, will be knocking on the door soon. At least he won't be pushing and panting on top of me and I won't have to look at his bloated face for his sixpence.' Nell sighed and bent down to unlace her ankle boots, looking at the worn-out sole of one as she did so. 'I could do with a new pair of boots, but I'll have to make do with these . . . Mmm, or perhaps I could run to buying a pair off Ma Fletcher off her second-hand stall? Although even she's a thieving old devil and likes to haggle.'

'Well, I've made you something to eat — fried bread and an egg on top of it. Mary is asleep and I pacified her with a teaspoon of gin after feeding her.' Eve put Nell's supper in front of her and watched as the older woman closed her eyes before opening them and looked at the scanty meal in front of her.

'I wish Maude and Stanley would take you back, Eve. We really could do with the money. It wouldn't have been too bad, but the doctor went with all my savings. I'd thought we could manage for a while longer than we have.' Nell looked worried as she picked up her knife and fork and started to eat her supper.

'I'm sorry, Nell, I'm nothing but a nuisance to you. I'll leave or I'll go looking for a job on the other side of town. I think I'm going to have to admit I'm wrong and give Mary up because nobody wants a woman with a baby and at least I could get a live-in job as a maid or servant of some kind if I didn't have her. I'll put her on the orphanage steps in the morning and then I'll leave you in peace,' Eve said quietly. She hated being dependant on Nell and, to make matters worse, she'd seen a new barmaid in the Black Swan, so she knew that she was no longer needed there. It was going to be a dreadful decision to make but best for everyone that she took it.

'You will not! I've looked after you and that baby this long and I'm not letting you give her away that easily. Indeed, I think I love her more than you do, bless her. Every time I look into those eyes and put my finger in her tiny hands, I think of the baby I gave away and regret every minute. So just clear your head of those stupid thoughts,' Nell barked. 'Something will turn up for you and I'll just have to keep on pleasing the odd gentry or two and charge that little bit more.' She pushed her plate to one side and warmed her toes at the fire, closing her eyes as the tiredness of the day came over her.

'I'm sorry,' Eve whispered as she took the dirty plate away to let her rest until she had to be wakened for her next client, Councillor Hargreaves.

★   ★   ★

Eve looked across at Nell; she looked pale and drawn as she slept and when the usual treble knock of Councillor Hargreaves was heard on the outside door she got up from her chair and decided to tell him that Nell was unwell and that he should return another evening for his pleasure. She walked quietly across the wooden floor and into what Nell called her entertainment room and opened the outer door to the councillor.

'Oh! Good evening, I-I was expecting Miss Nell.' The little elderly man looked bemused and somewhat embarrassed.

'I'm sorry, Miss Nell is unwell this evening and sends her apologies,' Eve said, looking at a man old enough to be her father, well dressed, with a bulbous nose as red as a strawberry.

'Oh, I see and she's sent you in her place, I presume. A new girl for me to spy on — and a very pretty one at that. I take it she's told you my little secret?' the old man said and grinned.

Eve stood for a minute and wondered what to do. Should she get Nell or should she do what he'd requested? After all, she wasn't anywhere near the dirty old devil; he'd only be spying on her . . . She closed her eyes and breathed in deeply before answering. Then, 'No,' she said, 'I'm sorry, but I'm not like that and you'll have to go elsewhere for your pleasure tonight. Now, please go. Nell will see you next week as usual.' Eve pushed the councillor back to the outside of the door and bolted it quickly behind her. She just couldn't lower herself to sell her body, no matter how hard times were. She'd more pride than that — but now she would have to face the wrath of Nell and she knew she had risked all in her life for the sake of her pride.

Without looking around from her chair, Nell spoke. 'I heard it all and I thought that you were going to give him what he wanted for a minute.' She kept her eyes closed. 'I've got a right one in you, haven't I? You had the chance to make some brass by just undressing in front of the old devil and instead you kept your dignity and pride intact.' Nell opened her eyes and looked at Eve. 'If it wasn't for that lil' baby through there, I'd probably throw you out. You do know that, I hope?'

'I know. My mother always used to say that pride would be my downfall. I'm sorry, Nell, I can't perform for men who don't love me, who only want me for sex,' Eve said and hung her head.

Nell sighed. Time and looks were starting to be against her and Eve would be a godsend if only she would sell her body too, but clearly there was no convincing her to do so. 'Never mind, something will come along. And don't worry, you're not out on the streets yet. I care too much for that baby — and you're not such a bad 'un yourself. Here, take a swig of gin and let's forget about it.' Nell sighed again deeply and passed Eve the gin bottle.

'I think I'll need more than this to stop me from feeling the way I do. I'm the lowest of the low and it's all my fault.' Eve swallowed and looked around her.

'Nay, you are never that low with friends that will stay by you no matter what. I respect you, Eve. You knew I'd not be suited when you turned the dirty old devil away but you did it to look after me and you were determined to keep your pride and dignity. The whore and the saint, what a bloody pair we are!' Nell laughed.

18

Eve sat in the sunshine and held Mary tight in her arms. She looked down at her perfectly formed baby girl with a mop of black hair that was growing fast. Mary, in turn, looked up and gurgled and smiled at her mother, her cheeks showing healthy dimples, flushed from the just-visible tooth coming through her aching gums.

'That's a nice toothy peg we've got coming through there, Mary. That's the reason for your sleepless nights of late. No wonder we're both shattered. I wouldn't blame Nell if she threw the pair of us out onto the streets, the way you've wailed and carried on.' Eve smiled and then held Mary close to her when she whimpered, as if her mother's words had reminded her of the pain she'd been feeling and she'd decided to have a moan. 'Shush, my little one, we've had enough of all this; you try and keep smiling a little bit longer and just give me a bit of peace.'

Eve placed her baby on her knee and tried to console her but Mary was not having any of it and she thrust her small, determined fist into her mouth to chew on to stop the pain that came on in bouts. 'I'll sing you a song, my little one, and you try and sleep in my arms while I rock you.' Eve smiled, looking down with a sudden rush of love at the protesting baby, and then sang, sweetly, the latest ballad that was being sung by the Irish immigrants who had filled the streets of Leeds.

> All the dames of France are fond and free
> And Flemish lips are really willing.
> Very soft the maids of Italy
> And Spanish eyes are so thrilling.
> Still, although I bask beneath their smile,
> Their charms will fail to bind me
> And my heart falls back to Erin's Isle
> To the girl I left behind me.

Her voice carried out across the Black Swan's yard, filtering through the inn's walls, making even the ardent drinkers rest their tankards and listen to the haunting lyrics that Eve was singing with so much feeling. It made them think of loved ones lost, of the love and hurt that they had once all felt. Stanley, behind the bar, looked startled as big men were nearly reduced to tears at Eve's singing and then listened to all the men demanding more when her song came to an end. He placed his dishcloth down and looked out thoughtfully at the young lass sitting with her beloved bairn on the bottom of Nell's steps. Perhaps there was something he could do for her — if she had the nerve. It would be a shame if she didn't because she'd been blessed with the voice of an angel.

Stanley watched as Eve held the comforted baby to her and climbed the steps to her room to put the child in its crib. When he'd done serving he'd go and have words with her, offer her an hour or two every other night, singing to his customers. Not only had she quietened the whole rowdy lot, she'd also made them drink more to forget their heartache as they remembered their families and loved ones. She'd be a real boon the inn but he knew he would have to work hard to convince her before counting the money he knew he'd make with her singing the way she did. He shook his head. He'd never heard a voice so beautiful. She just had to come and sing for him and his customers and she would fill the Black Swan to the rafters once word spread around the docks. She was going to be his golden goose and she had been there under his nose all along.

★　★　★

Eve sat on the edge of her bed and looked down at her sleeping baby, brushing away a tear. The singing of 'The Girl I left Behind Me' had made her feel so melancholy, her hopes of a better life slipping away. Her mind was also playing tricks on her, remembering only the good times with the dashing John Oates. Surely if he'd known that he had fathered a baby on her he would have returned and perhaps married her, she thought, and put her head in her hands. He had loved her, she knew he had; it was just he had been made to go and fight, else he would have stood by her. Now, in the gloom of the late afternoon, she felt dejected and lonely. It was only the love of her daughter and the support of her loyal and most loved friend, Nell, that kept her strong. If it wasn't for them, she'd have given up on life a long time ago.

'Go on, lass, when I heard you, shivers went down my spine. That voice of yours is a precious thing and you shouldn't keep it to yourself.' Stanley looked across the table at Eve and could see that she was giving his suggestion serious thought.

'I can look after Mary,' Nell urged her. 'If you go of an evening she'll hopefully be asleep in her crib even if I'm entertaining. Besides, you'll only be across the yard so you can keep bobbing back and seeing to her if you need to.' Nell placed her hand on Eve's arm and smiled. 'You do have a voice, lass. I've heard you singing to Mary and thought you should do something with it, only I couldn't see what.'

'I don't know . . . I don't know if I could stand up and sing to all the drinkers. What if they don't like me?' Eve felt herself blush.

'It takes something to make grown men wipe a tear away from their eyes — and that's what you did today, unbeknown to you. I'll pay you well for your time, Eve. And I don't give my money away gladly, so I must have faith in you, lass,' Stanley urged Eve. He knew he couldn't lose money if she would only come and sing in his inn. Dockers and wharf workers were worse than washerwomen for gossiping and the Black Swan would soon be full of folk coming to hear a voice such as Eve had.

'I suppose I can try it, just for one night, and then if they like me, I can come back. But Mary must be looked after at all times, I can't leave her to cry on her own.'

'She'll be looked after, don't you worry. You know I love the bit of a thing.' Nell smiled.

'Go on, lass, try it for one night and if you don't enjoy it then I won't make you do it again.' Stanley looked at Eve and hoped that she would agree to his offer.

Eve bowed her head and breathed in. 'Very well, then, I'll try it the once and see how I go. But I don't want anybody groping me or shouting things while I'm singing — I well know some of those that drink late in the evening get more than a little rowdy.' Eve looked squarely at Stanley. She'd no intention of being used like Rosie and Nell; she'd kept herself to herself since John Oates had used her and she was not going to let anyone take advantage of her ever again.

'I'll keep them in order and if Nell can't look after Mary then I'm sure Maude will enjoy nursing the little soul.' Stanley was determined that he would have Eve performing for him, come hell or high water, even informing Maude that, if it came to the worst, she would be babysitting Mary. 'Will Saturday night be all right for you? I'll spread the word and then we'll get a good crowd in for your debut.'

'I think that will be all right.' Eve felt her stomach churn — she had never performed in public before and she had no idea what to sing for a whole evening.

'Well, to put your mind at rest on your first night, I'll not tout for business for that night and will make Mary my business,' Nell said, smiling. She knew the first night would either make or break Eve so she had to be there to give her support. 'And I'll hunt you out a frock, make you look a bit special. The fellas will like that.'

'Saturday it is then.' Stanley rose up and looked at Eve. 'You have got the voice of an angel, lass, you'll be all right.' He left Eve and Nell looking at one another, at least one of them wondering if she had done right to agree to Stanley's request.

★ ★ ★

'Stop wriggling and messing! The sleeves are supposed to look like that; shows your shoulders and bosom off.' Nell looked at Eve as she tugged at the loose-hanging beaded sleeves of the green dress that Nell had appeared with for her from off the market earlier that day. 'Ma said that it had come from one of the finest houses in Leeds. She also said that if you didn't damage it and no longer wanted it after tonight, she'd give me my money back, so stop your bloody pulling on it.' Nell stood back and looked at her now gilded lily of a friend. 'Bloody hell, you scrub up well! You could charge God knows what if you went on the streets with me.'

'I'm not happy doing *this*, let alone walking the streets. You will look after my Mary, won't you? You'll come to me if she won't stop crying?' Eve looked over at the gurgling baby who had defied her usual bedtime, sensing something was afoot.

'No, I'll throw her in the bloody cut! What do you think I am? I think the world of this young woman, she and I will be just fine.' Nell smiled at Mary as Eve walked towards the door and made her way down the steps into the yard of the Black Swan. 'Sing like a nightingale, lass!' she shouted as Eve walked across the cobbled yard and stood for a brief second after turning to look at her with Mary in her arms.

★   ★   ★

'Lord give me strength,' Eve whispered as she opened the door into the bar she knew so well, but tonight it felt different; she was dressed up to the nines and the drinkers were there to listen to her. He smiled as the dock workers and labourers commented and whistled.

'Now, Eve, you start to sing when you're ready. I've cleared that corner for you and everyone's been told to behave.' Stanley took her arm and placed her in the corner next to the fireplace. He winked as he saw her smile wanly and then he looked around him as the room went quiet in anticipation. The pub was heaving, some of his regulars had even brought their wives, who were sitting together and looking at the woman that their husbands had talked about and told them to come and listen to as they enjoyed a drop or two of gin.

Eve felt uneasy as she looked upon faces that she had served over the bar when she was pregnant and she wanted to run. Why had she been so foolish to listen to Stanley and Nell? They knew nothing about how it felt standing there. One of the biggest dock workers that she knew to be Irish shouted out, 'Sing 'The Girl I Left Behind Me', Eve. It reminds me of a lass I left back home.' And then he put his tankard to his mouth and waited in expectation.

Eve shuffled her feet and felt her heart pounding in her mouth, then she closed her eyes and pretended that she was singing to Mary. The first few notes were a little wobbly, but with every breath her voice grew stronger and clearer and she could hear people whispering and saying how fine she sang. At the end of it, she opened her eyes and looked at the big Irishman who had encouraged her. Tears were running down his face and, as he wiped them away, he smiled at her and started to clap and everyone else joined in.

'Another! Another!' the crowd shouted.

Eve looked at the big man and thought hard about what next to sing, her confidence growing as she knocked back a generous swig of Stanley's special brewed gin, and she sang out clear and proud and flirted with her crowd.

Near by the swelling ocean,
One morning in the month of June,
While feather'd warbling songsters
Their charming notes did sweetly tune,
I overheard a lady

Lamenting in sad grief and woe,
And talking with young Bonaparte
Concerning the bonny Bunch of Roses, O.

'Oh, son,' spake the young Napoleon,
And grasp'd his mother by the hand:-
'Oh, Mother dear have patience,
Till I am able to command

I'll raise a numerous army,
And through tremendous dangers go,
And in spite of all the universe,
I'll gain the bonny Bunch of Roses, O.'

Your father raised great armies,
And likewise kings did join the throng;
He was so well provided.
Enough to sweep the world along.

But when he went to Moscow,
He was o'erpower'd by drifting snow;
And although Moscow was blazing
He lost the bonny Bunch of Roses, O.

'Oh, Mother, adieu for ever,
I am now on my dying bed,
If I had liv'd, I'd have been brave
But now I droop my youthful head.

And when our bones do moulder,
And weeping-willows o'er us grow.
Its deeds to bold Napoleon
Will stain the bonny Bunch of Roses, O.

The room burst into cheers as Eve finished singing, especially the Irish lads among them. Although many Irish had given their lives fighting with the English against Bonaparte, there was still a bitterness towards the English who ruled Ireland. This Eve had known and had sung it especially for them. They were the ones that had always spoken kindly to her and she knew how they felt, being so far away from

241

home. Eve had found her place in the Black
Swan and she was enjoying every minute.

★ ★ ★

Nell looked at the baby asleep in her arms and
laid her in her crib for the night. The singing
from the Black Swan could still be heard and it
was well after midnight. 'I think your mother's
enjoying herself, little one. She's found her way
in life at last.' Nell bent down and kissed Mary's
head. 'It looks like you'll have two mothers from
now on, two mothers who love you dearly.'

19

Riot and slaughter once again
Shall their career begin
And every parish suckling babe
Again be nursed by Gin.
Sir Charles Hanbury Williams

'By heck, she's growing up!' Nell looked at Mary as she attempted to walk around the yard of the Black Swan. 'Her first birthday, who would have thought it?'

'Yes, and it's been a hard year, Nell, but at least we have survived through many ups and downs, thanks to you.' Eve smiled at her beloved daughter as she kept her balance and stopped herself from falling as she negotiated the cobbled yard. Mary was a stubborn little soul with a mind of her own and if her head was set on doing something or wanting something, then that was what she would do. Eve saw a lot of herself in her daughter and hoped that, in the long run, it would not be a bad thing and that her life would be so much better than hers.

'Well, I can't sit here all day — unlike you, I have to walk the streets for my bread and butter.' Nell stood up and looked at Eve who, though she looked pale and weary, had more of a spring in her step now she was contributing to their lives because of her employment at the Mucky Duck. Three nights a week she sang there, once

Mary was asleep, but she was looking a little drawn with working long hours in the inn that hardly ever closed its doors now they had found a star on their hands. Nell watched as Rosie gave them a quick glance as she entered the Black Swan with a punter on her arm. 'I tell you what, Eve, Rosie sounded a bit annoyed the other day, saying she thought that I'd taken some of her trade and that everyone's eyes were always on you now. I put her right straight away and told her that I was choosier than her — and that you would never think of bedding anybody.'

'She had a go at me as well, saying that having a baby playing in the yard was putting her fellas off. I don't know why she's so bitter,' Eve said and stood up next to Nell.

'Well, she's losing her looks, lass, and her teeth are rotting, so she isn't as popular. And I'm sure she's going the same way as Tilly, riddled with the pox. Thank the Lord, I've kept clear of it! I turn away men that carry the vile disease, although they never tell you they've got it. I keep my eyes open as they're undressing and soon send them on their way if I think they're carrying it, though you can't always tell.'

Nell looked worriedly at Eve; she had taught her all that she knew, even though she knew it would be a cold day in hell before Eve took somebody to bed again in a hurry.

'Yes, I pray that neither of us will ever befall its terrible grip. I think you're right, Rosie is bitter with her lot in life and knows that death is stalking her. I do so hope that you never contract it, Nell, for I couldn't bear to see your life ebb away like Tilly's and Rosie's.' Eve kissed her friend on the cheek; she had become very fond of Nell, sometimes forgetting the dark side of her life and the dangers that she was a party to each day. 'Is Sergeant Jones coming to see you later?' Eve enquired, smiling. 'I don't mind looking after his son Toby while you lie together.' Robert Jones had been a constant in Nell's life for some years and since the death of his wife, he seemed to have become fonder and more caring of Nell.

'I think he is.' Nell grinned. 'He even comes and asks me out for just a stroll and we walk along the canal nearly to Rothwell, with Toby running in front of us. I sometimes dream that we are a true family.' Nell looked around her and sighed; she was getting weary of her life in the yard of the Black Swan and longed for a life of respectability now she was ageing — thirty-five was old for a whore. 'I don't charge him for these times, because we enjoy one another's company and I don't want money to spoil this friendship that we seem to be enjoying.'

'He should ask you to marry him; he could do a lot worse and you certainly could.'

But Nell shook her head and looked down at her feet.

'Nay, nobody ever marries a prostitute. Why should they? They pay for the pleasure and have no responsibility, that's what we are all about.' Nell smiled sadly. She did have feelings for her Sergeant Jones but she knew he'd never marry her and she was content as she walked up out of the yard to make her way to Briggate and The Headrow.

She'd not said anything to Eve, but she'd been touting for trade on Bert Bradshaw's patch a lot of late, not just occasionally as she'd done before. The men were of better class, not as rough as those down on the quayside, and Nell longed for an easier life. The years on the streets were beginning to catch up with her and now Eve was earning her way in life, she was beginning to be choosier with her punters. She pushed her way through the crowds and stallholders who were making their way home as the gas lights were lit and the evening began to descend upon the busy main market street of Leeds. Most of the stallholders yelled hello to her and grinned as she swaggered up to the top of the market.

'Are them boots still whole?' Ma Fletcher, who ran the second-hand clothing stall at the top of Briggate, shouted out to her as she folded the tarpaulin over her flat cart and waited for her old man to tow it home with his horse. 'You got a bargain with them. Came from a good house, did those boots.' She grinned at Nell. With her swishing skirts, long black hair and cheeks of rouge, Nell, like her, was in the business of servicing the good folk of Leeds, albeit in a different way.

'Aye, dry as a bone, Ma. Best sixpence I ever spent!' Nell stopped at the stall and smiled. 'Have you had a good day? Made plenty of money and seen and heard all the news?'

Nell looked admiringly at the old woman who looked as if she hadn't a penny to her name but she knew Ma's house on Speakers' Corner had taken wealth to buy.

'Can't complain. I sold a lot of my wares to

the wild lasses this morning and I've had steady trade all day. Now, Nell, putting that aside, I must warn you to take care for I heard on the grapevine that Bert Bradshaw is not happy with you. You're on his patch too often, my lass, and he'll tan your hide if he sees you up here.' Ma Fletcher shook her grey-haired head and looked at the prostitute that everyone liked.

'He'll not touch me, Ma — I'm no threat to his empire. He's got that many lasses on every street corner, I'm not going to make much difference. Besides, I go for the more refined gent nowadays, I like to be bedded properly.' Nell winked.

'Well, just you mind. I've told you, so watch out for the bastard,' Ma Fletcher said worriedly.

'He'll not see me on his patch for long tonight, cos I have an appointment with a regular. He books us into a room above the Turk's Head — a real gentleman he is, knows how to look after a woman good and proper.' Nell grinned.

'He'll be married and up to no good while his wife is left at home with a tribe of children. That's the sort of gentleman he is.' Ma shook her head and looked away at the sound of her husband and his horse coming along the cobbles of the market to take them home.

'Aye, but he's got brass, and you know and I know that's all that matters in this world.' Nell winked and then left Ma Fletcher and her husband to trundle home after a hard day's work. Her workday was ending but Nell's was just beginning as she made her way to see the man she had made her business for the last week or two. He was better class than her usual clients, insisting that she stayed with him until the morning and paying her well to do so, providing she asked no questions of him and provided him with what he required when it came to satisfying him.

Nell's paced quickened as she approached the ginnel leading to the Turk's Head. She was in Bert Bradshaw's part of the world and she couldn't help but notice two of his bully boys watching her and talking about her as she entered through the Turk's doors and made for the stairs that led to the room where she met her mystery man. She looked around her at the stallholders having a gill or two before returning home and the shop workers, still in their aprons. The man behind the bar didn't acknowledge her as usual as she flounced through and to the stairs at the back of the darkly lit bar.

'I don't think you want to climb those stairs tonight, Bonfire. Your boyfriend's just getting a good talking-to by one of my mates,' said a stout, dark-set man, stepping out of the shadows. 'This is our part of the world so he uses and pays for our whores, not old washed-up slags like you.' He blocked Nell's way and the cudgel in his left hand hit the palm of his right hand in a threatening manner. 'Now, we can do it the easy way and I can tell you to get off Bert Bradshaw's patch and you run along. Or you can make it hard for yourself, in which case I'll have to sort you out.' The man got hold of Nell's shoulder and pinned her to the wall.

'Get off me! You don't frighten me.' Nell

struggled and pulled at his muscled arm. 'Bert Bradshaw doesn't frighten me. He doesn't own me or this place.'

'He wouldn't dream of owning a trollop like you! But he does get annoyed when you take our best punters from off our girls. Now we can't stand for that.' The man put his face so close to Nell's that she could smell what he had eaten for his supper. She looked away and wanted to shout for help from the men and the landlord in the bar, but the brute put his hand around her neck.

'It's no good shouting for help, you're on Bradshaw land. The Turk's Head gets benefits from us so they'll not jump up and help you. Do you understand? There's no Sergeant Jones to help you here, not tonight.' The bully squeezed her mouth and chin and looked at her hard. He stopped as his partner in crime came running down the stairs and stood next to him.

'Jack, he's come around to our way of thinking. I've to send the two sluts from outside to him. I've told him they're on the house but in the future to do business with our molls if he knows what's best for him.'

'He better bloody had, else it'll be the worse for him! Go and get the slags and leave this one to me.' The man forced Nell out past all the men at the bar, who didn't even look up as she kicked and screamed her way onto the narrow passageway. They knew better than to cross Bert Bradshaw's men when they were about their business, especially the landlord, who valued the safety of his property too much.

She watched as the two prostitutes in Bert

Bradshaw's employment walked past her; they smelt of the cheapest cologne and were dressed in the flimsiest of dresses.

'Now *they* are class, not like you, old trollop! It's a wonder you haven't died of the pox yet as all those do down in the Black Swan's yard. Here, have something to take back to that hellhole with you — something that will put men off you for a while.' He lifted his fist and hit Nell in the face, bursting her lip and nearly breaking her nose before pushing her down onto the hard cobbles. 'Now piss off!'

Nell sat back on the ground and wiped her face with her sleeve, then spat at the bully in front of her. 'You don't frighten me. Bert Bradshaw is a bag of shite and I hope he rots in hell!' she shouted as she raised herself up onto her feet. 'He can piss off when it comes to threatening me.' And then she turned on her heels and ran down the cobbled gas-lit streets towards home as if the hounds of hell were on her tail.

★　★　★

'Nell, Nell, who's done this to you?' Eve cried, bending down and looking at Nell's bloodied nose and bruised eye. Without waiting for an answer, she quickly went into her bedroom and poured some water into her bowl on the washstand, then placing a towel and flannel over her shoulder, checked that Mary was still asleep in her crib and went to clean Nell's injuries.

'I'm all right, I'm all right. Never mind me.'

Nell reached for her usual bottle of gin to eliminate her pain and feelings while Eve wet a towel with water and found a bottle of laudanum for the pain. 'I'll not get rich looking like this,' Nell said, wincing as Eve patted her wounds and looked at the damaged inflicted on her friend's face.

'Hold still! Now, are you going to tell me who did this?' Eve stepped back and looked at Nell, who looked pale. Her lip was burst and a bruise was beginning to show where the bully had nearly broken her nose. 'You're going to have two lovely black eyes by the morning, Nell, but just be thankful your nose isn't broken — or at least, I don't think it is.'

Nell sighed. 'It was one of Bert Bradshaw's louts who was waiting for me at the Turk's Head. I've had a regular bit of business there, with a gentleman of some quality. He was a good payer and an easy ride. But he'll not be wanting me anymore, the bastards saw to that.'

Eve shook her head sadly. 'Well, you should have known better being up that way regularly. It *is* Bradshaw's patch, so you were just looking for trouble.' She gave Nell's face another gentle wipe and then put her flannel back into the bloodied waters of the bowl before sitting down in the chair opposite.

Nell shivered. 'Bert Bradshaw had bought the silence of everybody in the Turk's Head, nothing stands in his way. Not one single man came to help me tonight because they were all too frightened. The Turk's landlord watched me being dragged out, kicking and screaming, but he just kept wiping his glasses as if nothing was happening. I'm frightened, Eve. He's a hard man and he'll stop at nothing if he thinks I'm causing him bother. For the first time in my life I'm really worried about the bastard; he seems to be getting away with more and more.'

Nell shook with nerves as she tried to impress on Eve how dangerous she thought their situation was. Up until now, Bert had left her and the other girls at the Swan alone, but he was getting greedy in his old age. Leeds was growing and the dark underbelly of it was thriving also; he would look at wiping out any opposition to his dirty business — and that could include her and Eve. 'Perhaps you and Mary should leave, for your own safety.'

'And where would I go? I've still hardly any money and with a young child in tow, nobody would want me. What I live in hope for is a rich gentleman to see me singing and make me his wife — it's the only way out of my situation,' Eve sighed.

'We've all dreamed of that — and it'll never happen.' Nell shook her head. 'I'd go, Eve, and take Mary to somewhere safe. Another town, Wakefield or Bradford, just leave me here and take care of yourselves.'

'I will not! Because I don't want to leave you. I am my own woman and for the first time in my life I am my own person, albeit not wealthy, and I'm no threat to his business because I'm not a whore.' Eve looked at Nell and saw the fear in her eyes. 'Nell, he can't hurt us if we stand together and watch one another's backs — and you stay away from his territory.'

Nell bowed her head. Eve had never met Bert, but she had. Until now they had rubbed along, with him putting up with her. But now she had overstepped the mark and maybe he'd got his mind set on getting rid of her, whether she stuck to her own territory or not. She shivered. Things were going to change, she knew it.

★　★　★

Bert Bradshaw sat in his office, his feet up on the desk, enjoying his cigar. The heavily scented smoke swirled around him as he mused over what to do about the Black Swan's yard and the tarts that lived there. He'd always ignored Bonfire Nell, even come to an agreement with her when it came to the canal quayside, but she had overstepped the mark lately by coming up into town and stealing trade from his girls. He rolled his cigar in the ashtray, carefully leaving an inch of ash on its end. Well, his men had tackled Nell and warned her off doing business at the Turk's Head. The cheek of the bitch, she must have known that the Turk's Head was looked after by him and his boys, so any business done there was to be done by his tarts! She'd deserved a seeing-to.

'You all right, boss?' Bert's right-hand man walked into the office and helped himself to a whisky from the decanter on the sideboard. 'You decided what to do with the old slag down at the Black Swan?' He sat back in the chair opposite, crossing his legs and looking at his hard boss that no one ever dared cross.

'I have. It's a damn pity that she got greedy. Bonfire has always behaved herself until now, kept herself to herself and didn't cause me any problems, and Stanley Nelson's tart is past her best, so she's no threat to us. Let's see if Bonfire's learned her a lesson. I'll give her a week or two, see if she steps out of her territory again. If she does . . . well, Leeds is my town and there's only room for me and my girls in it.'

20

Nell walked down by the quayside, her lip nearly healed, her bruises turned to shades of yellow and purple. She felt edgy as she shouted and touted trade from the bargemen and dock workers. Eve had told her not to worry, but she hadn't forgotten the threats and the look of the big brute that had pummelled and beat her. She stood with her back towards the corn warehouse and lifted her small bottle of gin to her lips. She needed to keep her courage up if she was to make any money.

She swigged her drink and looked at the murky waters of the canal; it was at that spot she had first met Eve. A dark thought passed over across her mind: perhaps she shouldn't have talked the girl out of taking her life. Since Eve had come to live with her money had been tight and now she had her baby living with her too. Then she smiled. She couldn't help but love baby Mary, who reminded her of a life she could have had if things had only turned out right. However, touting for trade down by the canal made her little brass and the worry of Bert Bradshaw and his henchmen was always there now. She'd seen them watching the yard, of late, watching who went in and out and at what time of day; they were planning something and she knew it, despite Eve telling her that she was imagining things. She knew that she shouldn't have been as desperate as to go onto his patch . . .

'Hey, Nell, give us one for free! I've no brass, but I could do with a quick e'n with you,' one of her regulars shouted. He was black as the ace of spades, covered in coal dust from the collieries on the far side of Leeds at Rothwell, Methley and Woodlesford.

'Fred, bugger off! I can get your sort any day. Anyway, your missus will be waiting for you, with dinner on the table and your slippers by the fire,' Nell said and grinned despite her sore mouth.

'Will she buggery! She'll be waiting at the door with her rolling pin in her hand and a twined look on her face, especially when she hears I haven't been paid.' Fred grinned back as he walked beside the grey mare that pulled his painted barge, the *Florrie May*, which was loaded with coal for the factories of Leeds.

'Aye, well, buy her a bunch of flowers, make her think you've missed her,' Nell joked.

'Then she *would* hit me over the head with her rolling pin. She'd think that I'd been up to no good. Besides, like I say, I've no brass. See you later, Nell, when I've coppered up and got paid.'

'Aye, see you later, Fred, when you're a bit cleaner.' Nell sighed. Trade was very slow and she wished she had the nerve to go back up onto The Headrow, where it was always busy and she could easily find herself a willing client. But no, it wasn't worth the risk. She took another sip of gin, put her hand on her hip and raised her skirts to show her ankle, then sauntered along the canal-side.

★　★　★

Sergeant Robert Jones stepped out on his beat, hoping his path would cross with the prostitute that he was beginning to have deep feelings for. She might be rough and ready and have a mouth on her that put everybody in their place, but underneath all the hardness her heart was one of gold and she had been his prop since his wife had died. He also wanted to share his news with her — the news that he was in line for promotion, that he was being considered for the post of inspector. He was going up in the world and he wanted to share his news with Nell, despite the digs and jokes that his colleagues at the station gave him over his friendship with Leeds' best-known streetwalker.

He felt his heart flutter as he turned the corner down onto the loading docks and saw his Nell propped up against the wall in her bright scarlet skirt and laced-up boots, giving her usual lip to a bargeman. He watched as she took a swig of gin and lifted her skirts in one hand to show her ankle and attract trade. Why had he fallen for a common prostitute? She would bring him nothing but pain and he knew that while she was on the streets she'd never be his.

'Now then, Nell. Trade brisk this morning? Brisk enough for me to say move on?' Robert walked up behind his love and surprised her as she turned around and quickly put her flask of gin down the front of her bodice.

'I might as well never have left home this morning. I've hardly had anyone look at me, let alone ask for my services.' Nell smiled at Robert. 'Are you asking in your official capacity or as a mate?'

'Give over, Nell, as a mate of course! What they don't know at the station won't hurt 'em.' Robert looked at his love and noticed her healing lips and bruises around her face. 'Has somebody been giving you a hiding? Tell me and I'll sort the bastard out. You might be fair game, but there's no excuse for anybody to use their fists on a woman.' He stroked her face with his hand and looked into her eyes. In them, he saw sorrow and despair; his Nell was not as hard as she made herself out to be.

Nell pushed his hand away. 'Don't! You shouldn't do that, Robert, you've got your reputation to think about. Besides, you peelers can't do nothing about Bert Bradshaw and his rackets that he runs in Leeds. He keeps everyone sweet with his donations to local charities so that he can get away with his brothels and underhand dealings.' Nell could nearly have cried at the love and care showing in Robert Jones's eyes.

'So, it was that bastard, was it? Well, his time is coming to an end. I've wandered down this way to tell you that the inspector who's been covering Bradshaw's back at the station has been relieved of his post — and I'm hopefully in line to take his position.' Robert reached for Nell's hand. 'Bert Bradshaw's days are over, especially if I have anything to do with it. He's a bad lot, is Bradshaw, he needs locking up and the key throwing away. Are you all right, Nell? You do know that I'm there for if you need me?' He held

Nell's hand and squeezed it tight.

'The prostitute and the peeler — what a pair! It's a wonder you want to be *seen* with me, never mind anything else.' Nell threw her head back shaking her long auburn hair and trying to smile. 'I'm all right, just a little bit shaken up and scared of what Bradshaw might do next.'

'He'll not do owt! He'll be behind bars before long, if we have our way at the nick — and don't you worry about my reputation. I'm used to taunts and jibes; and besides, when I'm an inspector, they'll not be able to say anything to me.'

Robert smiled tenderly at Nell; she always thought the worst of herself when she was with him and yet, when he watched her from afar, he could swear she was as brazen and cocky as all the rest of the prostitutes in Leeds . . .

'What! You an inspector? Now that is something to be proud of. You'll not be honouring me with your presence, I'll be long forgotten when you get an office of your own and a peeler or two to do your bidding.' Nell could feel tears welling up in her eyes; she'd miss Robert, he was a good man and what had started out to be a shoulder to cry on had developed into a close friendship.

'Nay, I'd not do that. We've become close, you and me, since my wife died and Toby talks a lot about you as well. Perhaps you are not in a profession that's desirable to the force, but it's got nowt to do with them.' Robert put his arm around her. 'I'll still come for our time together, I'll not forsake you.'

'We'll see. Many a man has said that to me and then walked away.' Nell pulled her hand away from Robert's and started to walk down the towpath, grinning and giving cheek to the workers on the wharf.

Robert watched her as her skirts billowed in the wind. Damn it, if he didn't know better he'd have said he loved Bonfire Nell — she gave him hope and made his heart skip and that was an incredible combination . . .

* * *

'Right, Sergeant Jones. We have looked at your service with the Leeds Constabulary in great depth and my colleagues and I have come to a decision about your application for the place of Inspector at Leeds Central Station.'

Robert stood in front of the highly prestigious panel that was making the decision that would affect the rest of his life and make it a whole lot better, or so he hoped. He felt his stomach churn as he stood with his helmet under his arm and his uniform pressed immaculately. He believed he had made a good impression but had it been good enough? he wondered as he waited for their verdict.

The chairman looked at Robert over the top of his spectacles and viewed him up and down. 'You have all the right assets and qualifications for the position, Sergeant Jones, and your time in the force is without blemish. Inspector Crosby here says that you have a good nose for tracking down crimes and culprits and that you know

260

Leeds and its people like the back of your hand. In fact, from what I understand, perhaps you know some of the less savoury people of Leeds a little too well . . . Which leads me on to what I must say next.' The chairman stopped for a second and looked at Robert, dressed so sharply and proudly in his uniform, and thought about how to word, politely, what it was that bothered him and the panel. 'We would like to offer you the inspector's position; however, it comes with a commitment we need from yourself, one that you must honour for the respectability of this force. It is that that you no longer associate with the prostitutes along the canal at Leeds' wharf. We have been told that you are frequently seen visiting and walking out with the prostitute known as Bonfire Nell. For the integrity of the force, this must stop. I know it's permissible in society, and lawful, but I don't expect it of my inspectors. Therefore, I ask you to stop this relationship immediately. If we are to clean up the dirty dealings of Bert Bradshaw, my men have to be beyond reproach. Therefore, the position is yours once you have accepted our terms.'

The board of highly placed officers watched as Robert Jones thought about what their chairman had said.

Robert dropped his head while he thought through the thing asked of him and then, lifting his head, he answered firmly: 'Aye, I'll not be visiting any prostitutes no more if that's what it takes for me to secure a higher place in the force. Thank you for giving me the opportunity and for being so understanding.' He smiled.

'Good man! You are welcome, indeed, Inspector Jones.' The chairman rose and shook Robert's hand, then Robert, smiling, shook each of the other men's hands.

He nodded to himself. He would stick by his promise and would not be visiting Bonfire Nell for her services — or any other prostitutes — of that they could be certain.

21

'Just look at the queue that's building up outside!' Nell looked out of the grimy window onto the Back Swan's yard as Eve pulled the shoulder up on her latest dress and made sure she looked pleasing to the eye as she prepared for another performance at the Black Swan. 'Stanley should be paying you more than he does, he must be coining it in.' Nell glanced over at Eve as she bent down and kissed Mary, who was asleep in her cot.

'I've told him that I need more money. I didn't think I'd be that popular and now I can hardly move for the folk that come and listen to me. But you know Stanley: he says it's because he's serving different gin and beer and that these crowds are nothing to do with me.' Eve pinned a rose behind her ear and peered over Nell's shoulder at the crowd who were most certainly gathering to see her.

'He'll tell you anything, so tell him you'll up sticks if he doesn't pay you more. That'll make the old bugger think again,' Nell said and grinned.

'Nay, I owe him. I couldn't let him down, and I'm loyal if nothing else.'

'You might be about to think different. Here, come here and look who's in the queue awaiting you.' Nell pulled Eve back and made her press her nose at the window. 'Bloody hell, lass, now you *are* famous.' Nell slapped Eve on her back and chuckled. 'It's Charles Thornton!'

'It can't be him! And if it is, he's just passing by and fancies a drink at the Swan.' Eve stood back from the window and caught her breath, feeling her heart beating faster than a trapped bird.

'Give over, why the hell would the owner of the biggest music hall in Yorkshire come to the Mucky Duck for a drink? He's heard about you! He's here to listen to you — and you know it.' Nell grinned. Eve's voice had been the talk of Leeds for a while now, with even upper-class clientele visiting the Black Swan to hear her voice. 'Bloody hell, lass, you've got to put on a good show tonight for it'll be the making of you! He'll pay you more than Stanley ever would.'

'Oh, Lord, Nell, my legs are wobbly! I can't sing in front of *him*. Charles Thornton only employs the best at his music hall.' Eve's cheeks flushed as she peeked another look at the man below, dressed in a shiny top hat with a white scarf around his neck that made him stand out in the crowd.

'You go down there, lass, and you sing out loud and clear! Do it for that one over there, asleep. Make her proud of her mother; she'll not want for anything if you get signed up by him. The music halls are only just starting out and whoever makes it now will be famous for years to come.' Nell hugged Eve. 'Go and sing 'The Bonny Bunch of Roses' — that really makes people feel a lump in their throats and you look so genteel when you sing it. He's bound to lose his heart to you.'

'Oh, Lord, I feel sick at the thought of him listening, let alone having to talk to him! He can't have come just to listen to me.' Eve held her waist as she breathed in excitedly and looked at Nell.

'Well, there's only one way to find out. Go on, get a move on — go and entertain your crowd and no matter what time you return, wake me up and tell me your news. I'm sure it will be good — I can feel it in my bones.' Nell squeezed her young friend's hand as she left and prayed that it would be as she said. At least Eve might be due for some happiness in her life — but as for hers, there was very little to smile about. Sergeant Jones seemed to have deserted her and although she had not seen hide nor hair of Bradshaw's henchmen, she dared not make her living anywhere other than the wharf side, so times were hard and something would have to give.

★   ★   ★

Eve clutched her shawl tightly and said hello and smiled at those in the line waiting to get into the Black Swan who greeted her. She glanced quickly at the man she knew to be Charles Thornton but didn't dare approach him although she noted him watching her walk past him and hurriedly squeeze through the Swan's doors when Stanley unbolted them for her after she'd knocked for him to let her in.

'Lord, lass, we've got some folk waiting to come in tonight! Word soon got around about the new gins I've got — it's the best thing I've

265

ever done.' Stanley wiped his brow and looked at his newly taken-on barmaids to see if they were ready to serve the waiting crowds.

'So this lot is nothing to do with me singing here?' Eve turned, raising her eyebrows, and looked at Stanley.

'No, lass, they just know I've upgraded a little of late.' Stanley looked around at his partly refurbished inn, which of late he'd managed to spend money on due to people coming to listen to Eve singing — not that he would admit that.

'Well, that's all right then, Stanley, so you won't miss me when I go and work for Charles Thornton at his New Music Hall. Because he's standing outside in the queue, probably to hear me sing — or perhaps you are right and he's come for your gin. After all, they don't serve the best quality in his inn, the White Swan, do they?' Eve said sarcastically.

'Charles Thornton's standing outside? Oh, my Lord, I'm making him stand outside with the rest of the riff-raff! I'll have to open my doors and let everyone in.' Stanley, flustered, walked to the door and started to unbolt it. 'Now, don't you be going to work for him, Nell — we'll come to some arrangement, you and I. Perhaps I could pay you a bit more? Folk do seem to like you singing to them. We'll talk about it later.' He quickly finished unbolting the doors and watched as people started to flock into his small inn.

'No, no, you can't sit there tonight, that seat's for a guest.' Stanley grabbed hold of the Irishman who always came and listened to Eve and was her closest admirer, always sitting on the chair nearest to where she stood. He then turned to smile at Charles Thornton as he took off his hat and scarf and looked for a seat. 'Over here, sir, I saw you in the queue and I've reserved you this seat.'

'Why thank you. I've never drunk in this part of Leeds before but I keep hearing about a girl with the sweetest of voices who sings here and I thought that I would come and listen for myself.' Charles Thornton passed Stanley his hat and scarf and took the seat, glancing at Eve as she prepared herself by knocking back a gin at the bar.

'You mean our Eve? Well, she's all right. The wharf workers and dockers like her, but I doubt she'll be refined enough for you at your New Music Hall. Besides, look at her drinking — she likes her gin, does that one.' Stanley nodded his head in the direction of Eve and shook his head. 'She lives with a prostitute and all, birds of a feather and all that.' Stanley winked and then moved away from his rival.

Charles Thornton looked across at Eve and noticed her looking at him; he winked at her as she put her drink down and moved to her usual corner, where she stood to sing for her supper. He'd soon know if she was refined enough for his music hall . . .

*　*　*

Nell stood and cuddled Mary, who'd been woken by a nightmare. 'Listen to your mother, my darling,' she said. 'She's singing to change your lives. Let's hope that she manages it, because she deserves better, unlike me.' Nell, rocking back and forward in her rocking chair, with Mary asleep on her lap, bent and kissed the child's head as she closed her eyes to go back to sleep, listening as Eve's voice filtered into the room. Oh, she'd chosen some sad songs to sing tonight and Nell felt her heart aching as she looked down at the small child asleep in her arms.

If life had been different for her, Mary could have been her child and she might have been happily married and not touting for trade with every man who had enough money to pay her. Even her faithful sergeant had abandoned her and she missed him, because for once in her life she had broken her own rule and become attached to a man and now she was paying the price with a broken heart. Tears came to her eyes and a lump in her throat. She was no longer youthful and soon, no one would want to bed her; the workhouse would be her only salvation. Why hadn't she made more of her life?

Nell rose carefully from the rocking chair and placed Mary gently back in her cot. She'd have a good rink of gin to bury the pain and then be away to her bed. If Eve had worked her magic on Charles Thornton, the lass's struggles would soon be over; she'd be earning good money singing for him at his New Music Hall and Nell would be left to fend for herself again. She bent down and pulled the blanket over the sleeping child and watched her. What would life bring *her*, she wondered. She only hoped for her to have a good life, one where she was not dependent on men for a living, one where she was free of worry. As for herself, for now she'd bury her worries in the bottom of a gin bottle and hope that tomorrow would be brighter.

★   ★   ★

Nell woke suddenly, hearing the door of her bedroom open and smelling the perfume that Eve wore when she was out singing. She rubbed her eyes and looked up at the smiling Eve in the half-light of early morning.

'I'm sorry I've wakened you, but I couldn't wait to tell you!' she grinned at Nell, full of excitement, and Nell noticed that she was still dressed in the clothes that she had gone out in the previous evening. 'I've got to tell you about my night! I've only just come in from the Black Swan — poor Stanley and Maude gave up on us around three and left me and Charles Thornton still talking.'

Eve lay down next to Nell on the bed and squashed up near her, making the bed creak when she turned and looked at Nell to tell her the news.

'Squash me, why don't you?' Nell moved over for her friend and looked at the flushed cheeks and the sparkle in her eye. She had obviously been given a new lust for life after her night spent with Charles Thornton.

'Oh, Nell, I'm sorry, but I can't believe it! He's so handsome and so wealthy — and he's offered me a place in his music hall. Five nights a week and he's offering to pay me three times more than Stanley. He says he's going to make me famous and that I'll want for nothing!' Eve couldn't tell her closest friend fast enough as she put her arm around her with her face inches from Nell's. Eve's blonde hair spread out on the pillow beside Nell's long auburn locks and they looked at one another, both smiling delightedly.

'I'm glad for you, Eve. Didn't I tell you that he'd sign you up? That once he'd heard that voice of yours he'd know you were right for his spanking new place? Just don't you let him use you — stand your ground and don't let him push you around. Does he know you've got Mary? Who will look after her when you are working those long hours?' Nell stroked Eve's hair and ran her hand down the side of her face. She cared deeply for the lass who had come into her life by accident, but now it was time for Eve to move on.

'Don't worry, he's promised me he will look after both me and Mary. He promises that he'll get a nanny for Mary while I perform and he's even offered me a place of my own if I draw enough people in to watch me. I just can't believe my luck! This morning, everything has changed for us!'

Eve, bubbling with excitement, looked into Nell's almond — coloured eyes and noticed a hint of sadness in them. 'Oh, Nell, don't worry! You are coming with us, of course you are — I couldn't leave you here while I live like a queen.'

Nell shook her head firmly. 'No, Eve, you must do this on your own. This old lady of the night

270

will only drag you down,' she said quietly. 'I've seen the prostitutes that make their living walking up and down the aisles of the music halls; they are pretty and very young and I can't be bothered with it all. You seek your fame and fortune and I'll stay here in the Black Swan's yard.' Nell turned her head and fought back tears.

'But I need you, Nell — I can't leave you here!' Eve pleaded.

'No, you must do this on your own and I'll go back to how things used to be. I've not had the same trade since Mary was born because fellas don't like the sound of babies when they are having their way — Rosie was right about that,' Nell said sharply, knowing that Charles Thornton would not want her as part of the deal he had struck with Eve.

'You've never said anything before! I thought you enjoyed looking after Mary?' Eve sat up and turned her back on Nell.

'I do, but she's your bairn no matter how much I love her. And she needs her mother and I need my peace,' Nell said quickly.

'Well, it's a good job that Charles Thornton has come along. I hope that he finds accommodation for us quickly and then we won't be under your feet for much longer, if that's how you feel.' Eve stood up and looked down at the woman she'd thought her closest friend, who had now made her feel like a burden. 'By the way,' she added coldly, 'mentioning Rosie? She died inside the workhouse yesterday, screaming with pain from her syphilis, God rest

271

her soul. So there will be some of her regulars wanting a new whore.'

As Eve left the bedroom, Nell said nothing. She'd had to be hard, even though it had hurt; nobody would want a famous singer with a whore as a best friend so it was best that the lass went on her way without her.

22

Nell looked at the lad who had just thrust a letter in her hand.

'Inspector Jones says not to bother replying, but for you to wear your best and most respectable clothes and he'll be waiting for you under the clock as directed in the letter,' the boy said quickly and then left Nell watching him speed out of the yard, while she stood holding the letter on Leeds Constabulary headed notepaper in her hand.

Nell's hand trembled. Had she heard right? Did the lad call Robert Inspector Jones? If so, he must have got his promotion. Her heart fluttered as she opened the letter and read it. She thought that she would read that he would no longer be visiting her, but then again the lad said that they were to meet. As she read the words, she didn't know what to think.

My dear Nell,

I wish to meet you under the clock at the head of Briggate as a matter of urgency. I want to tell you of my plans now that I have been made an inspector. Please come. I look forward to seeing you at two o'clock this afternoon.

With warmest regards,
Robert

Nell looked at the letter. He might have written 'with warmest regards', but with his promotion to inspector, he would be wanting to meet her to tell her that she could no longer be suitable company for him, of that she was sure. He'd not shown his face for a while now, not even down on his usual patch; he had obviously gone up in society and would no longer wish to be associated with her.

'Ooh, a letter, nobody ever sends letters to either of us! It must be important,' Eve commented as Nell stood with it in her hand and contemplated whether to attend to Robert Jones's request.

'It's from Robert Jones, h-he's been made inspector and wants to meet me this afternoon.' Nell sighed and looked at Eve, who was full of life now that she knew she had an exciting new future to look forward to.

'Get yourself gone, then. See what he has to say for himself,' Eve said urgently.

'I don't know if I will. He even told the messenger lad to tell me to dress in my most respectable clothes before I see him. I think he is embarrassed by me, but at least he is going to be courteous enough to tell me to my face that he no longer wishes for my company. The sad thing is, I thought he really did have feelings for me, no matter how low in life I am.' Nell screwed the letter up and threw it on the fire before sitting in her usual chair and bowing her head.

'Nell, go and see him! He's the only man I've ever known you have feelings for. Finish it properly, leave one another as friends, even

274

though he'll not be knocking on the door at all hours of the day and night like he has in the past.' Eve saw her friend looked dejected and even though feelings between them had been cool of late, she knew that rejection by Robert Jones would hit Nell hard. And here she was, about to venture off into a grander life and poor Nell was going to be back on the streets without even her friendly sergeant to cover her back.

'I'll see, Eve. I don't know why he needs to see me to tell me what I already know. That I'm not good enough company for him anymore. That's just heartless,' Nell whispered.

Eve was right, she had hoped that Robert had truly felt something for her, but he obviously hadn't and he was going to tell her that he was washing his hands of her; it was as plain as the nose on her face.

★   ★   ★

'Well, I certainly look plain, I don't know about respectable.' Nell looked at herself in the mirror and pinned her long hair up in a tight bun at the back of her head. 'You might suit this sort of dress, Eve, but this high neckline feels like it's choking me.' She pulled at the high, buttoned-up collar of the plain blue dress that Eve had lent her now that she had been persuaded to meet Robert Jones.

'Stop fiddling! You actually look lovely, Nell. He can't fail to see now how refined you can look if you put your mind to it.' Eve stood back and grinned. Nell really did look completely different dressed in more ordinary clothes, rather than the gaudy, low-cut dresses that she usually wore. 'Now, go and see what he has to say for himself. At least you'll see him one more time before you part — and anyway, it might not come to that,' she said hopefully.

'Oh, it will. Men have only ever used me for one thing. Lord, I wish I was more like you and not so dependent on them — although this last day or two I've seen and heard you sighing and mooning over Charles Thornton. Take my advice, don't lose your heart to him! Well, here I go on my walk to heartbreak. I must be stupid to put myself through this hurt, but I'll hear what he thinks is so urgent and then I'll drown my sorrows in good old mother's ruin.'

Eve watched from the window with Mary in her arms as Nell walked out of the Black Swan's yard. She knew that, just for once, Nell was going to be hurt by the loss of Robert Jones as a friend and lover and she hoped that it would not mean her going into a downward spiral with her life. As for herself, she knew that better things were on the horizon, with her first night appearing at Thornton's Music Hall coming on Friday — and yes, the attentions of Charles Thornton, her new manager . . .

* * *

Nell listened to the clock of St John's strike two from across the busy street. She felt awkward in her mundane clothes, would have felt much more confident and at ease in one of her own gaudy dresses. Her stomach churned as she thought of seeing Robert; it would have been better if he had just disappeared from her life instead of meeting her for what she envisaged was the last time. In fact, he might even have thought better of it now, she thought, as the minute hand moved to five past two and there was still no sign of him. She glanced around her, not liking to be up here in Briggate, aware that Bert Bradshaw's men would be walking the street, keeping an eye on the prostitutes that they pimped. She was standing there, with the world passing by her, and open for them to assault her once more. However, she'd not seen hide nor hair of any of Bradshaw's men or their dollies and, to add insult to injury, dressed in her plain clothes, looking the height of respectability, she'd not attracted any custom.

★   ★   ★

'Nell, Nell, I'm here! So sorry I'm late. I had to go and sort Toby, who keeps running away from the school I'm paying for to go and help at the livery stable. I'm going to have to have strong words with him and tell him just how lucky he is to be able to go to such a good school.' Robert Jones had rushed up to Nell, his long black coat flapping in the wind and his bowler hat perched on his head, his face thunderous.

'Aye, he like his horses, he's always telling me and Eve how much he enjoys grooming them and helping out at the livery stable. He's a grand lad and growing up fast,' Nell said, smiling. Toby was ten and she knew that he hated school but loved working with the horses in the nearby stable.

'He might, but I want better for him, especially now that I've been made inspector. He should set his sights higher,' Robert snorted and looked at Nell.

'Is that what you're meeting me for today? To tell me that you're going to be setting your sights higher and that you won't be needing or seeing me anymore?' Nell looked at Robert and felt her heart breaking.

'On the contrary, I've booked us a table at the posh tea room at the top of Kirkgate, just over there. That's why I asked for you to wear something appropriate — and you have not let me down by the way you look.' Robert held his arm out for Nell to take and smiled. 'I thought that we deserved a treat.'

Nell put her arm through his and didn't know quite what to say as the tea room's doorbell tinkled and they were shown to a reserved table set back in an alcove away from the rest of the tea drinkers.

'I wanted us to have a bit of privacy, so I insisted that they reserve me this table. Oh, Nell, it's amazing the power that an inspector's badge can have!' Robert smiled at Nell as the serving girl made sure she was sitting comfortably before giving them the menu of delicious cakes to choose from.

'So, you are to break my heart over a cream cake,' Nell whispered. 'It's all right, Robert, I know that you'll no longer want to be seen with me now. I know why you're hiding me in a corner and are ashamed of being seen with me.'

'Oh, is that's so? Well, my dear, I think you are in for a shock.' Robert stood up from his seat and then went down on bended knee in front of Nell, with the whole of the tea room looking on. 'Eliza Wilson, my Nell, would you do me the great honour of becoming my wife?' Robert put his hand in his pocket and brought out a small box with a wedding ring within it. 'I think it's time a man made you an honest woman and hopefully, I'll be that man.' He held the box out in front of him and watched the expression on Nell's face as she held her breath in shock.

'This can't be real! You must be doing this as a heartless joke . . . ' Nell looked at him with tear-filled eyes.

'No, my dear, it is far from a joke. I want you to be my wife. If my job does not allow me to visit you in your current position, then I have no option but to make you my wife. Now, is it yes or am I going to stop down on my knees forever?' Robert looked at Nell and saw her tears, happy ones, falling down her cheeks.

'I never ever thought this would happen to me. I knew we thought a lot of one another but I didn't think that you cared enough to ask me to marry you.'

'Well, come on, what is it? Yes or no, and then I can get up off my aching knees!' Robert looked at the woman he had loved for some time; the woman he had known he could not give up for the sake of his work. So, it had been obvious to him that he had to marry her and make her his wife.

'I don't know, I'll bring shame on you.' Nell looked at Robert and then at the ring while the other diners in the tea room, unable to hear the conversation between the couple but knowing from what they'd seen what Robert's question had been, held their breath for the right answer.

'I love you and that's all that matters, please don't turn me down,' Robert said quietly.

'Then yes, Robert, I *will* be your wife. I will also be a good mother to Toby and keep your house clean and try not to embarrass you when you are at work. I-I can't believe what you have asked of me.'

Robert, beaming, took the ring out of the box and put it on her ring finger while Nell swept her tears away and the tea room erupted with good wishes and laughter. She, the hard-talking, hard-headed dock whore was to become a police inspector's wife and she could not believe it.

'Thank the Lord for that, else I too would have been broken-hearted as I was told to break all relations with you by my superiors. I knew I loved you too much to do that, but they can't do anything about it if I choose to wed you. I should have asked you some time ago when we grew close after my wife died, but like a fool, I didn't because of pride. Now I know I can't live without you, Nell. But there is one thing you must promise me,' Robert whispered as he got up from his knees. 'You will be mine and mine alone. No more walking the streets or down by the docks.'

'Of course! Oh, Robert, I'll have no need to with you by my side — and I promise to love and look after Toby just as if he was my own,' Nell said as she held his hand across the table and smiled.

'Good. Well, as far as he's concerned, you can start by talking some sense into him about schooling — perhaps he'll listen to you more than me. But for now, let us enjoy our tea and cakes and make plans for our wedding day. The sooner the better, I think.' Robert squeezed her hand and smiled at his bride-to-be as she looked down at the ring he was slipping onto her finger.

'I never thought this would happen to me,' Nell said, sighing happily.

'Well, it is, and I will be so proud to have you by my side, no matter what anyone says, my Bonfire Nell, soon to be Mrs Robert Jones.'

Nell looked down at the ring on her finger and started to pull it off to place it back in its box.

'No, don't take it off, leave it on your finger for now. Then I know that we really are to be married. In fact, leave the ring on your finger and come and live with me until we are married. It will give you a better life and get you away from the life you have led. The sooner you are with me the better,' Robert whispered.

Nell was slightly shocked at his suggestion. 'You mean *pretend* to be your wife and live over the brush?'

'Just for now, Nell, just until we have arranged a wedding day. It won't be for long, I promise you.' Robert reached for her hand and kissed it.

'All right, if you promise that we are indeed to wed. Eve, who lives with me, as you know, is to leave our home above the Swan, so we are both to start new lives.' Nell looked at Robert and started to doubt his intention, thought that he'd just put a ring on her finger to make her look more respectable.

'Good, because I don't want you to go back to that place once you've collected what's yours. Let's make this a new life for us both; we'll both be mixing in very different circles from now on and I need you to act like a respectable wife.' Robert smiled and sat back in his chair. 'The main thing is that I love you and vow to look after you until the day we are parted by the Almighty.'

Nell looked at Robert and couldn't help but feel a pang of doubt about his marriage proposal. If she wasn't beginning to need some security in her life, she would probably have told him what to do with his ring. But no, she knew that they both had feelings for one another and perhaps that was enough. After seeing both Rosie and Tilly die, with no one to look after them, she knew she needed someone by her side to look after her and hopefully, love her . . .

'I'll be happy with that, Robert, as long as you promise to look after me and treat me right,' Nell whispered.

'Of course I will. Now, let me treat you to a new dress or two — we can't have Mrs Robert Jones looking anything other than fashionable.' Robert pushed his chair back and offered his arm for Nell to take as he left payment for the tea on the table and they made for the door out onto Briggate. As they walked out of the tea room, the enchanted customers offered them their congratulations and Nell and Robert thanked them and smiled, not letting them know the secret relationship and agreement that they had just agreed to.

A happy man, Robert walked with Nell on his arm down Briggate. He'd managed to get the best of both worlds — and Nell had a ring on her finger for all to see.

Nell looked across at the start of the market and out of the corner of her eye she spotted a man that she recognised instantly. It was Sergeant John Oates, curled up on the ground, his jacket no longer pristine and scarlet, his hair matted and uncared for — and his face covered by the scabs and the sores of syphilis. No longer the dashing man who had taken advantage of many a young girl like Eve, he was dying like a dog in the street. She walked past him and gripped Robert's arm tight. It didn't matter if he never married her, she was away from walking the streets and all the dangers that involved. And as for Eve, she too had a new life, one that would bring her fame and fortune and soon, she would not want to know Nell anyway.

23

'You can have everything, Eve, I'll not be needing any of it.' Nell looked around her at the rooms that had been her workplace and home for as long as she had been living in Leeds. 'Not that you will be wanting it for long if Charles Thornton does what he says.'

'We've both landed on our feet, haven't we, Nell? A few weeks ago we were both rock bottom and now look at us! It just shows that you should never give up on life.' Eve hugged Nell tight. She'd been a friend, guardian and saviour to her and now she was walking out of her life.

'You'll take care, won't you? You'll look after Mary and yourself?' Nell held her friend at arm's length and looked at her. 'I'll try and persuade the old man to come and watch you — he can afford a ticket into the music hall, now that he's an inspector,' she added, laughing.

'The old man, indeed! You're not even married yet!' Eve wiped a tear away from her eye and smiled at Nell. 'I hope he *does* marry you, and I'll expect an invitation.'

'He will, in his own good time.' Nell walked over to Mary, who was sitting on the bare floorboards playing with dolls made out of dolly pegs contentedly. 'And you behave for your mamma, my little precious.' She kissed Mary on her head and then gave one more glance around her old home before leaving Eve standing there, feeling lost and alone. Nell was going to a new life, a respectable one, although knowing that her marriage to Inspector Jones would perhaps never happen but at least she would be looked after.

'Take care, I'll miss you,' Eve whispered under her breath, believing that if Robert Jones had his way she would never see her best friend ever again. She went and sat in what had been Nell's usual chair by the fire and looked at Mary. 'It's just me and you now, my love. And we'll be away from here before long to our better life. Tonight is my first performance at the Music Hall and I will have to prove my worth — and you will have to behave for the woman who's been hired to look after you while I perform. Let's hope that we both impress.' She reached for the half-filled gin bottle that Nell had left behind as a parting gift and took a swig. She'd need all the courage and help she could get if she was to give her best later that evening and now there was no Nell to back her up . . .

★   ★   ★

Eve stood in the dark passageway behind the stage of the noisy music hall. Dancers in their bright, scanty clothes ran past her, giggling and pushing one another in order to get changed for their next performance. She could hear the crowds in the auditorium laughing at the comedian who was keeping the audience on the edge of their seats. She was brought to her senses as the stage manager pulled on her arm.

'Have you not got changed yet? Somebody

285

take this baby and get it out of here!' The sharply spoken, hard-faced man stared around then gestured at a young woman who was instantly put in charge of the blubbering Mary and took her away as Eve protested and yelled instructions for her care. 'Here, get dressed in here,' said the stage manager. 'Put this on and get into the wings in the next five minutes — you're on stage straight after the juggler. The child will be looked after and you'll only be on for five minutes seeing you're new.'

Eve looked around the room she had been pushed into and noticed how dingy it looked, full to the brim with costumes and props. The main wall was covered with a long tall mirror and she looked at herself as she undressed and pulled on the long, glittering dress, so low-cut she was frightened that her breasts would fall out of the bodice. She had expected to be looked after, for someone to pamper her and get her ready for the stage, as Charles Thornton had promised her. Instead, she had been virtually ignored until the last minute and then instructed to do as she was told. As she put a rose behind her ear and pinched her cheeks to bring colour to them, the manager opened the door and yelled at her. 'Get a move on! The juggler's started.'

'I'm coming,' Eve said quietly and followed the man who had no time for anyone.

He looked her up and down as he waited in the wings with her. 'I suppose you'll do, I just hope you can sing,' he said with contempt in his voice. 'You'll survive if you can sing like Mr Thornton says you can.'

Eve's stomach churned and her legs felt like jelly as she heard the audience clap as the juggler ended his last performance. She was on next, on a stage that she had never even seen properly before and in front of the largest audience she had ever performed in front of. Would there be even one known face in it? If she could have turned and run, she would have done so when the juggler came running up to her, wiping his grease-painted brow and said, 'Break a leg, they're a bloody hard crowd tonight!'

Eve could have cried as she heard Charles Thornton announce her.

'She's our own Yorkshire linnet, with a voice that will enchant you and pull on your heart-strings. Please put your hands together and give local girl, Lydia Lovejoy, a warm welcome to our stage.'

'Lydia Lovejoy? That's not my name,' Eve protested to the manager.

'It is now, it's your stage name. Now shut up and get on, they're waiting for you.' The manager pushed Eve onto the stage, where Charles Thornton took her hand and led her forward, then he smiled at the crowd and turned and glared at her as he left the stage, leaving Eve standing looking out into the crowd, dazzled by the bright lights that surrounded the stage, as the crowd clapped and waited for her to start singing. Never had she seen so many faces waiting in anticipation of her voice. Terrified, she froze for a moment and the orchestra down in the pit, recognising she was struggling, started to play the introduction to her bestloved song, 'The

Bonny Bunch of Roses', to ease her on the stage.

Charles Thornton stood in the wings and put his thumb up as Eve looked around her, wondering if she should take flight. But no! She *had* to sing if she and Mary were to survive. The melody of her most-loved song came to an end and the conductor looked up at Eve to give her the cue — and she found herself opening her mouth and singing loud and clear in a voice that could be heard all around the hall. At first, she was a little shaky, but as the song progressed she managed to smile and look at the crowd she was singing to — and she couldn't help but notice the joy and tears on their faces. When it came to the second of her songs, she was more confident and started to relish the crowd and the bright lights, the rich velvet of the curtains and the highly decorated hall. The applause thundered out as she ended on a high note and Charles Thornton came out and grabbed her by the waist.

'Our lovely Lydia Lovejoy!' he yelled. 'Doesn't she sing just like an angel?' And he smiled and turned to Eve and whispered, 'Do you want to give them another?'

She nodded.

'She's willing to give us another! So what are you to sing for us, Lydia?' Charles Thornton asked and then encouraged the crowd to yell suggestions.

'Sing 'The Wild Mountain Thyme', no matter what they shout,' he whispered. 'The orchestra has been told that's what you are singing.'

Eve nodded and tried to block out the noise of the shouts from the crowd as she recited the words of the Irish ballad in her head. She nodded to the conductor once she knew she was ready and Charles Thornton left her to sing alone and keep her audience enthralled.

'You've got a star in the making there, boss,' the manager said as they watched from the wings. 'She really can sing, that one.'

'I know — added to which she's so innocent, and that's what they like. Have her sing something that pulls on their heartstrings and she'll have them eating out of her hand and filling our seats every night. There's brass to be made with this lass, of that I'm sure.' Charles Thornton patted his manager on the back and went back out onto the stage as the audience yelled for more as the haunting notes of 'The Wild Mountain Thyme' came to an end and Eve bowed to her loving crowd.

'Miss Lydia Lovejoy! She'll be back, I promise you,' Charles yelled to the roaring crowd and put his arm around Eve as he guided her off the stage. 'You were fantastic, my dear. The crowd loved you. I knew as soon as I heard you that you would go down a storm.'

'I was so afraid,' she said. 'All those people in their best clothes and they were all looking at me, just me. Then, when they started to sing along with me at the chorus, I knew that they had really enjoyed my performance.' She caught her breath and beamed at Charles. 'Thank you for giving me this chance; I'll be forever in your debt, and I know now that I will always love the bright lights, the audience, performing on the stage.'

'This is just the beginning, Eve. If you are

successful, folk will come just to hear you. We'll get your own poster advertising your name and dress you in the finest of gowns. And once you have got that far, I'll find you better accommodation and someone to look after your child. However, it is early days yet, let's see how you go.' Charles looked at her and smiled as they stood in the wings with the next act pushing their way past them.

'Oh!' she exclaimed, confused. 'I thought that you'd see to a new home for me straight away and I really wanted someone to look after Mary properly while I sang on stage. She just got handed to a girl whose name I don't even know.'

'That will all come with your success. Now, your daughter was given to Kitty, who helps with the costumes. She's a good girl — all the performers like her — and your little daughter will have come to no harm. In fact, here is Kitty, and your little one doesn't look any the worse for her ordeal.' Charles looked at the young girl with Mary in her arms and pinched Mary's cheeks. 'Your mamma has the voice of an angel and she's going to make us all rich. Speaking of which, talk to the manager and he'll pay you for tonight's performance before you return home — and we'll see you again tomorrow night at the same time. Kitty here will look after Mary again — her room is two doors down from where you changed earlier this evening. Now, tomorrow I want you to sing the same songs again. The Irish in the crowd are all homesick for the Emerald Isle and need to hear it sung to them in words, so they love you.'

290

Eve took hold of Mary, who looked as if she was about to cry. 'And the contract? You said that you would give me a contract,' Eve said as Charles started to walk towards the stage.

'Yes, yes, I'll see to it, keep reminding me!' he shouted back and then disappeared behind the heavy velvet curtains that had just gone down between acts.

★　★　★

Eve sat in the glow of the fire and candlelight and thought about her performance that evening. She had loved every minute of it, her nerves kicking in at first only for them to be quelled by the encouragement from the crowd and the feelings of elation and importance that she got as she sang her heart out. And the payment had been worth it as well; she might not have got the contract or the new home that Charles had promised, or even the nanny, but she did have the money the manager had given her and if he paid her the same every night, she and Mary would not be going hungry. She picked up the poker and stirred the coals. It was quiet without Nell, no men coming and going and no one to share a drop of gin with. She only hoped that Nell was happy in her new home and that Robert Jones was enough of a man to keep her satisfied.

Eve sat back and closed her eyes. Her head was aching again; she'd tried to ignore the fact that she had felt slightly unwell on and off for the last few weeks but now, as she sat by herself in the early hours, she realised that of late her chest was sore and sometimes she struggled for breath. Perhaps it was with singing so much, and all the worry, she told herself as she banked up the fire for the morning and swigged the last drop of gin down her throat. Tomorrow she'd wake up and have the evening on the stage at the Music Hall to look forward to — and her headache would subside now she knew she and Mary could afford to live off her earnings there. Things were looking good.

24

Eve walked up Briggate with three-year-old Mary chattering beside her. People nodded and smiled at her as she made her way to the Music Hall where she had made a name for herself and her little bit of fame had made all the difference to hers and Mary's lives. She gloried in the bright lights of the hall, in the applause and rapture that folk gave her after each performance. The Music Hall, with its plush seating, beautifully painted backgrounds and heavy luxurious curtains was where she found relief from the drabness of the Black Swan's yard. Although the place was home, she longed for the better living quarters that Charles Thornton, along with a contract, kept promising.

'Well, what do you think of that, then?' The manager of the hall stood back and turned to look at Eve as she and Mary came down the alleyway to the Music Hall.

Eve smiled at the poster that was being pasted to the brick wall. It showed an artist's impression of her dressed spectacularly in a gaudy pink dress with the words Miss Lydia Lovelace — Yorkshire's Linnet with an Irish Heart.

'If they did but know, I've never even been to Ireland, let alone have any Irish blood in me.' Eve looked at the poster and shook her head. 'I never ever thought that I'd see myself emblazoned on a wall. I thought that sort of thing only happened to the really big acts who travel the country.'

'Well, Eve, believe me the box office is taking really good money and it's all because of you. By the way, the boss wants to see you; he said to tell you he's in his office. You've made it, lass.' The manager winked and smiled; she had grown from a shy nobody to the Music Hall's star attraction but he knew Charles Thornton was having concerns over his new star.

'Hopefully, he'll have news of my contract at last and has got us somewhere nice to live, like he originally promised.' Eve felt excited. The poster seemed to suggest that this was the day she had been dreaming of for so long, that Charles believed she'd finally proven that her success was not a fluke, that she could draw audiences in every time she walked on stage. 'See you later,' she said to the manager, 'and don't forget I need a glass of water between performances.' Eve smiled down at Mary, who ran to Kitty as they walked through the stage door. The child loved being with Kitty while they watched her mother from the wings and wanted so much to join her.

'Thank you, Kitty, you're an angel. I swear Mary thinks more of you than she does of me.' Eve smiled as Kitty took her ward's hand and she urged her to go and play with her. 'I believe Mr Thornton is wanting to see me before I change, and I'll go to him in a second — I just need to take something for this sore throat that I can't seem to shake off. I think it's because I get so worked up before my performance.'

294

'Yes, he said I'd to remind you that he needs to see you urgently,' Kitty said as she picked Mary up into her arms.

'Oh. Then I'll not let him wait another minute.' Eve turned and left Mary and Kitty, heading up the steps to the dark interior of backstage where Charles had his small office that was always full of show props and posters and where he sat ensconced in his chair, smoking his cigars. She'd take something for her aching chest and throat after she had seen him, just before she went on stage; she only hoped that the cough that she'd been having of late wouldn't start as she spoke to Charles. She knocked on his door and waited to be summonsed.

'Enter!' Charles bellowed and looked up as Eve opened the door and stood in front of him. 'Ah, Eve, close the door and come and sit down. I'm glad that you've come to see me.' He looked at her closely as she sat down.

'Is it about my contract, now that I've been singing with you for over eighteen months? You must be happy with me, because I've just seen the poster that you've had pasted up on the wall outside.' Eve leaned forward eagerly only to notice that Charles Thornton seemed worried. But why?

'Yes, we are trying to promote you a bit more. But Eve, I need to know: is it worth my while? Because I think you have a problem. For one thing, my backstage hands say you like the gin too much and then I've heard you're suffering from a sore throat and we've all heard you coughing before you go on stage. You may have thought that you've been covering it up well, but nothing goes unnoticed here, everyone is waiting to step into someone else's shoes for the fame and the money. Last night I sat in the back of the auditorium and listened to you, and Eve, your voice is not as strong as it was and you stopped midway for a drink. Was that drink water or gin?'

Eve hung her head. 'I'm sorry, Charles, it's true I don't feel too well at the moment, but I didn't want anyone to know. I-I love singing here, p-please don't get rid of me because of a simple cough! As for the gin, I only have a sip to give me courage. I can stop having my nip at any time.'

Charles Thornton frowned. 'But some of us have noticed that you don't look as well as you did, Eve. Now, I need to know, are you in basic good health? I can't have one of my main singers drop dead on stage — the gossip would close the place.' Charles leaned back and looked intently at Eve. Yes, her looks were definitely declining. 'How about I pay for a doctor to look at you, see what this cough is all about? I owe you that at least.'

'I'm sorry, my throat *was* sore last night, Charles, and I was struggling, but I'll be fine tonight. However, if you would be kind enough to pay for a doctor's advice, it would put both our minds at rest,' Eve said quietly. She knew only too well that Charles was right: she wasn't singing on form and she did look pale, but she had put it down to the pressure of performing each night.

'Very well, I'll ask Dr Sanderson to come and

visit you at your home tomorrow afternoon. Will that be convenient for you or would you rather see him at his surgery? He's a good man.' Charles smiled.

'At my home would be more convenient, if he's able to?' Eve said. She hadn't wanted to admit to anyone that she had felt ill, not even herself, because life was just beginning to be rewarding and she and Mary had few or little worries and money — not a lot, but some — set aside for the future.

'I'll see that he visits you and as I said, I will pay his bill. I need to keep you on that stage of mine, especially now people are coming just to see you and you alone. I'm sure that he'll say you are in good health, maybe just need some more rest or a tonic. Now, go and give your all to those that are waiting for you. I'll be listening in my office tonight, I'm afraid, I'm snowed under with paperwork.' Charles looked at the young woman who the crowds had fallen in love with. He certainly wished that she was in good health, but as he scrutinised her features, he realised that she actually did look quite ill.

'Thank you for your concern, Charles, I won't let you down. And I appreciate all the time and money you have spent on me so far. Both Mary and I are thankful for your support.'

Eve breathed in deeply as she left the office. She stood for a moment behind his door as she closed it. She'd *have* to sing well tonight and she would have to do it without the prop of her tot of gin if she was to keep her job. She would also have to receive a clean bill of health from the good Dr Sanderson the following day — and she feared that would be asking the impossible the way she currently felt.

★ ★ ★

Dr Sanderson stood back with a solemn look on his face. 'What did you do before you started singing at the Music Hall?'

'Until I gave birth to Mary, I worked as a barmaid at the Black Swan and the Bluebell Inn on Walker Street.' Eve quickly buttoned her blouse up and looked at the doctor; though he tried to hide it, she knew from his face that he had found something seriously wrong. 'Then after Mary was born, I started singing at the Black Swan.'

'Have you always lived in Leeds? The accommodation here is not the best, but neither is it the worst that I've seen in Leeds, so what about before?' he said as he looked seriously at her and then around the room and at Mary, who was sitting quietly with her newly adopted cat from off the street.

'No, I've only been living in Leeds for the last few years, I'm originally from Rothwell.'

'And the father of your child? Who is he and where is he now?' The doctor folded his stethoscope into his bag and waited for an answer.

'He's a soldier. He left me pregnant with Mary when he went to serve Her Majesty out in Ireland.' Eve bowed her head and tried not to cry.

'Well, my dear, if what you say is true, I've

298

some bad news for you and your daughter. I'm afraid you need to get your affairs in order and take your child to its father or return home. After my examination I can tell you that you are suffering from consumption. I suspect, although you have not told me, that you have been spitting up blood — and for some time from how your lungs sound.' The doctor shook his head as Eve looked at him in horror. She had not wanted to mention the worst symptom of what she had tried to dismiss as just a cough.

'I can't have! I have to keep on singing!' Eve cried in despair.

He shook his head. 'I'm afraid it is true. You have all the signs. You are seriously ill, my dear, and there is very little I can do for you except give you something for the pain. That is, if Charles Thornton is willing to pay for a prescription once I tell him what ails you.'

Eve fought back tears. 'I don't deserve this!' she cried. 'What will I do with my Mary? I don't want her to face the world on her own.' She slumped down in her chair and sobbed.

'I can't answer you that, my dear. But the future — or what you have left of it — is not bright. I would make plans for her future care and enjoy what life you have left with her. Unfortunately, I will have to inform Mr Thornton of my findings, as it is my duty.' Dr Sanderson picked his bag up and looked with sadness at Eve. 'Disease and drink are the scourge of our society and, unfortunately, both are easy to find. I'm sure you have known many die from consumption and you will know what to expect and how it will end.'

Eve lifted her head. 'Indeed I do, sir, and I wouldn't wish it on my worst enemy, let alone suffer it myself.'

'Then God be with you. If Mr Thornton asks me to attend you and supply you with pain relief I will do so, but for now that is my duties done.' Dr Sanderson put on his top hat and left Eve and Mary, knowing full well that he would not be returning to the young woman and her child. Charles Thornton would not waste his money on somebody that was of no further use to him. She might be his latest attraction now, but in another few months she would not be alive, let alone singing for her living. It was such a waste of life, he thought, shaking his head. Hopefully, in the future, a cure would be found for the debilitating and fatal disease.

★　★　★

Eve sat and sobbed and her tears would not stop. She cursed the day she had lost her heart to Sergeant John Oates for their child would be left a penniless orphan and regretted, even more, leaving the safety and love of her home. Why had she not been satisfied with her lot in life? She could have been married to a hard-working farm labourer or estate worker with a home of her own and her parents proud of her, but now she was going to die, unloved and uncared for, and leave the love of her life, Mary, without parents, without anything. She knew that Charles Thornton would no longer want or need her, but she would beg him just to keep her on for a little while longer. She would need every penny to look after herself and Mary until her death.

'Don't cry, Mamma.' Mary dropped the stray cat from her lap and went and placed her arms around her mother.

Eve wiped her eyes and looked down at her precious daughter. 'I'm sorry, my little love, Mamma is just having a bad day today. I fear it will be the first of many and we will both have to be strong.'

25

'I'm sorry, Eve, I can't keep you on. Dr Sanderson says that you are suffering from consumption and that the outlook is very poor.' Charles Thornton looked at the woman whose dreams had just come to an end and felt a pang of guilt at not supporting her.

'Please, please, just keep me on for a while longer, Charles. My voice is still fairly strong and if I could just get some pain relief to help me through my performance, I'll try my best not to cough.' Eve found herself pleading with Charles Thornton; apart from the money, she didn't want to leave the music hall that she had found happiness in, didn't want to be thrown out of the world that she loved.

'I'm sorry, I can't, Eve, I need someone who can perform strongly every night and for me not to worry if they are going to make it to their next performance.' Charles pushed back his chair and walked over to his safe, opening it up to get Eve's wages. 'I'll give you an extra month's pay, which will help you and Mary out a little. I wish I could do more for you.'

Charles had listened to the doctor's prognosis and what Eve had said to him and had felt sorrow for the lass who had won many a music hall goer's heart. But business was business and he couldn't carry anybody who wasn't about to make him profit. He had to let her go.

'I understand,' she said bitterly. 'You want me gone before I get worse. Well, I thank you for your generosity and I'll be on my way now.' Eve took the money out of his hand and picking up the silent Mary, she turned to leave the office where dreams had been promised her, trying not to cry.

'I wish you well, Eve. Look after that little soul for as long as you can.' Charles Thornton felt his heart ache for her — and himself. She could have really been something if not for that dreadful illness.

As Eve walked out of the Music Hall, the manager's boy was scraping her poster off the wall, ready to replace it with a new smiling face with the slogan A Lass from Lancashire. So, she'd been replaced already; Charles Thornton's life rolled on while hers was about to come to a halt. With Mary balanced on her hip, she nearly ran down Briggate and the streets to her home. She didn't exchange pleasantries with the crowds, instead she imagined that she could hear them whispering that she was the singer that was dying from consumption — or perhaps it could be worse, they'd say, it might even be syphilis and the Music Hall was covering it up. After all, had she not lived with Bonfire Nell? So what else could she expect!

In all this it was Nell she missed most; she needed her to confide in, needed her to show her a little compassion — and she desperately wanted to ask her to look after Mary when the worst happened. She had not seen Nell since she'd moved out and had obeyed her wishes and had not visited her since she had left to live her new life with Robert Jones. However, now she had to. Nell was the only one who would have sympathy and hopefully take Mary in as her own. Tomorrow she would go and visit her and tell her that her life was ebbing away rapidly and hope beyond hope that she would take Mary. It was either Nell or the orphanage at the workhouse and she wanted better for her most precious daughter.

★ ★ ★

'You can stop your knocking on that door; nobody will hear you because they've cleared off,' a woman called down to Eve from her bedroom window as she knocked loudly on the large lion-shaped brass knocker of the home that she knew to be Robert Jones's.

'What do you mean? Where have they gone? I've got to find them. Did they not leave an address?' Eve queried the woman who was scowling down at her and Mary.

'No, not them, for Robert Jones has got bigger fish to fry now. He thinks himself God's gift since he's been made inspector — he forgets that we all know he married a common prostitute. Oh, his poor wife will be turning in her grave,' the neighbour said viciously. 'Common as muck she is, got a mouth on her like a sewer. I'm glad that they buggered off.'

Eve said nothing but turned, with Mary hanging onto her hand, and put her head down in despair. Where had Nell moved to with her new family and how was she going to find her? Nothing in her life was running smoothly. She sobbed as a pain in her throat gripped it like a vice and left her coughing and staring helplessly at the blood that she spat up into her handkerchief. She was dying and she had to find Nell.

★ ★ ★

'Go on, get out of it, we don't want any of your sort hanging around here,' the police constable said as Eve walked into the police station on The Headrow a few days later to ask for Inspector Jones.

Eve knew that she was looking worse than ever but she hadn't realised that folk could tell she was very ill. 'I just want to see Inspector Jones for a minute, I won't take his time for too long,' she begged.

'Well, he'll not want to see you. Besides, he's over at Yeadon this morning and he's got enough on his hands with the murder over there, without you touting for trade with him.' The peeler looked at her and grimaced, mistaking her for a prostitute.

'I'm not after his trade, I just wanted to pass a message on to his wife or ask him where they've moved to, seeing that he's no longer at his old address.' Eve stood stubbornly at the desk and glared at the young constable.

'Why, do you want to take that wife of his back on the streets with you? Because we all know that's where she came from. Just look at you! You *smell* of the disease that's eating you alive. Now get out of here before I arrest you for vagrancy.'

Eve hid her hurt and decided it was no good pursuing Robert Jones and Nell; she'd tried everywhere and nobody knew where they were living. She looked at the few coins that she had left in her hand and hoped that there would be enough to buy a loaf of bread and some dripping for her and Mary's supper. The money that Charles Thornton had given her would soon run out and her savings were small. How would she feed them, never mind pay the rent to Stanley and Maude? She looked down at Mary, who had stood quietly by her side while she had talked to the policeman, but now she was starting to pull on her arm and wanted her mother to carry her.

'Shush, Mary, we're going now. We'll walk down home and buy some bread and then Mamma and you will take a nap.' Eve smiled down at her daughter. God, she loved every inch of her and she was heartbroken that, not very far in the future, she would be leaving her without anyone to care for her.

'Carry me, Mamma, please carry me?' Mary held her hands up to be carried on Eve's hip the way she always had been in the past.

'I'm sorry, my darling, Mamma is unwell today, so you'll have to walk. It's not far.' Eve bent down and kissed the little girl who didn't know what was wrong with her mamma; all she wanted was to be held close to her. 'Perhaps I've just enough pennies left for a barley sugar twist — but only if you promise to be a big girl and walk home for me.'

Mary nodded her head and smiled. The deal had been struck — and although Eve could hardly afford the farthing for a stick of barley sugar, it was a way to get them both home in one piece.

* * *

The following morning, Eve counted what money she had and put part aside. She had to face the fact that she was dying and, if she was not being buried in a pauper's grave, she would need some money to see to her funeral. She put some of her coins to one side in a black box above the mantelpiece and the rest she put to one side to live on. There was not a lot, at most just enough to keep them fed for a week or so. She looked out of the window that she had gazed out of so often out in good times and bad and wondered if she dared ask Stanley and Maude if they could employ her, just for an hour or two a day, although she realised that they would not want her to serve behind the bar. Her looks had diminished so quickly since her diagnosis and the pain in her head made her unable to concentrate for long. She took Mary by the hand and walked down the stairs as she saw Maude and Stanley discussing how to tidy the midden pile, once it had been cleared.

'Aye, look at you, lass, you looked jiggered,' Stanley said as Maude looked angrily at him. She knew those were words that Eve did not want to hear, a reminder of how ill she was.

'I'm not that bad, Stanley. In fact, I was

hoping that I could ask you if you have any work I could do for you? I'll be honest, what money I have is nearly at an end.' Eve tried to smile and watched as Mary jumped up and down on the bottom step as she talked to the couple.

'Well, I can find you a bit of work washing the glasses and helping in the kitchen because you'll need something to keep body and soul together.' Maude smiled gently and tussled Mary's hair as the child came running to her side and then stood watching yet another stray cat prowl around the yard.

'Thank you! Anything that you can pass my way, I'll be grateful for.' Eve bent down to Mary and whispered, 'Go on, go and stroke it. It'll like that. But walk quietly, don't frighten the poor creature.' She watched as her little girl made her way gingerly to the scraggy tabby cat that looked up at her and purred as she stroked its fur.

'Just look at her face!' Eve smiled. 'I know I've not got long on this earth, that there's no hope for me, I just want to spend what precious time I have with my Mary and find her a home.' Eve's eyes filled with tears. 'Could I ask you, Maude and Stanley, to look after her after I've gone? I know she'd be looked after because you are good people. I don't want her to end up in the workhouse.'

Maude looked at Stan and closed her eyes and thought for a second or two. Then she opened them again and looked directly at Eve. 'Aye, lass, we're not in the first flush of life and we're not the wealthiest of folk. It just wouldn't be fair to her, for she'd end up losing one or the other of us before she was old enough to look after herself. We can't, lass, we can't. Look, why don't you go back to your father? His heart would surely melt, once he saw Mary, if he had anything at all about him. Besides, don't talk like that, you'll be with us for a while yet.'

Eve swallowed hard and tried to hide her disappointment. 'I understand, Maude; it was a big commitment that I asked of you. And I can't face my father like this; he'll not give me the time of day and, in any event, I wouldn't want to leave Mary with him. He'd treat her as if she was the devil himself, born out of sin as she was and raised in a brothel. Her life would be hell with him. No, I'll take her to the orphanage when I get too ill to look after her; it'll be for the best.'

All three watched Mary as she picked up the scraggy feline and sat down on the bottom of the steps up to her home and stroked and petted the now-protesting cat.

'I'll see you don't go hungry,' Maude said. 'We can always afford to feed an extra mouth or two while you are ill.'

'Aye, come on into the pub now and I'll pour you a jug of the old Geneva; it'll keep your pain and the reality away when the going gets tough.' Stanley put his hands in his pocket, feeling awkward; the lass deserved a better life and he felt bad about not taking her. But Maude was right — they were too old.

Eve fought back the tears as she followed Stan into the Black Swan. She understood why they couldn't commit to looking after Mary and they were right to say no. She looked around the old pub that, when she had first entered it, she'd thought the worst place that she had ever been in. Now, she knew different. It didn't matter what the place looked like, it was the people within it that made it. And here they looked after their own, no matter what. She knew Maude and Stan would look after her and be there for her as long as she needed them, with no questions asked.

Stan passed Eve a jug full of his own brewing of gin and reached for her hand. 'We'll be right with you, don't worry. I'll find you a bit of work. You'll surely be good for a few months yet,' he lied, looking at Eve and watching as she coughed and spat blood into her handkerchief. She'd been lucky to stay at work on the stage as long as she had, he thought; she must have been hiding the symptoms well.

'Thank you, Stanley. We'll be all right, I'm sure. It's just I don't want to leave my little girl.' Eve swept away a tear.

'She'll be right; she's a bright little thing and somebody will take to her and give her a good home. Now, you go and have a drink and play with her. Enjoy your time together.'

Stan watched as Eve left him and walked out into the sunshine of the yard. He'd watched death stalking the tarts of the streets all too often, but this time it was different. Eve had never lowered herself to a whore's level; she should not have left home in the first place, hadn't realised just how lucky she was compared to those who lived in the dark underbelly of Leeds, which she now knew all too well. 'God protect her and that lil' one,' he whispered as he went about his business, trying not to feel guilty about not adopting the little lass who looked so innocent and full of curiosity. She, at least, deserved a better life, a life away from the darker side of Leeds.

26

Mary sat on the bottom of the steps outside her home. Her mother had told her to go out and play while she talked to the stern man who had made her mamma cry when he had walked into their home. She didn't know what was wrong, but lately, her mother cried a lot and seemed to be so tired, and occasionally she cried and hugged her so close that she could hardly breathe.

'Are you all right, Mary?' Maude looked at the little lass sitting forlornly on her own in the yard as she threw some slops in an enamel bowl onto the midden that filled the air with its pungent smell.

'Yes, Mamma says I've to play out here for a while, just until she's seen to the man that is visiting her,' Mary said in her small voice and scowled at Maude. She was lonely and wanted to go a walk with her mamma.

'She won't be long, little lass. I hope that you are looking after her because she needs and loves you, you know?' Maude stopped for a second longer. It had been three months since Eve's consumption had been diagnosed and although Eve had started to look really gaunt and her hair was thinning, she was still managing to keep body and soul together by working for Maude when she could.

'I am, I love Mamma.' Eve threw a pebble and

312

looked stern, not bothering to answer all the questions that Maude asked, then watched as Maude smiled and put her enamel basin under her arm and walked back into the Black Swan, shouting back, 'She won't be long.'

Mary looked out towards the entrance of the yard, which her mother had told her was the boundary of her world and that she was not allowed further than the edge of the Black Swan. She'd always been kept away from the street, her mother warning her that it was a dangerous place, but the day had been a boring one and the noise and jostle of people were drawing her towards it. She could linger at the edge of the yard, couldn't she, and watch everything that was going on in the street? She found the carts loaded with all sorts of goods and the people walking past her fascinating.

'Rag-and-Booo . . . nes!' a man shouted, leading a cart filled with old clothes, pots and pans and anything else people had thrown out. His horse stood with its head down, just a few yards in front of her across the street, and Mary wanted so much to stroke it. She watched as the rag-and-bone man disappeared down one of the many alleys to knock on people's doors, leaving the poor horse on its own. Mary looked behind her; there was no sign of her mother, nor anyone else who could forbid her to go out onto the street. She wondered just how much bother she would get into if she crossed the road and stroked the horse . . . Then her need got the better of her and she set off across the street, weaving in between people's busy feet and wagons as she went to the horse, which looked tired and hungry as it drooped its head down and champed on its bit.

'Nice horsey,' Mary said and tried to hug the old dark brown horse as it snorted and looked at her before raising its head sharply, knocking her off her feet and right in front of an oncoming wagon.

'Mary!' A voice shouted as she lay crying in the street, inches from the wagon wheel that avoided her head by mere inches.

'Mary, stay there, I'll get you!' A young boy jumped lithely down from the wagon as the driver swore and pulled his horses to a halt. 'What are you doing here? You were nearly killed.' He picked her up, put her onto her feet and dusted her down, wiping her tears away.

Mary looked at the boy who had saved her. 'I wanted to see the horsey.' She smiled and wiped her tears away, glad to see a face that was looking kindly at her.

'Well, you nearly got killed, so never mind the horsey in future. Now, where did you come from? Is your mother still living in the Black Swan's yard?' Toby Jones looked around him. The little girl, she had grown a great deal since he had last seen her but it was definitely Mary Reynolds, the baby that he used to nurse when he was younger. The wagon driver, not having the patience to wait for the stable boy whose father did not like him making an honest living working with horses, whipped his team back into action.

'Mamma, I want my mamma!' Mary cried and

314

pulled on Toby's hand, leading him across the busy street to the Black Swan's yard.

'So, you are still living here.' Toby smiled as Mary urged him up the stairs to see her mother. Halfway up, they stopped as an official-looking man came out of Mary's home. His stomach only just fitted into his mustard-coloured waistcoat and he looked with disdain at Toby and Mary as they squeezed up on the side of the stairs to let him pass. Toby put his head down and followed Mary into her home. He knew all too well who the rotund gentleman who had just visited Mary's home was. It was the bursar of the workhouse, his stomach always full at the expense of the poor people within it.

Mary walked into her home and through the room that, in the past, had seen so much trade when Nell had lived there; now was empty and bare. In the sitting room she walked up to her mother, who sat with a glass of gin in her hand and tears running down her face. 'Mamma, this boy is here. I fell and he saved me.'

Toby looked at the once-beautiful woman as she lifted her head, her hair tangled and matted and her face drawn and skeletal. She was dying and Toby, even though he was young, knew it.

'Toby, I can't believe it's you! You are well and thriving, by the look of you.' Eve wiped her eyes and tried to smile. 'How's your father and how's Nell? Oh, I miss her so much!' Eve picked Mary up and put her onto her knee, looking sorrowfully at Toby, thinking that her Mary would soon be an orphan but now, at least, she had put something in place for her care. 'Where

315

did you fall?' she quizzed her daughter, who just put her head down and said nothing.

'She was out on the street, Eve,' Toby said quietly. 'The rag-and-bone man's horse knocked her over and she nearly ended up under the wheels of a wagon I was riding on. As for my father, he's well, but I get fed up with him nagging: he says being a stable boy is not good enough for me, that I should set my sights higher. But, Nell, she knows my heart is with the horses, so she sticks up for me.' Toby grinned.

Eve looked at Toby and smiled. 'That sounds like Nell. Has your father married her yet? Is she what she always wanted to be really, a respectable married woman?'

'No, not yet. He keeps promising but never gets on with it. She's enjoying life, though, and Father has just moved us into a new house. It used to be the old weighing house down by the quayside and it's made a lovely home. She loves it there. She's as happy as anything and says she's back where she belongs, but in style now.

'Father's rarely at home, he's so busy in his capacity of Inspector. The force is cracking down on Bradshaw and Father says it's only a matter of time before he's locked up and the key thrown away — or more likely, he'll hang, because that's what the bastard deserves.' Old for his years and kind, Toby smiled at Mary and then tilted his head to one side, thinking, as he looked around him, that Eve needed someone to share her worries with. 'I'll get Nell to visit you and she can tell you all the crack. Oh, she'll be glad to see you. There isn't a day goes by that she

316

doesn't talk about her days with you. And my father needn't know — besides, as I say, he's that busy nowadays he'll not know she's been gone.'

'I'm so relieved that she's well.' Eve smiled. 'Please, tell her to come soon . . . in the next day or two, Toby, else I might not be here.'

'Why, Mamma, where are we going?' Mary asked innocently.

'You'll see nearer the time, my darling.' Eve's face contorted as her body was racked with another bout of coughing.

'I'll tell her to come tomorrow,' Toby said. 'As soon as I get home, I'll tell her. But now I'll have to go, else my boss will tan my hide and I don't want to lose my job at the stables.' He bent down and kissed Mary on the cheek. 'You behave for your mother, now. No more going out onto that street.'

'I promise, I won't, Toby. Come and see me again and bring your marbles to play with.' Mary looked up at Toby, who she now could just remember — and his pretty marbles.

'I will. And you look after your mamma. She needs you.' Toby smiled and looked at Eve, seeing clearly how haggard and drawn she looked. He shook his head. Nell would have to come and visit her friend in the next few days else, as Eve had said, she would have gone to a much better place than the yard at the Black Swan, leaving Mary in the hands of the workhouse orphanage.

★　★　★

317

Nell climbed the steps that led to Eve and Mary's home, every step up the rickety stairs reminding her of her past life and the men that she had satisfied in her rooms. She had wanted to visit Eve on many occasions, but she knew that Robert would not have forgiven her for going back on her promise. Plus, she hadn't realised that Eve was still where they had both begun and was ill — according to Toby, at death's door. As it was, she'd had to be cautious because for once Robert had been home a lot at all times of the day and a week had gone by since Toby had told her of Eve's plight; she only hoped that she was not too late, else she would not be able to live with herself. She felt her heart beating fast as she knocked on the door and shouted 'Hello', pushing the door that was partly ajar.

No answer came and Nell walked through the room that she had entertained so many men in. She stepped into the main room, a hundred memories flitting back as she looked around the once-welcoming room; now the fire was unlit, the place uncared for and dark with the gloom that was filling the house.

'Hello!' she yelled again. 'It's Nell, Toby told me to come and see you.' She looked around the room again. Dirty plates on the table, the previous day's fire ashes spilling out onto the hearth . . . She looked into the darkness of the corridor that led to the bedrooms and saw Mary standing in the shadows. 'Hello, Mary, where's your mamma? Is she all right?'

'Mamma is poorly, she's in her bed. She said I

318

had to stay by her side until somebody comes and finds us.' Mary looked down at her feet, she wanted to cry but her mother had told her to be brave.

'Is she in here?' Nell looked down at the lost little girl and smiled. 'Let's see if we can do something for your mamma, make her comfortable and perhaps give her something to eat.' Nell pushed open the door of the bedroom that used to be hers and looked at Eve lying in her bed, her breathing laboured, her skin grey.

'Oh, Eve, my love,' she exclaimed, 'what's become of you?' Nell hurried across and sat on the chair by the bed, holding her friend's skeletal hand as Eve turned her head and smiled and whispered in a faint voice.

'I'm glad that you've come.'

'Toby said you were ill. Oh, I should have come days ago, but somehow Robert was always there or there was something I had to do. I'm here now, though, and that's all that matters.' Nell fought back the tears as she watched Eve try and push herself up to see her old friend better, only to rest her head down again when the effort became too much.

'Did Toby tell you that Robert is making a name for himself in the force? Oh, he's never kept his promise to marry me, but he's a good man for all that and we are both so happy.' Nell found herself rabbiting on, making conversation for the sake of it as Mary sat at the end of her mother's bed and Eve struggled for breath. 'Do you remember the times we've had together in this old place? And I watched you become famous in the Music Hall; you had quite a following.' Nell smiled tremulously and squeezed Eve's hand.

'Nell,' Eve said in a faint whisper, 'I'm dying. I'm not long for this world and when I'm gone, there's money above the fireplace for my funeral.' She stopped and held Nell's hand with all her strength. 'Nell, can you see that Mary is cared for in the workhouse orphanage? I've made provision for her and they promised they would take her in after I've died.' Eve looked at Mary with pleading eyes, her hair that used to be so long and blonde had all but disappeared and her face was so thin that it was just a bony skull.

'Oh, Eve, I'll see that your funeral is paid for, my dearest friend. But I'll not see Mary in the workhouse, not while I can do something about it.' Nell looked at the forlorn little girl on the end of the bed and smiled. 'I'll take her in as one of my own, of course I will. Toby has a soft spot for her and we've plenty of room — and Robert is not short of a bob or two now and I'll not have him say nay to this. That is, if you agree?' She smiled and watched as Eve breathed in deeply and wept tears of relief.

'If you do that for me, then I can at last finally rest, Nell. Mary is all that's kept me going these last few weeks. I didn't want her to go into the workhouse, but I'd no option. God bless you, Nell.' Eve smiled weakly and kept hold of her hand.

'You'll come and live with me and Toby, won't you, Mary? You can play with him any time, then, and you can have your own bedroom and we can watch the canal boats go up and down the cut from out of our front room window,' Nell said, smiling at Mary and saw her look at her mother.

'Will Mamma not be with us? I want her to come too,' the child wailed.

'She'll be being looked after up in heaven, little one. Because that's where your mother is bound. But she will look down upon us and be with us all the time in our hearts, so she will always be with us and we will never forget her,' Nell said quietly as she watched Eve close her eyes and squeeze her hand gently in thanks.

'You go with Nell; show her your clothes and put them together to take to your new home. Mamma is tired, my love, so very tired.' Eve turned her head and looked at her little innocent daughter. 'I'll always love you and I'll always be watching over you, just as Aunty Nell says. You go out into this world with my blessing, my darling daughter,' she whispered as she let go of Nell's hand and closed her eyes.

Nell rose from her seat and looked down at Eve, whose breathing grew weaker as she started to slip away from the world. Nell looked at Mary and fought back the tears. 'Now, little lass, where's those clothes that your mother said we needed? We'll let your mother rest in peace, for she's in good hands now.' Nell looked down at her closest friend as she took her last breath and whispered a prayer, before pulling the sheet over her face.

'Why have you done that? I can't see my mamma,' Mary cried.

'She's not there anymore, darling, she's gone to heaven,' Nell said as she put her arm around Mary, expecting tears.

'That's all right then, she can look after the cat that I used to stroke in the yard. We found it dead one day and Mamma said it had gone to heaven too, so Mamma can feed it and stroke it now.' Mary looked up at Nell and smiled.

'She can, my love, while I feed and rear you, your mamma can look after that cat, out in the countryside she should never have left, God rest her soul.'

★   ★   ★

Inspector Jones looked at the waif Nell had brought home with her, who had been the cause of many a heated argument. The last thing he wanted was to bring somebody else's child up. He was trying to better everyone's life and did not need another mouth to feed.

'She'll be no bother, Robert. Just look at her, she's such a bonny little thing and Toby already thinks of her as his sister.' Nell looked at Robert's stern face as he watched Toby and Mary play marbles outside on the garden path.

'As long as she doesn't grow up to be like her mother, Nell. You've moved away from that life, so don't be letting me down. When is her mother to be buried?' Robert growled. 'I hope that you are telling me the truth when you say she had left enough money to be buried with a bit of dignity in the churchyard at Saint Mary's. I'm not made of money and who's to say that we will not have any children of our own; I'd not see them wanting for sake of that 'en out there.'

'Be quiet, Robert! Our own children, should we have some, will always come first. Her mother's to be buried tomorrow, nothing special, not even a church service, just a committal, that's all she could afford.' Nell sighed and looked at the man who had rescued her from a life of prostitution but had little sympathy with those who were less wealthy than himself. He was a good man, really; he'd just conveniently forgotten how they had met. Although not to the point where he had married her legally — and he often reminded her of her past life and Nell sometimes wondered if he still visited the dark quarters he'd once frequented.

'Aye, well, I remember her mother, and she never sold herself from what I hear. However, I hope that you're sure that she died of consumption and not syphilis,' Robert snapped.

'Mary's the offspring of Sergeant Oates, the one that lay dying in the gutter when we came out of the tea room when you proposed to me. But Robert, Eve died of consumption, not syphilis, so you can get that idea out of your head. She always kept herself pure,' Nell said quietly. 'She didn't deserve to die . . .'

'Mary's father was a wrong 'un; I know from the gossip that he took advantage of many a young lass, and she wouldn't have stood a chance.' Robert shook his head. 'I suppose she'll not eat a lot and she'll be a help around the house when she grows older. Lord, I must be soft or daft or perhaps both — no other man would raise a child that isn't his own,' he said as he watched Toby and Mary laugh as Toby played a trick shot with the swirled glass marbles that Mary loved so much.

'You're a good man, Inspector Jones. She will be brought up right and proper, but I'll not allow her to ever forget her true mother. Eve Reynolds was a good friend who got the short straw in life and was perhaps a little too headstrong sometimes and should have listened to her parents' warning of the wicked town.' Nell squeezed Robert's arm and then kissed him.

'Then Miss Mary will be looked after by both of us and only time will tell us what her future will be. Eve can go to her grave in peace tomorrow and we will not let her down.' Robert put his arm up against the window and bowed his head. 'Lady Geneva has a lot to answer for, but it isn't all her fault: she just soothes the troubled mind for a little while. However, reality is never far away and you can't hide your troubles in a bottle forever. I bid Eve peace when she's in her grave, free from all worries, and we will raise her child as our own and give her the grace and dignity that was once her mother's.'

'Thank you, my love, you are a good, good man and Mary, I'm sure, will grow into a fine woman, a woman her mother would be proud of — we will both see to that.'

The History of Gin

The origins of gin can be traced back to the Netherlands in the thirteenth century. Back in those days, gin, known as Genever, was made by distilling malt wine to around 50 per cent ABV.

As one might imagine, the drink wasn't very pleasant to taste, so it was softened with herbs and spices and juniper berries. Originally, the drink was sold in pharmacies for medicinal use and it was discovered by the British after English soldiers encountered it while fighting in Antwerp alongside the Dutch against the Spanish in the Eighty Years' War of the late sixteenth century. They were known to drink Genever before going into battle and that is where the saying 'Dutch Courage' comes from.

English distillers began to make their own version of Genever, and when William of Orange, ruler of the Dutch Republic, took to the throne, his love of Genever was shared by his subjects.

Because the water in many cities and towns was of bad quality, distilled alcohols were filtered much better so were preferred by many. Also, with political strife between the British and French, the British increased levies on French brandy.

People soon shortened the name Genever to gin and the government encouraged the gin craze by reducing taxes and removing the licences to distil spirits. According to the eighteenth-century author, Daniel Defoe, in 1727 over half of London's 15,000 drinking establishments were dedicated to gin, making it a favourite with the poor.

Widespread drunkenness became epidemic, especially in the city of London. Magistrates in Middlesex refereed to gin as 'the principal cause of all vice and debauchery committed among the inferior sort of people'.

Finally, the government realised what they had unleashed by allowing the gin trade to flourish and they took action with the Gin Act of 1736, taxing it heavily and requiring brewers to carry a special licence to sell it. Unfortunately, this made gin drinking go underground and the illegally distilled gin was often more alcoholic and likely to cause poisoning. Juniper berries were often replaced by turpentine, which is a paint stripper.

In 1743, the government was forced to repeal the Gin Act of 1736 due to the sheer number of people flouting it. Also, informers on gin sellers were often the targets of violence. It was replaced in 1751 with a new Gin Act, lowering taxes and making it illegal to sell gin from any premises whose rent was less than £10 per year. This ensured that gin was only sold from reputable premises.

The gin trade began to wane and, in addition, a series of poor harvests increased the price of grain. This made it less affordable to produce gin. By the turn of the nineteenth century, the gin craze had all but ended, only to be revived again in 1826 when gin distillers, using the column still, created a new gin which came to be called 'London Dry Gin'. Gin was once more the public's favourite tipple.

Elsewhere, out in the British colonies, gin had found another use. Colonists used gin to mask the bitter taste of the quinine they drank to resist malaria. Quinine was dissolved in carbonated water to become what we now know as gin and tonic.

In response to increasingly cheap liquor licences for pubs, gin sellers began to consider what alternative experiences they could offer, the answer being the Victorian Gin Palace. These were cafes or bars, often tiled with large, elaborately decorated mirrors and gas lights. Gin palaces sold gin exclusively and became known for being brightly lit places, in contrast to pubs. Gin became the preserve of the sophisticated and remained popular until the late 1950s and into the early 1960s, when the import of Russian vodka became part of the British drinking culture.

In 1999, gin made another resurgence, with bespoke gin brands getting back in the game. The weight of the craft gin movement has led to a swell in numbers and kinds of gin out there and it has once again become a favourite tipple of the British.

We do hope that you have enjoyed reading
this large print book.

Did you know that all of our titles
are available for purchase?

We publish a wide range of high quality
large print books including:
Romances, Mysteries, Classics
General Fiction
Non Fiction and Westerns

Special interest titles available in
large print are:
The Little Oxford Dictionary
Music Book
Song Book
Hymn Book
Service Book

Also available from us courtesy of
Oxford University Press:
Young Readers' Dictionary
(large print edition)
Young Readers' Thesaurus
(large print edition)

For further information or a free
brochure, please contact us at:
Ulverscroft Large Print Books Ltd.,
The Green, Bradgate Road, Anstey,
Leicester, LE7 7FU, England.
Tel: (00 44) 0116 236 4325
Fax: (00 44) 0116 234 0205

THE CHILD LEFT BEHIND

Gracie Hart

Victoria Wild is only four years old but already knows about heartbreak, having been abandoned by her unwed mother when she was only a baby. Luckily her Aunt Eliza was there to take her in but times are still hard on Pit Lane and while Eliza does her best to make sure there is always food on the table, Victoria bears the stigma of her illegitimacy. But more trouble is around the corner — in the form of Victoria's mother, Mary-Anne Wild, who is finally coming home not to be a proper mother to her daughter but to exact her revenge on the man who ruined her life . . .

THE GIRL FROM PIT LANE

Gracie Hart

Can two young, coal-miner's daughters survive on their own?

Tragedy strikes a small Yorkshire mining town when Sarah Wild's husband dies in a terrible accident. Widowed and destitute, Sarah is forced to remarry to save her daughters, Mary-Anne and Eliza, from the workhouse. When their mother tragically dies, the sisters are left under the care of their drunken step-father. Unable to rely on him, they are determined to stick together. But things are complicated when Mary-Anne, the eldest, falls pregnant with the child of a married mine-owner. Scared and unsure what to do, the sisters try to hide Mary-Anne's pregnancy. But such things cannot stay secret for long . . .